Playing For Keeps

a Novel

First published in the United States of America 2023 by Lake Country Press & Reviews.

Cataloging-in-Publication Data is on file with the Library of Congress.

ISBN - Paperback: 979-8-9877391-2-9; E-Book: 979-8-9877391-3-6

Author website: www.tristencrone.com

Publisher website: www.lakecountrypress.com

Editor: Borbala Branch

Cover Art: Vivsketchess

Book Cover: Emily's World of Design

Interior Formatting: Dawn Lucous

Hello Reader,

I can't wait for you to dive in. Even though Playing for Keeps is a contemporary romance with a HEA, there are some content warnings we want to leave you with before reading.

Please note this list contains spoilers.

This novel contains:
- Alcohol Consumption
- Anxiety and Depictions of Anxiety
- Brief mention of Abortion
- Explicit Language
- Explicit Sexual Content
- Mention of Fatphobia and Fatphobic experiences
- Mention of Car Accident and Depiction of Minor Injuries to a Peripheral character
- Brief mention of a Peripheral character's Cancer Scare

To all the big girls who were told to hate their softness.
You are beautiful and your stories are just as worthy.

Six hours to go on this wretched Friday. Six hours of emotionally-draining work, a complicated commute, Midol, and a steaming hot shower were all that stood between Farren and the best part of her whole week.

Barely contained dark blonde curls started to slip from the hair tie as she bent over to fasten the kindergartener's shoes. The waistband of her pants dug uncomfortably into her soft stomach, and she longed for the forgiving leggings the school prohibited. The five-year-old was practically bouncing and ready to race off the second her hands let go of the light-up sneakers.

She'd been asked the same question at least six times by nine AM, despite her morning introduction during circle time.

"Where's Mrs. Wilson?" they'd chirped.

"What's a *sussitute*?" another asked when she'd introduced herself.

"What's 'maternity leave'?" a boy missing his two front teeth chimed in, and Farren worked hard to contain the groan that swept through her body at the prospect of explaining it to a bunch of wide-eyed children, who would no doubt share any tidbits they learned with their families. The last thing Farren needed on her first day at a new school was irate parents greeting her the next morning.

"I'm sure she spoke to you all about it. Mrs. Wilson had a baby, so she needs to take care of them until they're a little bit older. She's getting to know them, and in the meantime, I'll be here getting to know all of you!" Farren tried to be peppy. Usually, it wasn't too much of a stretch for her, but she'd recently finished up her first consistent chunk of subbing for a high school. They'd sucked the life out of her with their relationship drama, hormones, and attitudes so rotten, she'd done some deep breathing so she wouldn't walk out and not return.

You need the rent money. Farren chanted in her head like a mantra. *You **need** the rent money.* She could tinker with her game ideas and pipe dreams in her free time, but without steady cash flow, it didn't matter. The jagged envelopes of bills sitting on the coffee table came to mind. It was all that kept her going.

Farren filled small empty spaces, she plugged holes, a hermit crab hopping from shell to shell, keeping it warm for the permanent inhabitant, protecting herself in the process. It suited her. It did. Variety was the spice of life, or something, right? This way, she never got too tied down, and she could step out as needed.

She focused her energy on being what the kids in front of her needed: wiping snotty noses, and consoling tiny shaking shoulders. Farren administered band-aids, read stories, and drew shapes on the whiteboard to help them understand math problems.

Although it was draining and temporary, she treasured the feeling she got at the end of the day when one of the children turned around before walking out the door and gifted her with a little "See you tomorrow, Miss Davis!"

When the last child crossed the threshold, and Farren straightened the room back to normalcy, she turned the lights off and sighed.

A bus, the Metro, and two blocks later, Farren walked up the tree-lined street to her apartment, hips aching from standing all day in shoes that offered no arch support or comfort. If this substitute teaching thing was going to be long-term, she'd have to invest in better footwear. *If...* this was the first consistent job she'd found in a while. There was no if about it.

It made her feel like the associate's degree she'd muddled through wasn't a total waste. Her friend's referral had made all the difference. *Thank you, Luis.* After weeks of crappy dog-walking jobs waiting for the background checks and wading through interviews, she'd survived her first short-term placement and was onto her next.

Their row houses all looked similar, albeit with color variations between the buildings. The tall concrete steps outside were a bitch and left her feeling far older than her twenty-seven years. She greeted Gary, the neighbor who hung out on his tiny folding chair under a tree out front reading the paper, the same way he did every day. He lifted the rolled-up paper in response, and she pushed the doors open with a huff.

It didn't help her achiness that the elevator never worked or that mid-September in D.C. was still too damn hot. Skeletons were planted into the mulch beside the stairs, pumpkins hanging out by front doors. They were prepped and ready for Halloween, but it felt slightly ridiculous when the grass was green, and people still wandered around in T-shirts.

Her slightly heeled shoes clacked as she schlepped up the flights up to her home. A trickle of sweat made its way down her spine, droplets collecting on her forehead. *God*, she couldn't wait to get out of the Goodwill work clothes and rid herself of the kiddie germs clinging to the fabric. Clicking the lock, her keys jingled as she tossed them into the wooden bowl on the counter near the door. Farren was greeted with a slightly messy apartment, diluted light filtering in through the semi-sheer curtains.

Eventually she'd find time to mop the old wooden floors. It would probably be a good idea to fold up the fuzzy blanket she had bundled on the couch. And pack up the stack of games sitting on the floor. Still, she loved the feeling she got when she walked in after a long day. Cozy, messy and filled with things she loved. So, she would put up with the crappy commute and scrape the money together for rent, because this was her home.

Farren pushed aside the longing that snuck up every now and then, the niggle at the back of her mind reminding her how lonely she was. How aimless. But she was good at distracting herself. Despite the week she'd had, heck the *month*, it was Friday. Best day of the week and the one time she got to let it all go for a few hours.

She turned the window unit on in her bedroom, frigid air blasting out at her. Farren unbuttoned her blouse, letting the sides flutter as the air rushed over her, goosebumps rising on her skin, the blessed relief of her under-boob sweat finally cooling. If only she could remove them at the end of the day as well, toss them aside like house keys, pounds of weight gone. Maybe then the backache wouldn't be as bad.

Discarded clothes sat in a sad puddle on the floor, yet another thing she'd have to deal with later. For now, all she wanted was to be clean. Farren couldn't stand the sticky feeling of sweat clinging to her skin. She stood under the punishing spray of her shower, scorching water washing the last of her fatigue down the drain. She shrugged the stress of the day off, relishing the prospect of a well-earned weekend and the possibilities it held.

A shrill ringing cut through the steam of the shower, one of the few pre-programmed numbers to ring through her do-not-disturb, and Farren raced to her cell phone. She dug through where she'd tossed it onto the sheets and raised the screen to her ear before the call could drop, not bothering to double check the name.

"Hey!" she greeted, a little breathless.

"Hey, are you bringing 'Here to Slay' tonight?" Corinne's voice came through sounding frazzled as usual, clinking glasses and crashing sounds in the background. It was always chaotic on Corinne's end and Farren assumed she was unpacking the dishwasher while trying to keep Alison occupied. Subbing was worth it when it kept Farren off of Corinne's couch. The last thing Corinne needed was another stressor.

"I hadn't planned on it, but I can. Any other games you need me to bring?" Farren trapped the phone between her cheek and her shoulder, trying to keep it in place while she wrapped a towel around her dripping body, tucking the cotton into itself under her arm.

"Just that, Luis has a friend coming by who's really into D&D, and we were trying to come up with games with similar theming or such to make it a more enjoyable experience for them." Corinne's daughter, somewhere nearby the phone, let out a squeal and giggle which let Farren know she was up to no good.

"Okay, I can pack that. Tell Allie-Cat I say hi!" Farren tried and failed to keep the smile from her face as she listened to Corinne and Luis try to corral the feisty four-year-old.

"Auntie Farren says hello,"—more rustling and a dull thud as the phone was no doubt tossed onto the first soft surface. "Alison. *Alison*, get back here! *Alison!* You need to get your pants on before your grandmother gets here. Come on, do it for your abuela."

She must have acquiesced because a few seconds later a slightly breathless Corinne was back on the phone. "Sorry about that, she's a handful." The words ended in a sigh and Farren could relate after the day she had with the kindergarteners, though thankfully no one there shucked their pants and ran around bare-assed.

"This is what I get for not naming her after Luis's grandmother. My mother-in-law still gives me side-eye every time we call her Allie. She insists on calling her by her middle name, and loves to mutter about family and tradition." Corinne's voice was a near-whisper, the cultural differences between Corinne and her in-laws something Farren was familiar with after the last five years of listening to their family squabbles. It made something in Farren ache when she thought of how far away her own family was, and not just in miles.

"I'm sorry, I know how much that bothers you."

"I know I complain about it all the time. You're a freaking saint." Corinne was overly kind, as usual. Corinne confiding in her, needing her, was comforting. It was nice to be somebody to someone.

"That's what friends are for!" She frowned, recalling the mention of Luis bringing one of his own along. "Speaking of, is this person a recruit for the group or is this one of your thinly-veiled attempts to set me up with someone?"

Farren tried to keep the suspicion from her voice. She didn't mind, most of the time. Corinne was happily married and had seemingly made it her life's mission to lead others down the same path. It wasn't that Farren didn't *want* another boyfriend, or eventually a husband, but they usually didn't want her the way she was.

Farren was used to being fat. She'd gotten over worrying about being the biggest person in the room. It was too exhausting. But times like blind dates and set-ups were harder to ignore. She was tired of men who only wanted to hang out behind closed doors, with even fewer prospects wanting the 'real' deal. Those who did got serious far too quickly, and that in itself was a massive red flag. Farren was done being hidden, tired of meeting up with people, especially after a few phone conversations, and having the look on their face change when they saw her. She knew her worth and deserved better than that. There was a lot of her to love—her big personality, her overzealous laugh, her soft body that didn't fit *quite* right in a world built for a more acceptable size.

"No, I swear. I behaved myself this time. Besides, they're not into women. Luis is actually hoping to set them up with Cute Chris." Corinne's words sent a shiver of relief through her. Game night was her escape, it was where she could be who she was, enjoy what she loved, and not have to be "on" or performative. There were no squabbling kids, no bills piling up, no need to be anything other than what she was: an unapologetic board game geek.

"Okay, good. I'll see if I can help, but the moment Chris looks like he wants an out, I'm giving it to him. You know he's only recently single, the last thing he needs is pressure," Farren reminded her friend. Chris didn't need her help, not really. But she would have wanted someone to do the same for her if needed, so she kept the option open.

"Sounds good. I'll see you soon?" Corinne asked.

"See you soon!" Farren answered, and when her phone beeped to signal the end of the call, she left it on the bed to finish getting ready.

She fluffed her hair, body bent over as she scrunched curl cream into it to try and combat the sticky September humidity. Washington D.C. was a joke. Up north, people were already enjoying the leaves turning, crisp evenings after the sun completed its lazy descent under the horizon. Her mother had posted on Facebook about the new red hues outside their home. Rural New England was a world away from where Farren found herself now. Five years in D.C. was almost enough to make her a city-girl.

Leggings on, "Let's Connect" shirt eased over her curls so she didn't muss them, Farren slung her purse over her shoulder. Sneakers were tugged on by the door, her tote bag with games clasped in her hand. She ignored the bills and *that* box on the coffee table, and started the trek toward the coffee shop that hosted their weekly game nights.

Capitol Cafe—home to nightly events, artisanal baked goods, and mediocre coffee. The first place she'd found after moving here that actually made her want to stay, not tuck tail and run back home.

The coffee shop was always warm, and would be, even in the winter. The old wooden floors were scarred with years of use. The sage green walls were filled with local art. A couple of comfortable chairs were gathered around a nook in the back, replete with some books and magazines. Gamers occupied the tables in the middle while other cafe-goers sat by the long tables pressed against the floor-to-ceiling window, staring out at the city.

She grabbed her first drink for the night. Despite the lingering heat of the dying summer, Farren opted for a hot chocolate and headed over to claim a table, pulling boxes out to show she was here to play and open to people joining in.

Cute Chris was there, grabbing his own drink, and they exchanged a wave. Farren had no clue about the nickname's origin; he'd only ever been Cute Chris when anyone referred to him in private. Still, it made her laugh, so she carried on with the tradition.

He came over to her table, tight curls carefully styled, dimples cutting into his cheeks, smile bright and cheerful against his dark skin.

"Hey, how've you been?" Chris asked.

"Hanging in there. Started with a new class today after very little notice, so it's been a day. You?" She took a sip of her drink, relishing the sweet heat.

"Irate customers as usual. I need to get out of retail. I'm worried I'll eye-roll myself into another dimension if one more person asks me to 'go check the back,' as if we all have no idea of our own inventory and it's going to magically show up when we open the door. The only magical thing in there is the chair with the throw pillow we take turns screaming into when we need to 'check in the back,'" his words tumbled out, smile fading as frustration leached into every syllable.

Farren understood; she'd done her own stint in retail. Along with food service, babysitting, sales, and dog walking. "That bad, huh?" she sympathized.

"And more. I can't wait until I've finished my course and I can actually work in a field I'm interested in." He tasted his drink as he watched more people filing into the space. Farren swallowed her own sip to distract herself from the thoughts swirling in her mind at his comment, the dread and guilt she felt at the reminder of her failure to do the same.

"How long do you have left to go?" Farren asked, her attention slightly diverted by the people coming in, her eyes keeping a keen lookout for Corinne and the mystery guest they had planned for Chris.

He slurped his drink softly. "Forty more hours. I'm so close, I can taste it."

"That would be the coffee, actually," Farren replied with a smirk. Chris rewarded her with one of his aforementioned eye rolls, and they broke out into easy laughter.

"Want to get a game in before everyone shows up?" she asked.

"Sure, what did you bring?"

Square boxes spread out from her pile, a few smaller games, all different colors, vibrant and full of promise.

"Got some games for a bigger group, but as far as two-player games go, I brought 'Pink Hijinks,' 'Martian Chess'—which are both Looney Labs games. I also just picked up this one."

Farren lifted the little metal tin, shiny black and red illuminated under the lights. "It's called 'Niya'. The art on the tiles is super pretty, and I've heard it compared to 'Tic-Tac-Toe' or 'Connect Four.'"

Farren pushed all three games closer to him.

"I'm sensing a theme, a very strategy-heavy set of games here," Chris said and seemed to think about it for a moment before his hand wrapped around the little pink pyramid-shaped bag.

"'Pink Hijinks' it is!" Farren exclaimed.

"Better watch out, Davis. I'm coming for your record. I picked up my own set not too long ago, and I'm getting much better." He waggled an eyebrow at her, and it was on. Competition would drive her spirit and save the flagging energy she'd struggled with after the work day. Chris pulled out the tiny three-by-three cloth grid and stacked the clear pink pyramids on top of each other, largest to smallest.

They took turns trying to push pieces into each other's spaces, stealing pyramids the other wanted. For such a simple game, it seemed to take a decent amount of time, but by the end of it, Chris emerged triumphant with a line of three medium sized pyramids in the row closest to him. Although Farren should have probably been more sour about her loss, it was worth it to hear his little whoop before he punched his fist into the air.

"Good job. I hope you're ready for a rematch at a later stage. I have a reputation to uphold, after all," Farren joked, and Chris agreed.

"Perfect timing!" Chris said, and Farren turned to see her friends approaching.

Corinne looked harried, cheeks pink and her dark hair a little messy, as if she and Luis rushed to make it over in time. Knowing Miss Alison, that was most likely the case. Behind them was a new face, and after the usual hugs and greetings, Luis gestured to his friend.

"This is Braxton. They work in the admin department at school. It only took a few weeks of bringing games into their office to convince them to give it a try." Luis's words were teasing, but Braxton took it in stride and raised a hand in greeting, one corner of their mouth lifting up in a shy smile. They had a shock of blue hair, short on the sides and swooping back from their forehead. It reminded Farren of Pigeotto from Pokémon. They also had one of those dimple piercings she'd seen online but never had the guts to try.

"Don't worry, we don't bite," Farren tried to soothe.

"Much," Chris added, and Farren knew there was nothing to worry about when it came to Chris and his comfort zone. He already gave a cheeky smile to the newcomer.

Luis set his own bag down on the table, its protruding sharp edges attesting to how fully he'd packed it. He did that every time. Even though they only had a few hours in the coffee shop, he always packed as if they were on the verge of running out of games to play. The newcomers took their seats, and Farren rose from her own when Corinne gave her 'the look,' the one that told her there was something to gossip about in private.

"I'll be right back. Getting our drinks," Corinne said for Luis's benefit, but he was already engrossed in discussing a new game he'd picked up earlier in the week.

Farren followed her friend toward the growing line, contemplating a little something to go along with her drink.

"What's up?" Farren asked.

"She made a comment about the house, about how we should probably look into getting someone to take care of it now that I'm back at work and Alison's in daycare." Corinne's brows pinched, and her eyes got a little too bright. "I *just* cleaned!"

"I'm really sorry," Farren lamented with her friend, letting her vent about the hardships of mothers-in-law. Not something Farren had to worry about. Not something she'd *ever* have to worry about, if her track record was anything to go by. Farren interjected with all the properly timed noises, some agreeing, some frustrated, as Corinne ranted on. It was all Corinne needed—an outlet.

The line was pretty long, busy with the evening rush as people grabbed a small bite after getting off work or settled in for a fun Friday night. The press of bodies felt a little claustrophobic, and when Farren tried to take a step backward so her chest didn't press into the person ahead, she bumped into a solid, warm body.

"I'm really sorry," she threw over her shoulder, moving back into her small, relegated space. Farren got a brief impression of darkish hair, a frown over the screen of his cellphone. He looked vaguely familiar, probably a regular.

Corinne diverted her attention again, this time worrying about missing milestones in Alison's life now that she was back from her maternity-leave-turned-sabbatical. She loved working at the Anacostia Museum, but the guilt she felt at returning to work was understandable—especially when it meant less time to try and tame Alison's wilder antics. Farren tutted in understanding, assuring her friend that Alison wasn't worse for wear. Her boisterous energy wasn't unusual for her age.

Freshly ground coffee, sweet baked goods, and something else, something dark, musky and reminiscent of bonfires surrounded by evergreens filled her nose. It didn't take a genius to figure out it was the stranger behind them, so close, she could practically feel the heat pouring off his body.

Corinne must have noticed her distraction, mischief lighting up her features as they did that unspoken thing, something gained after years of friendship: the uncanny ability to communicate without actually speaking. Pointed eye movement, a sly smile. Farren shook her head and urged her friend to drop it. A scoff followed by a shrug that seemed to say 'fine, your loss,' before Corinne was called up to the register.

Her friend shot her one more look, getting a good eyeful of the stranger. Corinne's order was ready quickly, and she gave Farren a raised eyebrow and a smile before she headed back to the table.

Two registers opened up at the same time, Farren and the stranger walking up to the counter, standing beside each other now. She could see out of the corner of her eye that he was tall, dressed as if he'd come from the office.

"Back again?" the barista asked, and Farren's attention was drawn to the task at hand.

"Yeah, I figured I *had* to have a baked goodie to go with the hot chocolate." She peered into the glass case beside the register, taking in the offerings.

Croissants, cruffins, pinwheels. Savory, sweet, and everything in between.

One jumped out at her, its flaky golden exterior, sumptuous filling and crumble top practically whispered her name through the glass.

"Can I have the... honey lemon twice-baked croissant?" she asked, reading off the name from the little tag. The barista reached into the display with her gloved hand, tucking the pastry into a little wax paper bag. The man beside her asked for something to eat, coffee, and the same dessert she'd just ordered. His voice spread over her with a honeyed buzz, and part of her kicked around the idea of getting back in the dating game.

"That's going to be four-ninety-five," her barista said at the same time his apologized, "I'm so sorry, it seems we've sold the last one."

Farren slid her card into the chip reader, the little machine beeping happily as it ran her transaction, and she risked a look over at the man beside her, a scowl twisting his handsome face into something intimidating. It never occurred to her that she'd ever experience a look of such malice over pastry and lemon curd, but there was a first time for everything, apparently.

His hazel eyes were narrowed, lips pulled down in displeasure. What might they look like when they're soft and smiling? He was good looking, in a regular sort of way. Neatly trimmed hair and beard, clothing still surprisingly unwrinkled despite a whole workday. Something in her belly seemed to wake up, curling in recognition of the attraction sweeping through her. His frown cut deep lines between those dark brows, and the second he opened his mouth and that velvety voice grumbled at her, he ruined the whole thing.

Sebastian

Friday mornings always dragged. A cup of coffee cooled on his desk, too many tabs to count on his computer screen, and Sebastian's boss was heading over. There was no way this could be good. He'd barely scraped by this week, so he highly doubted Andrew was coming over to give him kudos. He plastered a smile onto his face and swiveled around to face the music.

"Government needs us to stay late, Clark. We need to make sure they re-up the contract next year, and we're gearing up for the new presentation." Sebastian's *favorite* phrase. The constant, looming doom of his job security being threatened, despite all the overtime he'd already put in, nullified and forgotten as soon as another big project came in. *This was what you wanted. This is what you moved here for.*

Which was how he found himself staring at dual screens all day, blinking away the dryness, and praying he could keep the momentum going into the evening. His swivel chair bit into his thighs, the back unyielding. Gray carpet seemed to blend into the walls, a dull and blank space to encourage focus.

It was a necessary evil. It was a stepping stone. It was the way things worked. Sebastian repeated the words until they became somewhat of a mantra. On days where he'd worked over the forty hours his contract stipulated—something that happened more often than not—it meant he could ignore the niggling voice at the back of his mind saying it was *wrong*.

Some days it was hard to pinpoint whether the voice was burn-out, or just the broken record of his parents replaying over and over telling him life was for living not working. Or the spite that drove him here not being enough to keep him grinding. Dream jobs were an oxymoron because nobody dreamed of working. Childhood conditioning like that was what he'd done his best to buck. They didn't get it, and probably never would. Instead, he focused on a different voice.

"If you work these extra hours, it will look really good. You know we're trying to land another project, and if you prove yourself with retention, that pitch could be yours." The words from his current superior echoed in his mind, the placation insincere, but he indulged it anyway, choosing to believe what Andrew said was true... that his hard work was noticed, and it would make a difference to his future, even when most days, he felt like a faceless name in a database.

So, he sucked it up. He pushed aside the fatigue that seemed to cling to him with a relentless grip. Even when he'd worked a full day and then some, he found himself on his bed staring up at the ceiling, eyes adjusting to the early hours of the evening, debating whether he should slink into his home office and get a head start on the next day.

He probably would have, if it'd done any good. Instead, he focused on his breathing, trying to slow it down in order to calm his racing heart, waiting for the coffee from a few hours prior to leave his system. It made him jittery and barely did anything for his tiredness at this point, but he'd gotten used to the bitter heat of it, the cups a way to measure time passing by.

One cup in the morning to get started. One around lunch while Sebastian worked some food into his body and caught up on personal emails. Another a little before five, if he was staying at the office. Or closer to six if he took work home with him—that was his favorite one. It was a break from the monotony, a chance to breathe and feel the city's energy outside an office's walls.

It didn't hurt that the coffee shop he frequented, the one between work and home, had fantastic food offerings. He found himself asking to work from home instead of staying at the office more often so he could swing by there for dinner instead of the same-old delivery options near their building, or worse still, the paltry choices of the vending machine on his office floor.

But it would all be worth it. The late nights, the lack of sleep, the acrid stress burning in his chest and rising up his esophagus—because in a few weeks, that promotion would be his. He would go from software developer to project manager, then program manager, and eventually a directorial role. Hopefully within government so his retirement would be set. And Ashley could fucking choke on it. After what happened in Ohio, he'd mapped out all of his career. *This* was where he had to grind, put in the work to ensure his future, and make sure nothing got in his way again.

So what if it meant he didn't have as much time for himself, or the inane dance that was dating in the city? He'd never gone to a Smithsonian Museum, or walked the Mall, or saw a show at the Kennedy Center... none of that touristy shit that people came to the city for, it didn't matter. Those things could wait.

So what if he didn't make it over to visit his parents in Ohio because he worked weekends and couldn't justify the hours of driving? *Or are you just avoiding home in general?* The thought pissed him off. It had been months. He should be over it. He *would* be over it once he'd reached his goal.

Some of his colleagues dicked around, peeking out from the sides of their cubicles to make conversation, eager for the week to end, but there were a few like him, working toward the goal of a promotion.

Keith: UMD grad, a year older and far more outgoing. Everyone knew his name, if not necessarily the quality of his work.

Rachel: two years younger, but she'd been working at the company since interning during her time at Georgetown. She'd built a rapport, fingers on the pulse of everything going on, ambitious and not willing to step aside without a fight.

Sebastian felt like nothing but a loser from out of state with no friends, or family, or connections in the area. Thirty-one approached with rapid speed. Ohio left his work reputation less-than-stellar, and he was still clawing his way out of student debt. He'd worked for everything he had with barely any support. Ashley pretended, quite prettily, but it was a lie. His parents watched him with the same question on both of their faces when they bothered to look up from their little corner of the world: *Why?*

Why bother? Why, when so much else mattered more? The earth was being pillaged. Poverty held countless generations in its unrelenting grip. What was the point of lofty career goals when you might be dead tomorrow? What's the point of missing out on your whole life for the sake of a job title?

Sometimes he had no answer for them. Sometimes when the insomnia caused dry-eye and his anxiety ramped up to a level that left him doing crunches and pushups in the middle of the night on the floor of his bedroom just to stop the itch under his skin—he couldn't really say shit. Because although he held onto the assurance that one day, it would be worth it, *one day,* he'd have achieved everything he set out to do and his success would speak for itself, he couldn't argue with the fact that today wasn't that day.

Today, he lived in a one-bed apartment part of a duplex with a lovely view of a parking lot, three metro stops and a couple blocks of walking away from his office. His car sat unused most of the time, and it would no doubt be covered in leaves within the next few weeks before it rested beneath a light blanket of snow at the end of the year.

He'd driven it to D.C. from Ohio, and left it parked since. It waited there unless there was an extenuating circumstance or the once-a-week trip around the block to keep the battery from atrophying. Sebastian should've sold it and let go of the past. Right now, it served as a reminder of the world he'd tried so hard to step out of and stolen moments in the back seat. It was a mid-size sedan, an unappealing beige that seemed prevalent in the early 2000s, with over a hundred and fifty thousand miles on the odometer.

In a way, Sebastian supposed there was a direct link between him and the used car he'd chosen back then, leaving for college —it was serviceable, plain, and it got the job done. There was a decent amount of wear on it, but he tried his best to take care of it despite an unforgiving environment. Not much had changed at all.

Sebastian worked until almost all the other screens in the room blinked dark, well after their government liaisons left for the day to enjoy the rest of the weekend.

It wasn't until Andrew told him to get out of there for the night that he finally shut down the monitor, packing up his work laptop and the cooler he used for his lunch. He tucked a thermos under his arm and slung the laptop bag over his shoulder.

Andrew was friendly, or at least he tried to be. He had a tendency to over-exaggerate the severity of what the government side of their division said in his meetings with them. He was also the one that tended to dangle those threats and promises under their noses as incentive. But on nights like this one, he relented, telling Sebastian to call it for the rest of the weekend. The work he'd done that day would have to be checked against the parameters in place which could only happen on Monday.

So, he found himself in his apartment a little over forty minutes later, unsure what to do with himself. Shoes shucked at the door, thermos and lunch bag washed, everything still tidy from when he'd stress-cleaned it two days ago... Sebastian was stuck with that funny feeling that came with not knowing how to exist outside of work.

In the few months he'd been in D.C., he'd yet to make friends. He didn't have the time or energy for it, but it was something that would have come in handy right then.

He sank down into his sofa, stretching onto the cushions to try and relieve the ache that built up in his neck and back from bending over a keyboard all day. Sebastian scrolled through his phone, the bright glow on his face and the sun's slow descent toward the horizon the only lights in the place. It created a subtle haze and dulled the edges of how empty the room was, even with him in it.

Facebook (which he kept only for his parents' benefit) and Instagram were full of his peers and their milestones, acquaintances he'd met in high school, college, and further on—a collection of names that at one point floated around his periphery. He had a few of his colleagues on there now, but only because they'd requested, so he'd accepted. Endless engagement rings, promotions, silly prattle about media being consumed en masse. Scroll, scroll, scroll.

Then, almost a boon on Facebook, a bright reprieve from feeling like he was drowning, falling behind—that coffee shop, the one he usually went to on the way home, posted their new featured dessert. Decadent, the description was enough to get him back on his feet even without the picture, which looked positively sinful. It could be something he did tonight: a quick pop over to Capitol Cafe for dinner, a mere precursor to that dessert. Sebastian would do his best to savor it, and this would be what made his Friday *more...* something. Just more than the sad space he took up right now.

Filled with a renewed sense of purpose, he slipped his shoes back on, wallet in the back pocket of his chinos, phone in the front. He walked it by memory, the ten minutes it took enough time for him to soak up the night around him.

The sun started slipping down in the sky earlier and earlier these days. The air was still humid, but the temperature dipped in degrees with the sun. A few stars glimmered in the sky, not as badly obscured by light pollution as New York City on the few instances he'd gone there for trips and interviews. It seemed so separate from Ohio, especially the small town he grew up in with its narrow-mindedness and the disconnect that seemed to exist there. That became *more* apparent the further he moved from home. D.C. was a little stuffier, a little more polished, a little more like him. *A little lonelier?*

The thought was shoved aside, bitterness leaving an unpleasant taste in his mouth. Better this way. Less chance to get screwed over this way.

So, he found himself among townhomes and apartment buildings, restaurants and bars tucked between very official looking buildings, as much of a melting pot as the people filling the city. The warm glow of the cafe spilled out onto the sidewalk outside, people coming in and out, some sitting in the window immersed in their own lives.

Sebastian stepped inside the cafe and took a deep breath, the aroma of butter and baked goods—cheese, garlic, and other spices mixing together in the most delicious way. As usual, the line to the counter was decently long, so he parked himself behind a growing line of people.

People sat grouped around the main tables, conversing

animatedly, boxes spread out around them. Board games. He'd noticed them a few times when he happened to stop by on the right day. Part of him was jealous of their laughter and camaraderie; the more significant side scoffed internally. *How silly*, he thought, *such a waste of time*. Mere steps up from comics and action figures at best, childish at worst. Sebastian no longer had time for games.

He tapped his foot impatiently, digging his phone from his pocket in nervous habit, waiting for emails that weren't coming. Fighting the agitation built up in his chest left an ache behind his sternum. Logically, he knew it was a stress response; his inability to be 'still' was a product of the environment he found himself in daily. Sebastian could have justified it any which way, but on a soul-deep level, he was harried, frayed at the edges, and had little patience as a result.

Two women stood in front of him in line, one yapping her head off about her family drama, dark hair bobbing around her chin as her gestures punctuated what she was saying. So animated, so loud. Her friend interjected at all the correct times, but something was off.

She was on the shorter side, generously proportioned, but her T-shirt accentuated rather than concealed the soft curves of her body. Her dark blonde hair tumbled down her shoulders and back in spirals and waves. Watching her, paying attention to the exchange with her friend finally shut off the "work brain" that followed him everywhere. This stranger and her soft "oh wow"s and "seriously"s gave him a tiny bit of amusement to set his frustration at bay.

He saw something of himself in the exchange. There were multiple conversations at work where he'd done the same.

And when she stepped back, trying to find relief from the press of bodies in line, she collided with him. Her body was warm, her skin and hair carrying the tiniest hint of lemon sage which reminded him of the bubble bath he'd bought on a whim and never used—an indulgence he couldn't afford when all his time went to more important matters. Slowing down was not an option. Slowing down meant he had to deal with stuff.

She looked up at him through lashes dark with mascara. Freckles on her nose and cheekbones were unimpeded by other makeup, and her dark eyes widened as she offered up an apology. Her friend blinked up at him as well behind dark-rimmed glasses she pressed up onto her nose before the women engaged in some weird mute communication he could only guess at. The blonde seemed a little stiff, tense, though he supposed the same could be said about him.

So he didn't try. He focused his attention back to the task at hand: choosing a good dinner, ordering a sandwich and that croissant he'd seen on their business page, and maybe a hot drink to finish it all off. Sebastian's eyes roved over the chalkboard above the counter where this week's offerings were carefully displayed through a mix of calligraphy and cute drawings. By the time he'd settled on what he wanted, the line had made significant progress. The dark-haired woman was at the register, and her friend—her gorgeous, indulgent-smelling friend—stood right in front of him.

The baristas called them forward almost simultaneously. Both registers were happily unoccupied. Sebastian tried to ignore the warmth of the blonde's voice as she placed her order, like the honey he couldn't wait to enjoy as part of the croissant. She ordered his pastry, and his stomach did a stupid little jump at the thought that she liked the same thing he did.

So when he tried to place his order—a coffee, a Monte Cristo sandwich with a side of blackberry maple reduction, the brightness of the sweet dip perfect to offset the smoky ham and spicy mustard—and *that* honey lemon curd twice-baked croissant...

only to be informed they'd sold the last one, it was incredibly hard not to lose his shit.

This was the whole reason he'd come here. The one goal he'd set for himself tonight. The one thing he'd been looking forward to within the monotony threatening to pull him under even on a good night. The barista gestured to the side, to the woman and the wax paper bag holding what he wanted.

Sebastian watched her pay for the pastry, her eyes flickering over to him when she heard his barista talking about her order. He ignored the warm brown eyes, her open expression one of curiosity. He dismissed the stutter in his chest when she looked at him, *really* looked. It was more than a passing glance. She paid attention. She made eye contact in a city where most people just glossed over his face. He ignored the voice telling him to mind his own damn business.

Instead, he opened his big, dumb mouth.

"That's my pastry."

The words were overly loud, even in the din of so many people talking, his tone too dark given the innocuousness of the statement. She shook her head in confusion, lifting the bag as if to say "no, clearly it's not," but no words left her mouth.

"Your total is fourteen-sixty-eight." The barista drew his attention back to her and the lit-up display of the card reader. She handed him a numbered placard to keep at his table for them to bring out his order.

"I'm not done with you," he said to the pastry thief, turning to shove his card into the receptacle, glaring at it until it beeped for him to remove it. "No receipt, thank you," he said to the barista before he turned to the offending party.

She stood in her silly 'Connect Four' shirt, a dumbfounded expression on her face, as if she couldn't believe he'd even opened his mouth in the first place. Logically, she'd gotten it split seconds before him, and the pastry was hers. Rationally, it was a dick move to berate her for taking it and unloading his stress onto her.

But Sebastian felt neither of those things. Instead, he was poised on the edge of breaking. All he had to hold himself together was the tiny ember flickering in his chest along with all the fucking heartburn.

"How much for the pastry? I'll pay you for it." His voice was firm, business mode activated.

Her stunned expression gave way to ire, slowly building but there, nonetheless.

"Excuse me, you are *way* out of line," she scoffed, walking away from him and the registers.

Sebastian followed her out of the way, his hand reaching before he could think about it, a gentle grip on her forearm. She stopped suddenly, the look on her face impossible to read, and he tried to ignore the lick of energy that shot up his arm at the contact.

"Seriously, I'll pay." Sebastian pressed, not willing to let this go, not willing to fail when he felt so fragile.

It was a joke, really. The power one pastry had over his day, over his mood, over the ability to go through another hellish week of work without walking out.

"Seriously, back off and get your hand off of me. I bought it. It's mine." The edge to her voice should have been enough warning, would have on a regular day. He'd overstepped massively, and he must have looked like such an asshole. Sebastian dropped her arm but pressed on with his mission.

"Look, I need this pastry. I doubt you'd understand, you and your *gaming* friends and the frivolity you surround yourselves with. But I've had a week from hell at work. This was the one thing I looked forward to this weekend." It was honest, maybe overly so.

Her frown deepened at his dismissive comment about her

hobbies, slightly softened by the latter half of his statement. Perhaps it was the desperate tinge to his voice... Maybe she was just a better person than he was because she seemed to be considering it.

"What's your name?" she asked, and he was taken aback. It was forward, but he'd crossed the line of decency when he touched her without permission.

"Sebastian." *God,* he sounded pathetic. Why the hell had he given her his full name? No one but his parents still called him that. At work, he went by Ian to seem more professional. *And to distance himself from who he'd been in Ohio.*

He waited for the comment he'd come to expect. She was in the proper age range. It should land any moment. Only it didn't, not a word about an animated Jamaican-accented crustacean. Instead, she reached her hand out as if to shake his, an offering of sorts. He obliged, his palm swallowing hers.

"Sebastian," she repeated, and the name somehow felt different coming from her mouth. "I'm Farren."

Farren... unusual, he'd never met a Farren before. She seemed to be waiting for something as well, and her features seemed to relax more with each passing second.

"Nice to meet you, Farren?" It came out as a question, his anger slowly fading, and he realized he still had her small hand clasped in his. He dropped it, as if a second longer would burn his skin.

"Tell you what, I'll make you a deal." The tone of her voice left him uneasy, her brows furrowed as she thought about it. "Since you have some crap to say about me and my friends, and how we choose to spend our spare time... I want the opportunity to prove you wrong."

Her face was resolute, and a twinge of guilt twisted in his stomach for being mean about it. When he opened his mouth to apologize, she lifted a hand to quiet him. "You seem like you could use some unwinding anyway."

He couldn't argue with it, but there was still the matter of the pastry.

"Where does the croissant come in?" he asked and was surprised to hear her laugh softly at the question.

"You're like a man possessed," Farren chuckled. "I'll play you for it. I have a new game I haven't tried, and it'll be a good way to make this fair. If you win, you get the pastry," she said, and it sounded easy enough.

"What's in it for you?" Sebastian asked, doubting her kindness extended so far she'd give it away with no potential benefit.

"If I win—" She considered for a moment, and Sebastian tried hard not to think about what possible punishment awaited him for his rudeness. "If I win, you have to come back here next week and join in the game night."

Sebastian sputtered, disbelieving. Why on earth would he have any interest in joining something like that?

"Unless you're worried you might lose? I guess the pastry isn't that important after all." Her cheeks stretched with a smile, brown eyes alight with mischief. Her generous lips turned up at the corners, and Sebastian was astonished at what flashed through his mind. He pushed it aside before it could bloom, left with vague curiosity about how the pastry would taste on her lips.

"No." The word was a whisper, choked by the sudden tightness in his throat from the inappropriate thought. "No, I'll do it, even if it is on your terms. I'll get my pastry," Sebastian vowed.

Farren gave him a look, her eyes wandering over him slightly, assessing before she smirked. "We'll see."

Farren

Corinne gave her a pointed look, eyebrows raised in question as Farren and Sebastian walked over to the table, as if she hadn't been hoping for this scenario in the first place. Though Farren was sure Corinne didn't picture it happening because of an argument over a pastry. Sebastian hung back a step, one hand buried in his pocket, the other holding his order number, brow furrowed. She could almost hear him thinking.

Farren's imagination filled in the blanks, surmising he had no idea how the heck he'd been roped into something like this. He screamed all-business with his rigid posture and the shadows under his eyes telling their own story. Even though he'd been sort of a dick, even though he made a scene in the cafe, he looked like he could use a little bit of lightening up. Farren considered it a public service. The next person he went off on might not be as understanding or gracious.

"Just grabbing my drink and this game over here," she said, and Cute Chris handed over her takeaway cup of hot chocolate in response. She wrapped her hand around the cold tin of the Niya box.

"See you all in a bit. I've got a game to win." Farren made sure it was loud enough for Sebastian to hear, unable to keep herself from teasing him.

Her friends watched, various expressions across their faces, only Braxton seeming indifferent given their newness to the group. Farren knew her friends would be ready to grill her when she came back to the table for more games later.

"Come on," she said, tilting her head toward a small table out of the way, against the window.

Sebastian followed without a word, dress shoes clipping against the wood floors before he settled at the table. The table and chairs were bar height, and Farren had to add an extra little jump to seat herself. Bar stools were not necessarily built for bigger bodies, but she could endure for as long as it took to beat him.

He was still scowling, his order number on the table, and Farren wondered how much of his grumpiness was his personality and how much was due to the fact that he was probably hungry. She'd find out after he ate.

She pulled out the small pamphlet inside the tin, with gameplay and rules displayed.

"Okay, we're going to set out these Garden Tiles into a four-by-four grid at random," she said, lifting the beautiful painted squares. Imperial Japanese imagery was simple but pretty—birds, cherry blossoms, maple leaves, rain clouds.

Farren laid out the player tokens, the feel of them similar to poker chips, one set of black, the other red, each with their own clan person depicted.

"Pick your clan," she said, gesturing to the tokens. Sebastian eyed her with caution. "It doesn't change anything, it's just preference."

His hand reached out and wrapped around the black pile.

"Okay, so... how it works is we each take a turn to claim a Garden Tile. The win-condition is four of our own-colored tokens either in an uninterrupted row—straight or diagonal—or a square," Farren read off. "Similar to Connect Four or Tic-Tac-Toe in that way."

She put out a few tiles to demonstrate a practice turn.

"Whoever goes first gets to pick their starting position on the board by claiming a tile. Each Garden Tile has two elements on it, so either a bird, sun, or a tree, etcetera. The player that goes next has to choose a tile with one of the elements from the previously claimed tile." Farren demonstrated by capturing a square with a sun on it, depositing her red token in its place, and then took one of Sebastian's black tokens to capture another piece on the grid with a sun as well.

"Got it? Do you have any questions so far?" she asked, finally glancing up from the game and the booklet.

Sebastian's hazel eyes were intense, his mood still decidedly sour, but there was a concentration there. It seemed as if he'd absorbed everything Farren said, bound and determined to trounce her on the first go.

"I'm ready." His voice was firm, still deliciously deep, and with a warm tone Farren thought would translate well for singing. Did he like music? She didn't think he'd be receptive if she started asking him personal questions right then.

She shuffled the tiles, laying them out at random, trying not to let her mind wander on possible moves. Farren wanted this to be fair. She'd played a good deal of strategy games, so it didn't seem right to try to predict where things might go before the first token had even been placed.

"You can claim the first tile," she said, giving him a small smile of encouragement.

Sebastian went for one of the tiles closer to the center; not a bad move, setting himself up for a good number of options. He claimed a piece with maple leaves and a sun on it. Farren found one near the end of the grid with leaves. And on it went.

The waitress brought his food and coffee. He thanked her

with an offhand comment but didn't touch either, forgotten or ignored as they played. The scent was savory and delicious around them. Farren eyed the prized croissant, her own hunger growing by the second, but Sebastian was laser-focused on the small tiles between them.

He seemed to really consider where he was going to place his tile, and despite Farren's best efforts, she found herself making contingency plans based on where he might lay down his token. It meant her moves were much quicker, more decisive than his.

They were down to the last two tokens each. Farren could see what action would guarantee the win for him, but she'd noticed Sebastian was only thinking one move at a time. So, when he claimed the wrong tile—the one setting her up for victory—it took everything she had not to react and let the game play out to completion.

Realization crossed his face when he placed his last tile, his long lashes shooting up as he opened his eyes in mild horror. Farren claimed the final tile, her grouping of four the only ones on the board.

Something in him seemed to deflate. The competitive glint that had been there just two turns before snuffed out as he resigned himself.

"Best two out of three?" Farren offered, not eager for it to end, especially not with him looking so defeated. It was supposed to be fun, a way to get him to peek out of his hard shell.

Sebastian perked up, sitting upright in his chair and taking a bite of his sandwich, a little moan escaping his mouth at the taste. Farren's cheeks flamed at the sound. He was cute, good looking in a way that wasn't alienating. He wasn't perfect, he wasn't arrogant, he took care of himself, and it was weirdly attractive to her. His nose was a little crooked, eyebrows dark and thick; his beard was neatly trimmed if a little speckled with early gray that had yet to reach his brown hair.

But those eyes. There was just something about the mossy green swallowed by a dark ring, whiskey brown growing from the pupil. They looked sharp, the wit behind them evident. Sebastian looked at her, and it seemed like nothing else existed outside that gaze. He really paid attention, absorbing when she spoke, his eyes not wandering around the room. There was no glazed, out-of-focus look on his face.

She sipped her hot chocolate, although it was more like chocolate milk by then, and dared to make small talk as they reset the board.

"So, do you work in the area?" she asked, even though she guessed the reprieve he needed was *from* work. It seemed like the blandest conversation starter she could come up with and stay impersonal.

"Yeah, on I Street, but I live in the area. How about you?" he said between bites, taking time to swallow before talking.

"Same, although where I work changes."

Sebastian's eyebrows rose in what she assumed was a question, a little "hmm?" from behind his lips as he chewed, confirming her suspicion.

"I'm a substitute teacher. I go where the District needs me." Farren shrugged. It wasn't weird for her, though she supposed some people wanted stability, knowing exactly how long their commute would be on any given day, with a routine keeping them on track. Sometimes she thought it might be nice. Mostly, she enjoyed seeing new faces, and the challenge of a different school subject outweighed the comfort of routine.

"Wow, working with kids seems like it would be a lot," he said, most of his meal devoured, leaving only the last few sips of coffee.

"It can be. I'm doing kindergarten at the moment. Today was

actually my first day with that class. The kids were a riot, but so tiring. I've never seen so much energy in one room. There *has* to be caffeine in their Uncrustables or something. It's not where I'd hoped to be placed. Middle school seemed like the safest bet, but there was a last-minute emergency with one of the teachers, and she knew of me through a friend, so I was requested." Farren knew she was babbling, her excitement spilling over as she spoke. She genuinely enjoyed the kids today, so sweet, so young, so many voices talking over each other.

"Why substitution? Why not teach full-time?" he asked, making her pause. It'd been ages since someone asked about her career beyond the perfunctory opening questions. Everyone she spent time with or spoke with was generally within her friend group and knew her propensity for yearning... she supposed— her inability to stay still when there was so much more out there to explore.

No one within the school system asked because it was sort of a personal question in a way, and they were just happy she was there to help in a pinch. Sebastian, on the other hand, didn't seem to have a sense of boundaries, even here.

He must have seen her bristle at the question because he jumped in quickly with, "Not that there's anything wrong with substitute teachers."

It was a poor attempt at editing what he'd already said, but Farren chose to believe good intent when it came to most people. She was sure the question wasn't meant to be rude.

"I like the variety. Plus, I don't have a proper teaching degree, only an Associate's degree. So there's that," she said, waving her hand in a dismissive gesture, even though she felt insecure telling him. He probably had a serious degree. Men of his age, dressed in "business casual," usually did. It wasn't like it used to be in her parents' generation where experience was enough to go by.

These days, in this city, in this *economy*, a degree of some sort was a must for all entry-level positions unless she wanted to work in retail, food service, or jobs even more thankless. Again.

He nodded in understanding.

"I'll take the red tiles this time, maybe that's the key to winning," he said, a small smile carving itself into his cheeks, and her spiral of self-doubt was cut off almost immediately.

He let her place her token first. They danced around each other again, watching the other closely to try and figure out the next move. Sebastian learned quickly, and it seemed like he tried to use more foresight this time... Which worked because he won the second game, despite Farren giving it a good go.

She couldn't help being distracted by him and the way he rolled up the sleeves on his button up so they bunched just above the elbows resting on the table, his chin in his palm as he leaned forward. A few small muscles in his forearm jumped as he moved, and it was strange how something so small could be entrancing.

"One each. Are you ready for the last game?" Sebastian asked, his face more relaxed, the tension in his body less evident as each minute went by. His good humor was aided by him winning the second game. The light was back in his eyes. And Farren wanted it to stay. She wanted it to be there again next week, so there was only one thing for it.

Farren had to get serious.

"You're on!"

They both leaned over the little table, practically glaring down at the grid, occasionally looking up at the other to try and gauge where this was going to go. The perfect game of cat and mouse—exhilarating. Farren loved playing games, loved the adrenaline rush that came with wanting to win and trying your best to do so. She also loved victory, and making new friends.

They didn't speak, didn't do anything but focus on the game, and those ten minutes passed incredibly quickly. Sebastian's scent tickled her nose, the lingering notes of deodorant or body wash, or simply him. As distracting as it was—as delicious as it was—Farren stayed on her task, the game ending with no one winning. At least not outright. Farren didn't have the heart to tell him that the person to set up a stalemate was technically the winner. She wanted it to feel fair. They'd both focused so hard on sabotaging the other, neither set up for a clear win.

Sebastian chuckled at the useless result with a slight shake of his head.

"I—I'll give you the pastry," Farren said in a near whisper, reluctant but she knew he needed it more than her. Playing with him had been worth it, even if she never saw him again.

His eyes widened, and although he shook his head, she could see him seriously considering it. "One more round, please?"

"Fine, since you asked so nicely. I can't believe you're risking your precious pastry," Farren teased.

"You set the terms; I intend to honor them. Now, pick your color!" It was said without much heat, a smile off-setting the command.

This time, they took their time and chatted a little throughout. Farren shared she was one of seven kids, smack dab in the middle. Sebastian responded that he was an only child. Neither of them skimmed too far beneath the surface. Farren didn't tell him how she'd always felt a little invisible in a big family, she didn't tell him that was why she loved game night so much and the friends she'd gotten to choose... the ones who saw her.

Was his family like hers, or did being the only child mean a sharp spotlight? It wasn't something she'd ever considered. Farren loved her siblings. Even if they were all so different, a life without them fell outside the scope of her imagination. The unbidden thought of her sister sprang to mind, those fraught days when Lindsay had been sick as a child, and Farren fought an unexpected shiver. Best not to think about the past. Lindsay was fine now.

The night outside spread toward them, black, inky darkness swallowing the edges of the trees and buildings. Light pooling under street lamps and spilling from buildings gave some relief from the shadows. The stars weren't as visible here, not the way they were where she grew up, and sometimes she missed them. Like she did right now.

This last game had the least heat out of all of them, and Farren got to enjoy the journey, trying to balance setting up her own victory with preventing his. It was a misstep on Sebastian's part that handed her the win. He seemed disappointed but gave a little half grin as he accepted his fate.

"So, that's it then," he said, shrugging.

"We could keep going if you'd like, best out of five?" Farren offered sincerely.

"No, no. I'll accept my loss," he said with reluctance. Was he used to losing, or did this chafe more than he let on? "But next week, I *will* beat you!"

"I look forward to it," she said, giving him a smile before something occurred to her.

She reached into her purse, rooting around for a pen. Farren wrote her name and number on the outside of the wax paper bag holding the croissant, careful not to crush the pastry.

"Here." She held out the bag to him.

"But, that's not what we agreed?" He seemed to be warring with taking what he wanted from her and keeping his word.

"Really, it's okay. You earned it. It clearly meant a lot to you." Farren urged him to accept it by reaching the bag further out toward him. His large hand wrapped around the bottom of the bag, a light grip to keep from smushing it. "But I'm expecting you to keep to the other part of the deal." She tried to sound stern.

He gave her a solemn nod.

"It starts at seven, same place next Friday. If something comes up or if you have any questions, you have my number." Farren pointed at the black ink on the bag, and Sebastian inspected it in his hand.

"I guess I'll see you around, then?" he asked as he stepped down from the stool, looking between Farren and the door.

"Sounds good."

Sebastian started toward the door, no more than two steps away when Farren spoke again, unable to let go of the stolen moment with him. It seemed to suck the world out and leave her in a bubble of competition, excitement, and the faint, familiar scent of the woods.

"Hey, Sebastian!" It wasn't quite a shout, but enough to draw his attention back to her. "It was nice meeting you."

He seemed to glitch, his eyes blinking as if he had trouble computing what she'd said. "It was nice meeting you too, Farren. I'll see you Friday." His smile was brighter than she'd seen it all night, plush lips stretching over white teeth, and her answering one stretched her cheeks.

He gave a little wave and then escaped into the evening, walking by the cafe with one last look through the window before he disappeared from view.

Farren made her way back to the line at the register in a little bit of a daze, hunger slowly seeping into the cotton wool fuzz that was her brain. She stepped up to the counter when it was her turn, placing an order for a Monte Cristo after how delicious it looked in Sebastian's hand, and another hot chocolate.

She rejoined her friends at their table, order number in hand, and when she sat down, four sets of eyes turned to her with unspoken questions.

Corinne, predictably, was the first to launch into questioning.

"So?" she asked, dragging out the vowel, punctuating it with a raised eyebrow and a gleeful glint to her eye.

"So, his name is Sebastian," Farren said, still trying to absorb everything that had happened. In the last few years of gaming, of meeting new people in this very cafe, she'd never been as off-balance as right in this moment.

"And?" Luis joined in.

"And he's kind of nice." A server placed her hot chocolate in front of her, and Farren took a sip that seared the front edge of her tongue.

"When do you see him again?" Braxton asked.

"Next Friday, at game night." The words came out a little jumbled, each syllable tripping over the last as she rushed through the answer. They must have been able to make it out though because the table erupted into an excited little whoop and a bunch of follow up questions.

Farren answered, her mind only partially engaged in what was happening around her.

The smile he gave her as he was leaving didn't make her feel like he was opposed to their deal; for someone who lost, he seemed way more chipper than when they first met.

Her friends finished out the games for the night, and Farren lost every single one, but somehow, she didn't mind. She was already looking forward to the next game night. Corinne tried to pump her for more information, but she'd divulged mostly everything she knew—the relevant parts, of course.

Farren didn't mention how his scent clung to her memory, something she knew she'd be thinking about for a while even if this went nowhere. Even if she saw him next week and then never again. Somehow, she knew his aroma would be hard to forget. She neglected to mention how tethered she felt when he looked at her like he was paying attention, as if he *saw* her.

Farren kept those close to the chest. Later that night, in the comfort of her apartment with the window unit rattling on low, she stared up at the shadowy ceiling waiting for sleep which refused to come. Her phone buzzed, dancing across her bedspread, and when his text came through:

Hi. It's Ian.

Sebastian.

Just checking the number works.

...she kept that to herself as well.

Sebastian

Sebastian definitely didn't "wait up" for her text that night, he was just up late folding laundry. Nor did he feel a frisson of something in his chest when she did respond. Those few black words on the brightly lit phone screen didn't mean anything.

Neither did the few that came his way the next day, and he especially didn't smile or laugh when she sent him silly memes and TikTok videos, appalled when she heard he'd never ventured over to the "clock app." In Sebastian's mind, it was for teenagers, the youths, the Gen-Z'ers who seemed to discover some facet of 90's culture every week as if it were something new.

No, he was stoic. Sebastian was a paragon of indifference.

He had to be, at least outwardly, because he was uneasy about how quickly she'd managed to worm herself into his day with her text messages. It was alarming how dread no longer slapped him in the face whenever his phone beeped—expecting nothing but work. Instead, he hoped it was something from her, something to look forward to. Sebastian held onto the little semblance of control he had left. He tried to wait a while before responding. It wasn't especially hard to do given how inundated he was with work, but it was difficult not to feel bad about it.

In the evening, when his computer screen went dark and all

that awaited him was dinner and sleep—it was harder to ignore the need to respond immediately, to not get lost in the gray and blue bubbles popping up between them on the chat screen. It was all surface-level stuff, but still way too much, way more than he'd bargained for.

Sebastian hadn't entertained this possibility. In all his careful planning and working toward what he wanted—it never occurred to him someone like her might derail all that. When he swore off attachments after the betrayal last time, he vowed not to let himself get carried away again. He worried about what awaited Friday night.

It was silly to expect it to be like the week before, just the two of them amped up on a game and the stakes enough to keep him invested. This time, he'd be in a group—all Farren's friends, in their comfort zone—with him the odd one out. He'd have to make small talk. The insecure part of him, the part he carted along with him since childhood, dictated he'd have to make them like him. He had to make *her* like him.

Even though he didn't have time for it.

Even though this was the exact opposite of what he was supposed to be focused on.

So, he lied. To himself mostly. He told himself he was only going there to defend his honor; Sebastian wasn't a man who lost often and never took it well. In a way, it was accurate. It did sting, losing to her. But somehow, it was easier that it was to her and not someone else.

His competitive streak would have to be enough to see him through another night. Sebastian couldn't deny he'd been more relaxed leaving game night than any other that week. He'd slept well without having to exhaust himself first.

But as the week dragged on, more and more work got piled onto his plate, until the threat of having to work late or come in on the weekend appeared more likely. His supervisor called them into their daily meeting, reaming them out, reiterating how the contract hung in the balance and it took precedence.

"The client comes first" should have been emblazoned on the front of the building instead of the company name. It was a creed, a lifestyle they'd all signed up for. For the most part, it would have annoyed him a little bit, but Sebastian would do it without questions asked. He had vowed to put work first, to avenge his reputation.

But on Friday, when his boss informed him no one would be leaving until the project was sufficiently handled, it irked Sebastian more than usual. Somehow, over the course of the last week, over the numerous text messages they'd exchanged... he'd gotten excited.

Something in his stomach gave a sour curl, displeased at having to bow out. Canceling made it seem like he was going back on his word. Sebastian didn't like that one bit. His intent after he left Ohio was clear. It wasn't a new concept, and it would continue that way. He'd already seen his work derailed once, so dedication to seeing it through this time was paramount. It hadn't chafed too much until now.

He pulled out his phone after the meeting. The little clock in the corner of the screen lit up with four-thirty in the afternoon, less than an hour until he usually would have gotten off work— less than an hour's notice from his boss to say they would all be staying late.

Pathetic.

Unacceptable.

Unavoidable.

Sebastian pulled up their chat, fingers hovering over the phone keyboard as he thought of what to say, of how to keep her from being disappointed in him.

When he accepted there was no avoiding it, he sent the message.

> Hi Farren. We just got told we all have to stay late. There's a massive project and the government is on our asses. I'm really sorry to have to miss out on tonight.

Her response came less than five minutes later. His chest was incredibly tight, and it took everything in him to check the message when he wanted to bury his head in work, and forget all about his brush with her.

> I get it. You just don't want to lose to me again

Sebastian couldn't contain the chuckle bursting from his lips at her text. So sassy, so upbeat. Farren seemed like everything Sebastian wasn't. And he found he very much wanted to see her again, to bask in her smile in person. Because as much as he hated to admit it, the hour with her—or however long it was— had been the lightest Sebastian felt in years.

> Let me make it up to you.

He sent it before he could rethink and talk himself out of it. Logically, it was a bad idea. Farren would be nothing but a distraction, eating away at what precious little time he had. The pace in his field was relentless. Somehow, they'd all consumed the same lie: there would be plenty of jobs waiting in the IT field after college. People like him flooded the market, developers angling for their shot. Developers like Ashl—No. He wouldn't think about her.

If he wanted to progress, he had to be sure to stand out, to focus.

She'd make your time worthwhile. The thought came unbidden, and a little unwelcome, but it wasn't wrong.

So, as he sat there, eyes bleary and stomach growling its

displeasure at not being fed for over six hours... Sebastian put some thought into how exactly he intended to make it up to her. He barely ventured out into the city in the time he'd lived here. Trendy restaurants and fun activities were low on his list of priorities, and a flare of panic bubbled in his chest at the prospect of making a mistake.

He already felt like he'd failed her by not keeping to his end of the bargain; he couldn't afford to fuck this up as well.

By seven-thirty, most of the work was done, and his coworkers all looked decidedly peevish at the intrusion into their weekend. For the first time since he'd gotten this job, Sebastian commiserated wholeheartedly. They wrapped it all up by eight, Andrew thanking them for their time and work, promising overtime pay Sebastian knew was unlikely.

Salaried employees rarely had that luxury. Full-time meant forty hours—minimum. Their bosses promised floating holidays to compensate, or offered workers the opportunity to put it toward their P.T.O., but rarely—if ever—did they see overtime pay. The only time Sebastian could remember was when the shifts were grossly over, or he worked a holiday.

He tried to ignore the bitterness welling within him. It was almost the end of their agreement with the government, suspense date looming; things should theoretically calm down once it passed. All he needed to do was keep his head down and grind a tiny bit longer, then he could entertain the possibility of whatever this was he felt toward Farren. It was still a fledgling flame in his chest, nothing concrete, nothing more than a slight breathlessness and an uneasy coil in his stomach. In other circumstances, it might have come across as anxiety, but it was accompanied by joy, so he allowed it.

Sebastian trudged out of work, the Metro stops and his brief walk to the apartment passing in a blur. Night claimed the city, streetlights and some overeager fall enthusiast's Halloween lights lit his walk home. People mulled about on the sidewalks, conversing, deciding the rest of their weekend plans. The emptiness of his own brief reprieve from work loomed ahead.

As soon as we meet the suspense date and the SLA is over, it's vacation time—no ifs or buts. For the first time in a while, Sebastian's 'inner monologue' was something he agreed with. It had been so long since he'd gotten a break from work. Maybe he would come back refreshed, ready to jump back in and claim the job he'd been working towards.

He got Nando's delivered through Uber Eats, and the slightly spicy scent of Portuguese-style grilled chicken filled the apartment. The roll was pillowy as he bit into it, the perfect amount of char on the mild meat. He finished it off with a pasteis de nata —cinnamon custard and flaky layers lingering on his tongue long after he'd savored it. Some inoffensive TV show played off the cable he needed to stop paying for, and Sebastian searched for ideas on how and when he could see Farren again. She hadn't responded to his text yet, probably already at game night and absorbed by her peers, but Sebastian hoped.

And he'd always given in to the saying that by failing to prepare, you prepare to fail. So he would have a plan ready. He'd have multiple ideas ready and take the time to get to know Farren better so he made it worth her while.

When she did respond, it was much later. Sebastian lay in bed staring at the static gray on the ceiling as his eyes tried to adjust to the dark room. He'd showered, tried watching more television, but his mind just wouldn't shut down. Usually, it would have been work related, everything yet to come or, worse still, things he'd done wrong that day. Tonight, his mind was on her, regretting not being able to join her, trying to brainstorm ways to see her again.

Logically, he knew he could try and swing by the next game night, but there was no guarantee he wouldn't be working late again. He didn't want to set an unrealistic expectation and disappoint her all over again. So, Sebastian hoped she had some free time within the next two days. It was the only uninterrupted time Sebastian could be sure of, and even then, there was a niggle of doubt.

I'm listening.

She'd texted, letting him know she was open to hearing him out, or possibly seeing him again.

We're in the middle of a big deadline right now. Guaranteeing work nights is going to be difficult. But I'm free this Saturday and Sunday. If you're available, I could take you out somewhere?

Nerves ate up his chest, building up like soap bubbles under a harsh spray of hot water. It fizzed inside him as he waited for Farren's response. He set his phone on the bed beside him, face down, to avoid refreshing the chat every couple of seconds. It was silly. It was juvenile. Sebastian never wasted too much time on this inane back-and-forth. There'd been a few hookups in college when his acquaintances dragged him out to events on Greek row. Surface-level. Encounters which only left him feeling guilty after because they didn't mean anything to him besides physical release, but he hated the thought of hurting someone else in the process. When he'd opened himself up last year, his fledgling attraction cost him everything he worked for. It drove him away from Ohio and away from the vulnerability of a relationship.

Isolation was comfortable, if lonely, but an existence he was accustomed to. It was easy enough to ignore during the day when work took up all the mental space he had available.

He worried his thumb and forefinger together, rubbing them along each other in an attempt to have the physical sensation quiet the anxiety running amok inside him.

It was the longest five minutes ever waiting for his phone to buzz on the bed beside him.

I could move some things around. Tomorrow?

It bubbled up his chest, effervescent happiness spilling over the low simmer of anxiety, and it came out as a surprised laugh, astonished at his luck. Or her grace. Either option was more than he deserved.

Works for me. One question for you…

The urge to try to make this perfect for her was overwhelming, but Sebastian knew how he could get it. Knew his need for control, his stupid rigidity, could get in the way.

Yes?

He tried to fight his programming.

Would you like to chat about it this evening and figure something out together? Or do you want me to cook something up myself?

Please choose option one. Pleeease choose option one.

Since you owe me, let's make this interesting. Surprise me. Just tell me where and when. I promise not to Google what it is.

Fuck.

Of course, she'd want the more challenging option out of the two. Sebastian hadn't gone on a date, an actual honest-to-good-ness first date in over a year, and it'd usually been dinner and a movie. Somehow, he doubted that would cut it this time. Besides, sitting in a darkened movie theater always felt fraught with tension, not close enough to take advantage of the shadowy intimacy, but still super aware of the person beside you.

Farren probably wouldn't mind the movies. She seemed like a fun-loving woman, but it was basic, even for him.

He pulled up his search bar again, relying on the internet to impart something. Anything. His mind raced with all the potential pitfalls: did she have food aversions, did she drink?

She was competitive, he knew that much. She enjoyed board games. But Sebastian was garbage at it. Gaming was her world, something she was far more versed to show him. Perhaps something in a similar vein?

He stumbled across something he thought was low-key enough to be able to talk, but still included an activity to keep them occupied in case his conversation skills absolutely failed him.

Sebastian texted her the address and the time. Five PM. It was plenty of opportunity for her to change her mind if she desired. Enough time to practice getting his foot out of his mouth before he saw her again. He could run some errands; not that he had many, but the fridge was pretty bare.

It would give him time to tidy the little mess he made tonight, on the slim likelihood they might wander back here. It would also be a chance for him to start the car and ensure it was in running condition so he wasn't just relying on the Metro.

Farren sent along her assent and a silly GIF of a cat putting on sunglasses with the text "I'm ready" following soon after.

It made him laugh, a little bit of those nerves dissolving with the plan in action, diminishing because he knew how he would pass the time between now and then. Sleep claimed him after he sent Farren a goodnight text, deflating, stress seeping from his muscles.

Sebastian woke to a sunny day, no pressing work emails, and that tiny buzz of excitement he slowly realized belonged only to her. He took the car for an oil change and had them check the battery since he didn't do much but start and run it weekly. He even sprung for a car wash. There was a particular kid-like enjoyment at the large brushes scrubbing up along the car's sides, the suds accumulating on the windshield, frothy and sweet-smelling.

Grocery shopping came next. When he got back, he ran a mop with diluted Pine Sol over the floor until it was pristine and the room held the fine scent of the forest. By the time he'd finished—showered, dressed and sitting on the sofa bouncing his knee—it was a little after four PM and about time for him to head out. She'd been quiet all day, but he sent over a text, letting her know he was getting ready to leave.

Farren responded with a "see you soon," and he took a few deep breaths before he started the car and headed out toward Penn Square. Sebastian got there embarrassingly early, sitting in the parking garage for ten minutes before going inside. Once there, he wondered if he should have worn something else.

He knew what the place offered, knew what they served, but somehow it eluded him to check what it looked like. He was in jeans at least. Dark jeans with a button up. And dress shoes. Stupid. Stupid. Who wears dress shoes to a casual date?

Skyward, the ping pong place he'd chosen, had definite warehouse-vibes. Not in a bad way. In a shouldn't-have-dressed-up-this-much kind of way. He had no time to think it to death because he had to grab a table for them before she got there. It wasn't too long after his own arrival, and she looked freaking gorgeous.

Her cheeks were pink, as if she'd been out walking, her dark blonde hair slightly windswept from the thick braid coiling its way over her shoulder. She wore jeans, the fabric hugging the thick curve of her thighs, sneakers, and a pretty shirt. A sweater or cardigan of some kind was draped over her bag at her side. When he caught her eye, Sebastian was awarded with a huge smile, and before he even thought about it, before it could be anything other than voluntary, his cheeks stretched in an answering smile.

"Hi!" she said, a little breathless, once she'd made her way over to the table. Farren lifted onto her toes and wrapped her arms around his neck in a quick hug. Sebastian had enough time to snake an arm around her waist, give the briefest squeeze, and was assailed by the sweet spice of her shampoo before she stepped back.

"Hey. I'm really glad you could make it," Sebastian said, and although it was generic, he very much meant it.

"I'm glad you reached out. You missed out on a good game night, but I get it. Luis used to work as a SharePoint contractor for the Army before he pivoted into teaching, and it used to drive Corinne crazy." The names meant nothing to him; perhaps if he'd made it over there last night, they would have.

She seemed to realize it not long afterwards because she jumped in to clarify. "Corinne was the friend in line with me at the cafe last week. Her husband is Luis."

He could picture dark hair, the vague impression of her during the silent exchange Farren had with her in line, but that was it. Sebastian nodded and smiled though, relieved she wasn't too put out by his last-minute cancellation.

They sat, the table between them, and a server came over shortly to give them both menus and glasses of water. Upon second inspection, Skyward looked almost hipster-y. The place was distressed brick and dark metal, artwork and music adding a level to the atmosphere in a way that kept it from feeling run down or overly cavernous.

"So, ping pong?" she asked after they'd both taken a sip of water and pretended to look at the menu.

"You told me to surprise you," he said, trying not to have it sound defensive.

"You did good." The words washed over him, and Sebastian was a little uncomfortable to realize how much her praise meant to him.

It's because you so desperately want validation from work. That's all. You're like a plant left out in the elements for too long without a drop of rain. Desperate. At least that's what he told himself, and it wasn't wrong. Not really.

"I figured since you like games, and seem fairly competitive, it might be a good way to hang out without it being too redundant—given I missed last night."

"I'll never say no to another day of playing board games, but this is a good change. Hopefully you didn't bring me here to decimate me with your table tennis skills?" He knew it was teasing, and he smiled.

"Nope," he said, enunciating the "P" so it popped when he said it. "I haven't touched a paddle since I was a freshman in high school at a friend's basement birthday party."

"Well, then I might have some more experience. Or at least some more *recent* experience. One of my brothers got a table when he moved out after college. So, it's been this decade at least." Farren's laugh was warm, soothing the last of the nerves bouncing around inside him. Her brown eyes were alight, face open and happy. Something within seemed to give way, melting under her warmth.

"I remember you saying you were one of seven. Seems like a lot to deal with in one house." Sebastian found himself wanting to know more about her, more about where she came from.

"Heaven help my mother. They still live on the land we grew up on—a couple of acres outside a small New England town. When I came along, my mom was already drowning in kids. But they're Catholic, so..." Farren shrugged as if it explained everything. Sebastian couldn't relate. His parents were older, born on the tail-end of boomers, and very much flower children in their youth. Religion wasn't ever prominent in their household.

"My folks are still out in Ohio. Like I mentioned last week, it was only the three of us growing up. They hadn't really planned on kids, especially not since my mom was nearly forty by the time she had me, but oh well." It wasn't ideal, for any of them.

His parents were often caught up in their own world, Sebastian feeling like an outsider, so different from them and what they wanted for him. Where they flowed free, he was rigid. Where they occupied themselves with fleeting moments, Sebastian kept his gaze turned forward on his aspirations.

"Do you visit them often?" she asked, and part of him wished she could take it back. There never was an easy way to answer it. To tell her he'd avoided home for ages. They didn't like to wander over to the city, content with their little slice of perfect impermanence, and Sebastian had to work. All the time now.

Without religion, there was little need for Christmas. His parents didn't adhere to the national decree that families had to spend Thanksgiving together, always quick to point out it was a colonialist holiday erasing the suffering the invaders wrought on the native population at the time.

Anyone who met his parents would probably have loved them, called them woke or whatever the word was these days for people that actually cared about others. He carried those values with him, but it was a quiet belief. Where they protested loudly, Sebastian merely boycotted. Liberal but not loud about it. His tangent ran a little too long in his mind, and Farren tilted her head as she waited for his response, a little amused smile on her face as if she could tell he'd been overthinking her question.

"No, it's uh… it's been a while. You?" He cleared his throat uncomfortably, taking a swig of ice water to drown down the guilt sitting on his vocal cords.

"Not really. Most of my family stuck around the area, and my youngest sibling still lives at home, but I kind of wandered over this way and don't go back except for the holidays."

"What brought you over this way? It seems a decent distance from wherever you grew up in New England." He couldn't talk though, since Ohio was probably just as far.

Her cheeks pinked up, the tips of her ears that he could see peeking through her hair doing the same. The red flushed out some of her freckles, and his curiosity piqued at her response.

"I uh—" She swallowed and rolled her eyes. "I followed a guy out here. Not that it lasted very long. But I'd met Corinne in the meantime, and she convinced me to make the city my own. So, I stayed. It's been almost five years now."

"You and Corinne obviously remained close, even if the guy didn't work out."

"Yeah, she's my best friend. I've crashed on her couch too many times to count, and I'm her daughter's godmother… which pissed off her mother-in-law, but that wasn't hard to do." Farren laughed at the statement, and Sebastian remembered bits of their conversation in line, her friend complaining about her mother-in-law.

"Sounds nice though, having people." Sebastian didn't think before he said it, but should have because her expression let him know she'd noticed something in it. Her mouth drew together in concern, her lips thinning slightly.

"Do you?" she started, worrying her lip between her teeth for a second before she added, "Have people, I mean?"

And what could he say? How could he explain it was just him, his bitterness, work, and little else?

He shrugged, his mouth twisting into a little rueful smile.

"Sebastian..." So much wrapped into his name, so much he wanted to avoid, even more he yearned to unpack. The way she said his name, the way it did things to him.

It had been ages since someone called him that; his mom still did in phone calls, but no one outside of Ohio knew him as anything other than Ian. He still didn't understand why he'd volunteered it that day, or why it wound something up inside him that felt spring-loaded when it left her lips.

The server saved him from having to answer the question in her eyes. They both placed their pizza orders, the moment gone —thankfully.

But it made him wonder what it would be like to have "people?" What it would be like if *she* was his person?

Farren

arren couldn't deny she'd been disappointed on Friday. Not in him. Not really. But when the text came through, letting her know he wouldn't make it to game night, some spark of excitement for the evening dimmed. She tried to tell herself it didn't matter. It was better this way. Farren tended to jump into things too quickly—and out again with just as much speed. Perhaps this time, she'd spare herself the little heartache and they'd leave it at a great evening between strangers, a fun story for the future.

Then Sebastian sent a message asking to make it up to her, and it took a few hours to decide what the heck to do. Because she wanted it. Because it was a little scary wanting something. Although Farren had a habit of getting ensconced in things, flitting between them like a butterfly before her wings could be plucked... somehow, she knew this wouldn't be as easy to disentangle herself from if it went south.

She was getting older. Her friends were all mostly settled. All her older siblings were as well. Even Toby, her younger brother —the one she'd been closest to growing up—was engaged to someone from their hometown. A girl Farren could only picture with braces and muddy brown hair, the way she'd looked when she lived with her parents.

Farren existed between these little spots where she found a

temporary home before moving along. But she couldn't outrun time. It raced toward her with relentless fervor and Sebastian—

Well, everything about Sebastian screamed serious. At least from their first encounter. He seemed to dance along a thin edge, the same graceless walk she'd seen others in this city make. It was bleary eyes, early mornings, and days stretching so long, they gnawed into souls. He had that twinge to him, lonely and whittled down.

And fuck if Farren didn't respond to it.

Her stupid inner monologue refused to shut up about the idea of him more and more as the week progressed. Every message flickering across her screen pulled her deeper into the hole she was digging. Farren found out he was actually pretty funny. Sweet too.

So, although it took her a few hours to shut the rational part of her brain up, she did finally say yes to him. Her sneakers slapped against the sidewalk as she walked the distance from the Metro stop, whispering to herself how stupid it was, how she should have gotten an Uber. Now she was going to show up flushed and sweaty. It did nothing for the nerves skittering under her skin, an irritation that wouldn't abate.

He was there when she arrived, looking cool and collected compared to her frazzled mess. Unfairly good looking, his eyes crinkled at the corners when he smiled at her, and *god,* something in her stomach flipped right over. She'd been surprised when she saw the sign outside, more so when she stepped inside, given how Sebastian didn't seem like the type for ping pong—or the purposefully distressed and eccentric energy of the space. He was tight-laced, removed from trends and the stream of society pushing people along. No way was he a hipster.

They delved a little deeper, scratching the surface of what she realized was probably a touchy subject for both of them:

family. Farren couldn't forget the look he got on his face when she asked about who he had to look out for him. Or the relief sagging across his body when the server interrupted to take their order and he didn't have to answer.

She tucked it away for later, scavenging for little bits of him to keep.

They ate their pizza and conversed easily about inconsequential things, but it lightened her spirits, nonetheless. Sebastian seemed to relax more and more as time went on, and she realized he must have been nervous about this as well, though perhaps not for the same reasons.

Farren was scared of falling.

If she said something to put him off, or they turned out incompatible... well those were easier to deal with compared to the threat of wanting to let him in. She was friendly, approachable in an easy way. Only her close friends knew how surface-level it all was. Even after years, Corinne still examined her with an inscrutable look on her face sometimes, as if trying to piece together why Farren was the way she was. After this long, she'd learned not to ask.

Farren didn't dwell. So what if she had trouble staying grounded? So what if her last relationship ended because he wanted to meet her family and she realized he was in so much deeper than she would probably ever be?

But Sebastian cracked jokes, dove for the tiny white ball with all intent of winning despite them both playing abysmally, and it was endearing. He was so clearly outside his comfort zone for her, and Farren wasn't immune. No matter how much the part of her that valued self-preservation wanted her to be.

They both took turns losing, though it had little to do with skill this time, and her sides ached with laughter by the time they decided to take a break. He'd unbuttoned the top of his shirt, his hair a little mussed from playing, and it was damn sexy in a repressed kind of way. It reminded her of the historical romances she used to read as a teenager, going through her Keira Knightley/Pride and Prejudice phase—where the mere mention of a bare ankle or soaked shirt would practically send the characters into vapors.

So, her cheeks were a little hot at the image of him disheveled, and she tried to ignore why. She wondered how much messier she could get his hair if she ran her hands through it while they kissed.

When he rolled his sleeves up over his forearms, it became a little ridiculous. There was no reason such an innocuous action should entice her. Again, she wondered at how he managed to look so strong when she knew he worked a desk job. He didn't say a word about the gym, and most guys would have been all over that. Then again, Sebastian wasn't like the guys she usually found herself with.

Farren attracted disasters. As a disaster herself, she recognized the signs. Disasters were easier to step away from, simple. When you dated guys who were bigger messes than you were, you could content yourself with knowing you were "good for them" and you left them slightly better off than when you found them.

Like with Travis, who she followed from New Hampshire to Jersey (because living in New York City was too expensive but he had big dreams of making it as an actor.) At twenty, she'd been starry-eyed enough for both of them. Farren spent those few months bolstering his confidence, his biggest cheerleader. It worked until it didn't. The haze faded. Farren realized she hated living with four other people in a six-story walk-up and having her boyfriend out most evenings and weekends.

Then there was Aarón. When she broke up with Travis, she'd needed a place to live. Aarón had one. His apartment was listed on Craigslist (back when it was dodgy but still got used), and she just wanted out. The two of them danced around each other for quite a while. They made it almost a year once they were official, including a move to D.C. for his work before they couldn't cut it anymore.

His family wanted more for him, and he succumbed under that pressure. At twenty-two, she wasn't ready. So, she bowed out.

There'd been more scrapes over the years. This past year was the driest of the lot. Maybe she was growing up. Maybe her disaster magnet broke. She could only hope because she couldn't afford another mess, but Farren wasn't sure she was ready for the real thing either.

Sebastian asked whether he could get her a drink, and this time, she opted for something alcoholic. The man had her flustered and reminiscing about her crappy love life. She needed something more substantial to dull the edge of her thoughts. He joined her; the copper cup of his Mule frosted with condensation. She opted for a daiquiri. Sweeter drinks were always her preference.

They were two drinks in, sitting at one of the booth tables, and she could see the sun doing its lazy stretch over the horizon through the windows. Her tongue felt loose enough to get her into trouble, and she didn't bother trying to filter herself.

"So, is this a date?" Farren asked, strawberry-tinged alcohol warming her chest.

Sebastian choked on his sip, recovering quickly to give her a quizzical look, considering her question before answering.

"Yes. Yes, I hope it is."

His answer surprised her a little. A shiver shot up through her body, icy drink in hand and the fist of desire settling low in her abdomen.

"You're single then?" It sounded stupid, should have been

redundant. Farren hoped someone in a relationship wouldn't be taking her out on dates. But she'd been bitten before.

"Yes. You?" He took another sip of his drink, and for once, Farren wondered what he'd look like under the beard. Would his cheeks be as flushed as hers probably were?

"Yeah."

Play it cool, Farren. Don't shoot your mouth off.

"It's been a while," she said.

Fuck. Fuck. Fuck! Why did she go and admit that? Now she looked all pathetic and weird. Little anecdotes from others— voices from her past—floated into her head, berating her for making herself seem too available, too desperate, too lonely. Small town boys could be really cruel. Between being fat and a blonde, it was like she was a walking target for sharp remarks about laziness and stupidity. She cursed herself for not being able to act more aloof, for always being too quick on the draw.

"For me too," he said, and it disarmed her, having him reciprocate something like that. She only said it because her mouth was quicker than her brain, but he had time to think it through before responding.

"How come?" It was prying, it was perhaps a little too intrusive. It came across almost like an interview question, the one where they asked you why you left your last job or to explain the gap in employment on your resume. But curiosity won out over propriety.

He grimaced slightly, and Farren jumped back in to ease his discomfort.

"You don't have to answer anything. I'm too nosy for my own good." She chuckled at herself, and it seemed enough to make him smile, if only slightly.

"Work, mostly. I've been so consumed with trying to prove myself as a developer, climb the ladder and all that. I haven't really been on a date—a real one—in quite some time. As you've already seen, it can be demanding and takes up a lot of my time." Sebastian shrugged as if it was no big deal, as if he'd accepted his lot long ago. Her heart ached a little at the idea of him feeling like he had to choose.

Before she could say so, before she could jump too far ahead of herself, he turned the question around onto her, and this time, it was Farren's turn to feel blinding panic build up in her chest. What could she say, really?

I'm terrible at choosing the right people. The thought of stopping long enough to get tangled in something real makes me want to dry-heave with anxiety? It was too deep for a first date. Farren hadn't even delved too far into it herself, mollifying herself with the notion it would sort itself out in the end.

"Just hasn't worked out, I guess? So, I stopped trying for a bit. Took a break from online dating, SPANX, and trying to make a good impression." It was mostly true. In the most immediate sense, it was true.

He laughed, his dark chocolate tone spreading heat up from her stomach to her throat. "Glad to know you're not concerned about making a good showing with me. Though I suppose I kind of ruined that when I made the worst first impression possible." Sebastian gave a little groan, shaking his head and running a hand through his hair in a way she suspected was a nervous habit.

"Yeah, I think it would be an understatement to say I wasn't expecting it, or you. But I'm glad. We wouldn't be sitting here otherwise."

"I'm still sorry, though. I shouldn't have... acted the way I did." His gaze was pleading, his lips narrowing into a displeased line. "It was uncalled for, and I'm not usually pushy—or that much of an ass."

He really seemed unhappy, guilty perhaps. How could she

explain it may have riled her in the beginning but playing games with him was the highlight of her night?

"Well, I appreciate you saying so. Even if I don't think it's necessary. I do, however, still expect you to make it to one of the game nights. Since those were the terms we agreed to." It was cheeky, meant to sound teasing, but Farren did mean it. She wanted to see him there, share something she loved with him.

"And I will. I'm a man of my word. Work's making it difficult at the moment." Work again.

"Do you have any hobbies outside of work?" It was supposed to be a harmless question, but his hand tightened around his drink, his lips thinning, and Farren realized she may have upset him by asking.

"Not really. Not at all, if I'm being honest, unless you count Netflix."

"Netflix counts! What do you like to watch?" She leaned forward, elbows on the table, eager to find out more about him.

The conversation continued on for quite a while, though Sebastian switched to water since he'd driven. She learned he liked watching documentaries (not surprising) and movie musicals (definitely unexpected). He blamed it on his parents, saying they were huge music lovers. He grew up on a steady diet of everything from ABBA and the Bee Gees, right through to Joe Cocker and Hendrix. They were a product of the era they grew up in, and he hinted at them being hippies.

Farren shared that her music taste was a mishmash of every season in her life. Like with every other aspect, she'd bounced around different genres. Right now, she was in that "fall feeling" even though it was still sticky and warm during the day, so today had been a Fleetwood Mac kind of day.

They played a few more rounds of ping pong, neither of them improving much by the end of it. They made their way outside, ready to walk in opposite directions—Farren to the

Metro, Sebastian to his car—when his hand shot out to grab hers.

She threaded her fingers through his and looked up at him in question.

"Let me drive you back?"

Don't give him your address on a first date. The careful part of her warned.

Invite him inside when you get home.

Her thoughts warred within her. As usual, the more devious of her natures won out.

She squeezed his hand in hers and smiled, electricity skittering under her ribcage as her heartbeat sped up at the prospect of more time with him.

"Sure."

It wasn't too far, less than a whole block to the parking lot, but he held her hand the entire time, his thumb brushing against the back of her hand in tentative touches. Only letting go once they stood at the car, the rear lights blinking when he unlocked it. It was neat and clean, as expected. Sebastian was consistent. Farren truly believed the night at the cafe was an outlier for him.

Streetlights passed in a blur, his phone mounted to the dash, dark mode lighting the way home. The silence seemed fraught with energy neither was ready to acknowledge, so Farren reached forward to turn on the radio. A faint thrum from the speakers gave her something to focus on besides the proximity of his body to hers. His shoulders were broad, his arm almost touching hers as they sat beside each other, and Farren tried her best to keep her cool.

It wasn't like she hadn't gotten physical with someone quickly before. There were a few one-night-stands in her time. When it felt right, Farren was happy to jump in on the first date. Somehow, she knew Sebastian might not have the same propensity for it. So, she held back, letting him set the pace, because the last thing she wanted was to scare him off by coming on too strong.

For the first time in a long time, insecurity bubbled up inside her. She'd spent years learning to love and accept her body, and she did. It took years to take proper care of herself, instead of trying to punish her body for not looking the way she wanted it to or working the way she wanted it to. Her hypothyroidism threw her off for a long time, influencing her confidence and the way she felt on a daily basis. Farren had come far from the little fat girl who hid behind chunky sweaters and wore T-shirts to the pool.

It rankled now, to have that small part of her pipe up, inching its insidious way into her head. She wondered if he even wanted her in that way. Conversation was great, the vibes were immaculate, but he made no move during their date, nothing besides holding her hand to the car. For the first time since she'd met him, she wondered if maybe she just wasn't his type.

It didn't last; and it genuinely didn't matter. Sebastian didn't determine her worth or her sexiness. If she wasn't for him, then that was his choice and held no bearing on her as a person. But she hoped.

Because she wanted him.

Every repressed, midwestern, shy inch of him.

They pulled up to a spot in front of her building, the inky night interspersed with pools of light from the street lamps. Little rectangles of yellow luminosity threw shapes onto the sidewalk from between curtains people neglected to shut. The hum of the car faded, the slight vibration gone from the seat, and the song playing on the radio was silenced with the turn of his key.

She looked over at him, fighting the nerves in her stomach in order to ask.

"Walk me up?"

Sebastian merely nodded, unfastening his seatbelt and stepping out onto the tar. He walked around the car quickly while Farren gathered her purse, opening the door for her, and fuck if it didn't make her want to jump him right there.

His hand wrapped around hers again, and this time, she noticed the tiniest tremor.

They walked the distance to the door, and it was thankfully too late for her neighbor to be out and about, but the light up Jack-o-Lantern in one of the windows illuminated the main steps. He followed her up the stairs to her apartment. Farren let go briefly to try to fish her keys out of her bag, and she slotted the cold metal into the lock, hesitating before she turned it.

She looked back at Sebastian, and his face was drawn in an expression she couldn't read. It was intense, almost a little intimidating, with his hands fisted at his sides. Farren knew it was now or never.

"Thank you for tonight. I had a really good time." It was barely above a whisper, the staircase around them abandoned, the sound bouncing across the tile, just her door behind her and Sebastian ahead.

"I did too." His voice was deep, a little husky, and he frowned for a moment before he stepped forward, crowding into her space.

The door was cold against her back, Sebastian so close, she could feel the heat radiating off his chest. She clutched her purse for dear life, the other hand reaching out to touch his chest. His heartbeat thrummed a tattoo under the fabric of his shirt, her fingers holding on slightly to pull him down the rest of the way.

It was sweet, brief. The slightest of impressions when his lips pressed against hers, and something in her chest burst free. It seemed to rush through her entire body, nerves and desire mingling until it roiled inside of her. Sebastian didn't seem unaffected, either.

Resting his forehead against hers, not ready to pull away completely, his breath was harsh against her cheek. Farren felt his heart thunder under her hand and risked another touch, reaching up to cup his cheek.

Sebastian looked down at her, seemingly at war with himself, and she wondered which part would win out—the strait-laced man she'd come to expect, or something else entirely.

She was answered by a slight growl. His thick thigh pressed between hers, his arm wrapping around her, the other hand framing her jaw and tangling into her hair. Sebastian's lips claimed hers again. There was the vague realization she must have dropped her purse because her other hand was suddenly free and splayed through his hair just like she'd wanted to earlier.

The scent of cologne filled her nose, those dark and misty notes reminding her of the woods near where she grew up. Sebastian's body braced hers against the door, and *the way he kissed her*, the fervor with which he touched her, left no confusion as to whether he wanted her.

Farren had no idea how long they stood there in the dim landing to her apartment, but by the time he was through, when he finally pulled away and she could see his lips swollen from their kisses... she wanted nothing more than to invite him inside and lose herself in his arms.

His gaze was heavy, drinking in every inch of her, before he leaned back down to pepper some kisses across the column of her neck. Farren was slightly embarrassed at the moan that escaped her throat, a little put out when he pulled back from her, almost panting.

He ran a hand through his thoroughly mussed hair, taking a step away from her.

"Sebastian," she started, the question on the tip of her tongue, the invitation plain.

"Farren." It was almost a plea, interrupting her before she had the chance to get the words out.

She looked up at him—heart in her throat, thighs quivering to keep her upright—her legs leaden and jelly-like as if she'd been running.

"This has been a phenomenal first date." His words were sweet, but they felt like an end to a conversation, not a continuation.

"Sebastian..." She tried again, and this time, he held up a hand, a light chuckle working its way up from his chest.

"Please, I'm trying to keep my head about me here. I have to go, before this gets even harder to walk away from."

Logically, she knew he was right. On paper, it was the smart move. Emotionally, she was a mess. A shaky, lustful mess. He must have seen something on her face because he dared another kiss, one on her forehead this time.

"I want this. I do. I... I don't want to rush into it. But I'd very much like to see you again. Is that okay?" he asked, looking down at her, and something about his expression gave her the impression he was as thrown off as she was—and perhaps even more insecure.

"I'd like that very much. Just... uh, text me. We'll figure something out." Farren's breath shuddered out between her lips, and she licked them absentmindedly, the slight bite of ginger beer somehow still there from his kisses.

"Goodnight," he whispered against her lips, an all-too-short kiss burning against them before he turned back toward the staircase. One last look at her and then he disappeared from view, the faint echo of his feet against the tile overly loud to her ears.

Farren turned to unlock the door, hand shaking, and she thanked her past self for getting the key into the lock earlier because it would have been a mission now. She lifted her purse from the ground, stepped into her apartment, and turned on the light that stung a little too brightly.

The click of the door shutting behind her was final, and Farren made her way over to her couch on weak legs. Sinking into the soft cushion, she exhaled heavily, finally taking a deep breath to try and still the calamity within her, sure of only one thing.

Sebastian wasn't as cool, calm, and collected as he seemed on the outside. The way he'd kissed her... her fingers rose to touch her swollen lips, a shiver going through her at the memory.

Well, he was far more than she'd bargained for.

Sebastian

The drive back to his place was frantic. Between the way his body responded to hers and the images still flashing through his mind, it was a miracle he hadn't run a red light or hit a curb in his haste to get home. It felt like a demand, a heat under the surface that wouldn't abate no matter how much the car growled beneath him. When he got back to his empty apartment with its clean grays, plain and dark, it was hard not to imagine what hers would've looked like if he'd allowed himself to go inside.

Don't kid yourself, her interior design choices were the last thing on your mind.

Sebastian would be thinking about it for a long time... about her and the way her body molded to his in the most delicious way.

She was hilarious, confident, and so alive. Farren Davis was trouble. She threatened the status quo he'd instituted after the disaster that was Ohio and Ashley, and the path he adhered to with strict, unwavering conviction since. Sebastian questioned the yearning to progress—his pressing need for success a little over time, when he was burned out—but it was easy to convince himself the promotion was worth it when it would cement his worth. He wanted out from the shadow of Ohio and his past.

Now that he wanted Farren as well—it could prove a problem.

What was he going to do? How could he keep his composure when she threatened the control he'd worked so hard to hone? It would probably be best to start distancing himself now, to step out gracefully before it got too tricky... before it became hurtful. He could be a good guy and stop misleading her; he could be clear about his priorities before things got too difficult to pull away from, because it would inevitably happen.

Sebastian was married to his work. Being available, sacrificing "play" time was a cornerstone on the way up to the top. He worried about her expectations, the time she was worth and how he would be unable to provide it. He should warn her, back away from her.

But we're not going to do that. His thoughts were as dark as the barely banked desire in his core—tendrils of smoke obscuring the more rational part of his mind.

No, he wasn't going to pull away. Even though he should. Even though he knew it would only complicate matters further if he didn't. Because he'd gotten a taste of what it could be like with her. The laughs, the serenity flooding through him from just holding her hand... the seething want he couldn't shrug off, even now, more than an hour since he left her there in her doorway. Sebastian wasn't ready to let that go.

He took a cold shower to try and shock his system back to baseline. When it didn't work, when he had to touch himself to get rid of the buzz burning under his skin—he couldn't even bring himself to feel embarrassed by his response to the image of her falling apart beneath him. He knew she'd desired him just as much. Farren would have swung the door open to let him inside if he hadn't interrupted her. Instead, he'd run all the way home, afraid of wanting, and getting what he wanted.

Sleep was fitful. Sebastian woke in twisted bedsheets,

covered in a fine sheen of sweat. He checked his phone, disappointed to see no new messages, merely a crapload of work emails. Rational Sebastian was in charge today; in the harsh light of morning, he tucked away the remnants of last night and sat down at his laptop to answer emails. He put in over six hours of work before he stopped to eat, before he dared another look at his phone.

This time, a message waited.

> Thanks again for last night. I had a really good time. xxx

He let it sit for another hour, finally shoveling lunch into his body while watching an episode of something on Netflix, so distracted he could barely register what was happening on-screen. When the feeling inside of him became too much to bear, begging to be unleashed, he finally responded.

> Leaving you last night was the hardest thing I've ever had to do.

He cringed a little at the message, but he'd already pressed send. No amount of fretting could pull it back out of the internet. Her response came seconds later.

> It seemed like leaving wasn't the only thing that was hard. Or was that my imagination?

Sebastian inhaled a little gasp, almost choking on his own damn spit at her sassy message. He envied her, the openness with which she seemed to navigate the world, the way she said what she was thinking. There was once or twice where it seemed like she was shocked by what she herself said, as if the words tumbled right out from her brain with no process or filter.

He didn't know what to say and was hesitant to continue this line of conversation. He was sure it would leave him hard and aching for her again, his mind addled with images of her body, and incapable of impartiality. So, he opted for diversion. She seemed to respond to that last night, to him being self-deprecating or trying to deflect anything deeper than surface-level for his own comfort.

I can neither confirm nor deny. I can only say that you looked gorgeous in that doorway and I can't wait to see you again.

It was true, as much as he wished it wasn't. Maybe he could make it work. Maybe they could keep it casual and he could ease his way into the idea of them.

He pocketed his cell phone and wallet into his sweats, grabbed his house keys, locking up behind him and heading out for a run to clear his mind. Anything to work off some of this pent-up energy which seemed to have doubled between work and her. Sebastian ran until his ribcage rattled with gasping puffs, hands braced on his knees as he tried desperately to catch his breath.

He'd run past the cafe, which only spurred him on further. By the time he stopped, he'd done a fair number of miles. Every step was a little wobbly, the slight burn of his muscles being pushed a little too far past their brink making every move heavier. Sebastian sank down onto a park bench nearby, waiting for his heart to return to a regular rhythm. The trees had the barest hints of fall to them, and he could sense it in the air. D.C.'s summers were unexpectedly humid, and the moisture in the air seemed to have abated somewhat.

Maybe now that the weather's getting better I can run along the Mall and not just the sidewalks around my building? It might be nice to sink into the soft, manicured grass and watch people soak up the city. I never did get around to the whole tourist thing.

But when would he find the time?

Daring a peek at his phone, his hands shook along with his whole body. Farren's response waited.

You let me know when and where.

What could he say? When he had no idea of either. They were gearing up for the end of their suspense date for their SLA and multiple projects they were trying to push through the pipeline before their deadline. Sebastian couldn't guess what waited tomorrow, let alone next weekend. There were two options: he could ask her to be patient and hope she'd understand, but he'd risk the chance of losing her totally. Or, he could try to make it work. Sebastian could attempt to balance these parts of his life and hope he didn't come up wanting.

Unwilling to let her go so soon, unwilling to choose, he ignored the message for now.

He made it through the night, exhausted by his run, only taking the time for dinner and some television before he passed out. Morning came with a sharp ringing alarm and the normal ribbon of dread slithering inside his belly.

Sebastian made it to the office on time, kept his head down, checking and rechecking his work before he submitted it. In their daily meeting, he listed off everything he'd worked on the day before and this one. His boss seemed impressed, applauding him for sacrificing his personal time. Andrew praised the quality of what he'd submitted, reiterating it was only a few more weeks, and if they could all rally the way he had, then their contract would surely be renewed.

"We're down to the wire, folks. I'm spread thin, as I'm sure most of you are as well. In addition to the contract we're trying to keep, we have the opportunity to develop an app for a new client. I'm thinking of having a little friendly competition between my top contenders. Ian, Rachel? What do you say?" Andrew's question was unexpected, but not unwanted.

"I—I'd be honored," Sebastian responded, trying not to look over at Rachel, not to feel the echoes of the last time he was in this situation. Only a different company. A different girl.

"Great! If you could stay a few minutes after this meeting, I'll get you both set up."

It didn't reverberate through him the way it usually would have, on another week, one from before. He would have let those words seep through his bones and bolster him through the next sleepless night and impossible project. Somehow, today, it didn't have the same shine. Still, this marked one step closer to what he wanted. It occurred to him Rachel wouldn't go down without a fight, but in his shock and glee at being closer to his goal, he didn't have the presence of mind to dwell on it.

Sebastian hoped this opportunity wouldn't make his job harder, an assumption he suspected was imminent, especially when he walked back to the cubicles after his meeting with Andrew and the tension in the room felt thick enough to choke on.

Andrew laid more responsibility at their feet, stressing the importance and size of the contract at their fingertips. Rachel soaked every word up, her gaze intense and focused. Notating most of it, Sebastian worried if he didn't write it down, it would prove to be a figment of his imagination. This way, there was proof. It didn't come with a pay raise, just an increased work-load. Still, it would look good on his resume. It would be precisely what he needed to edge out his peers. If he landed this pitch, he would be a shoo-in for the promotion.

The urge to share his good news was surprising, and it quickly deflated when he realized he had no friends in this office to share it with. No one was going to be cheering him on here. His parents probably wouldn't give two shits about it, especially not when it'd been a few weeks since he last called them. The only person he could share it with, the only person he *wanted* to share it with, was Farren.

So, even though he hadn't responded to her message about their next date, even though it was letting her into a part of his life, sharing it with her—Sebastian pulled out his cellphone to type up a quick message. She'd still be in class, he was sure.

> Sorry for not responding last night. As soon as I have concrete time off I will let you know! I got a really promising opportunity at work. It's not the big one I'm working toward, it doesn't come with a pay increase, but it will give me the edge when the time comes. I just... I wanted to share it with someone.

He sent the message, already worried about bothering her, unsure if it was the right move. Sebastian was surprised when his phone vibrated a few minutes later.

> YAY! That's so great! Congratulations! We should celebrate!

Warmth spread through him at her words, at her sharing in his joy and validating him. It was new and different, having someone be happy for him.

> I didn't want to bug you at work. I wanted... to talk about it with someone I guess. Thank you.

He didn't want her to feel obligated to do something with him to celebrate. Especially something this small, even though, in the scheme of things, it was what he needed.

> Not bugging me at all! I'm serious. Let me know when you get off work tonight and I'll meet you. You worked hard for this!

He relented, folding into his sentimentality far too quickly. Sebastian warned Farren it might be late, he might not get out of the office at regular time since Andrew dropped extra work in his lap, and he was wholly unprepared.

She didn't care.

When he clocked out that evening—after an afternoon of admin work and unwavering looks from his competitor—Sebastian shot her a text message with his ETA and his address.

They probably should have agreed to meet at a bar or something in the vicinity, but he didn't have it in him to be in a big crowd of people tonight. His mind whirred with far too much, and having Farren there was going to be a lot to handle as it was.

He stepped off the Metro, walking the distance to his apartment, slightly taken aback when he saw her waiting outside his duplex in the fading daylight. Farren leaned up against his car with a bottle of Prosecco in her hand.

"Hi," he said lamely, the day wearing him down.

"Hi," she responded, a little shy, which he thought seemed out of character. She seemed to get over it fairly quickly because she pushed off of the hood and walked over to where he waited.

"Congratulations!" she beamed and rose up onto her toes to press a soft kiss to his cheek. Something inside Sebastian's chest throbbed at the contact, at how sweet it was of her to do this, to be here for him.

"Thank you."

The words were soft, slightly choked up with an emotion he had no name for, and he wrapped her up in a big hug, relishing her warmth and the soft give of her against him. It was his turn to walk her up to his apartment. For once, he was happy his anxiety demanded a clean environment, given it would be her first impression of his place. They shucked their shoes inside the door, and he noticed her socks were covered in multicolored books, his own plain navy blue looking sad in comparison. Not unlike his apartment.

Sebastian knew it needed personal touches. After how long he'd been here, it was a little embarrassing that the most effort he'd put into making the space his own was putting up a rod and curtains over the blinds that came with it. The rest was furniture he'd accumulated over time, understated but comfortable. He wondered what her apartment looked like, kicking himself a little for not going inside when she'd invited him on Saturday night.

It was probably like her: loud, personable, with a bunch of different colors. He hoped he'd get the chance to see if his assumption was correct. They stood in the kitchen, part of the wall open to the living room, divided by the breakfast nook and bracketed on each side with the wall. She still held the bottle in her hand, raising it slightly and asking, "Glasses?"

Sebastian pointed to a cabinet near where she stood and watched her place the bottle on the fake-marble-but-actually-laminate countertop, rising onto her toes to search for them. He knew he didn't have any wine flutes, nothing besides regular old drinking glasses.

"Sorry, I don't have any stemware," he admitted, shifting slightly, uncomfortable because he didn't know how to act.

The last time he'd had a woman in his place—not this one, back in Ohio—was for a middle-of-the-night pitch prep for the biggest project of his career. There hadn't been time to get to know the contents of his cupboard. Farren was the first woman he'd let into his cabinets.

She went with it, no complaints, nothing besides a smile tossed over her shoulder when he spoke and her hands wrapping around two glasses to set them down on the counter. Farren held the bottle out for him, a silent question of whether he'd like to pop the cork, but he shook his head. It was fun to hang back, enjoying her energy and watching her move around his space. Farren leaned over the sink, trying her best to prepare.

Her thumbs poised against the cork, pressing slightly, her face scrunched into a bit of a grimace before the sound even happened. She closed her eyes, more force behind her press, and finally it burst free with a loud POP. A slight yelp escaped her mouth as frothy sparkling wine trickled down her fingers and into the sink. Farren giggled at her own reaction, and Sebastian was helpless, following her in her mirth. She was adorable. Incredible. Too goddamned stunning standing in his kitchen with wine dripping down her hand and her smile so bright, it made something in his chest give way.

Sebastian didn't stop to think, didn't give his brain a chance to catch up. Stepping up to her, freeing her of the bottle, he set it aside on the counter and turned her hand over in his palm. He pressed his lips to the pulse point at her wrist, a kiss followed by a bit of a taste, sweet wine and her, already too intoxicating for his own good. Part of him wanted to keep going, savoring the heady combination, especially when he heard that slight inhalation at the back of her throat at the contact.

He should probably behave, especially since he wasn't sure whether it was a good idea. Better to mitigate risk, and so it was prudent to keep it out of the bedroom.

There's plenty you can do outside the bedroom, his desire spoke up, pushing through the part of him that was focusing on anything but the feel of her hand in his—slightly sticky and saccharine. He let go gently, stepping aside to pour them each a portion, bubbles fizzing, and he took a sip to try and still the fight inside of him. Farren ran the faucet, rinsing the alcohol from her hand, her cheeks flushed against her pale skin.

"Thank you again for this. It's really sweet of you." More than he deserved, especially from her.

"Of course. It's a big deal, and I'm really happy for you!" She lifted her glass, clinking it against his own. "Congratulations, Sebastian."

They each sipped the cool liquid, not quite chilled but still good regardless, and it wormed through him with a slow-spreading heat. He hadn't eaten anything since lunch, hours ago, and although he wasn't quite a lightweight, his empty stomach would not help matters.

"Have you had dinner yet?" he asked.

"Not yet, just some snacks since lunch. You?"

"No. Would you... uh, would you like to stay for dinner? We can order something?" Technically he could have cooked, he'd gone grocery shopping, but he wasn't mentally prepared.

"That would be great!"

She wandered over toward the living room, not waiting for him to lead the way. Farren sank down onto the couch, tucking one of her legs under the other and sampling the Prosecco. When he sat down a slight distance away, she giggled at him.

"I won't bite. You know that, right?"

Sebastian took a page out of her book, blurting it out before he could overthink it to death. "It's not you I'm worried about."

She raised an eyebrow at him, her gaze roving over his body before she took another sip of her drink. "Well then. Let's focus on food."

He relaxed at the suggestion, pulling out his phone, and she did the same, both scrolling through their options.

"Is there anything you like, or dislike even? Any allergies?"

"No allergies, but not a huge fan of olives or jalapeños. You?" She looked up from her phone, paying attention to his answer, the screen highlighting the dusting of freckles across her nose and cheeks.

"Not really. I mean, cilantro kind of tastes like soap to me so it can ruin a meal real quick, but I'm not allergic or anything." Sebastian shrugged, more focused on her than the task at hand.

"So, what I'm hearing is no Mexican food?"

He huffed out a chuckle and nodded, returning to his scrolling, stealing glances of her as she frowned in concentration. So damn cute. So damn detrimental to his carefully crafted life.

"There's a Japanese place nearby that does delivery," she suggested, and they scooted closer together to go over the menu. They placed their order: shrimp tempura roll for her, katsudon for him, and were left with a sense of "what now?"

Luckily for him, Farren seemed content to take the lead, relieving him of the mental burden of trying to make a good impression after a crazy long day at work.

"Any shows you're watching at the moment? We could probably get an episode in before the food gets here, and then I'll head out once we're done eating. I know it's been a long day for you, so I want to make sure you get to bed at a decent time!" It was said teasingly, as if she knew he struggled to sleep. He was struck by her kindness, by how she considered what he needed and seemed content to see it through.

Sebastian owed her, big time. First for his no-show at game night, and now this.

"You pick, I'm not really in the middle of anything." It was a lie, he was four seasons deep into his Criminal Minds rewatch, but he doubted crime shows were the most romantic backdrop for dinner.

"You're going to regret saying that," she said, hand held out for the remote.

He deposited it into her palm with only a small amount of trepidation; whatever she had in mind would be worth getting to be with her.

"Remember you asked me to pick, okay? I don't want to hear any complaints," she warned as she clicked onto the show, a huge red rose and golden letters filling up the screen. He tried his best not to groan out loud. Sebastian knew the show only by reputation, but it was not something he ever would have chosen for himself.

The host came up on screen, introducing them to this season's Bachelor. Farren settled into the couch, bringing her other leg up so she reclined against the arm, her sock-covered toes resting against the outside of his thigh. She made it seem like the most natural thing in the world, taking sips of Prosecco as they watched. Farren seemed to get very involved in the action onscreen, making little comments about each contestant's entrance, explaining how the show worked.

Not that it would have been necessary, the host did a fine job of outlining each part of the evening to both the women and this season's Bachelor. Halfway through the drama, in the middle of the first night's party, the buzzer went off letting them know their food was there.

Sebastian answered and tipped the delivery person, grabbing cutlery on his way over. She helped him by splaying the food across the coffee table and pulling it closer to them. They ate and watched one woman get far too drunk, jumping into the pool in her fancy dress, the others making catty remarks behind her back. Farren assured him it wasn't a proper season unless one of the contestants made a comment about either not being there to "make friends" or being there for the "right reasons" when referring to someone they thought wasn't.

Had it been a drinking game, they both would have been wasted.

By the time the host announced it was the final rose for the night, the food was long-gone, Farren was curled into Sebastian's side, and his heart was at peace. She was addictive. Her slightly spiced scent, her soft curves against the hard planes of his body, felt too right. The way she made him feel seemed like too much and not enough all at once. He breathed her in, his lips pressed to her temple.

"Thank you so much for this. Really. I appreciate it." The words were whispered into her crown, his arm wrapped around her shoulders, and she snuggled against him briefly, fingers holding onto his shirt.

"Anytime, seriously." Her body shifted. When she made a move to try and tidy up, he stilled her by pulling her into his embrace.

"Do you want me to give you a ride home?" he asked, kissing down her cheek, along the edge of her jaw.

"No, I'm fine to get there." It was breathy, her body canted toward his, capturing his lips before he could speak any more. Her mouth tasted sweet and salty. Her lips were soft and generous against his own. They kissed for a short while, not working up the same heat as before. This was slow, savoring.

She pulled away from him with a sigh, and Sebastian already mourned the closeness of their bodies. When he was with her, he felt so much more than he'd allowed himself. It had been so long since he existed outside of merely getting up in the morning, working, and yearning for sleep that didn't come. He didn't realize how heavily he'd relied on his numbing routine to get him through the day, not until she breezed in like a stiff wind and ruffled everything inside him to the point he barely recognized it.

Nothing changed, not really. His job was the same, the expectations, goals, and day-to-day unchanging. But somehow this was different. Sebastian couldn't quite pinpoint exactly when it happened, but she was there now, on the edge of his subconscious.

It scared him, more than a little, because he could tell just how easy it would be to tumble into her and get lost in her orbit.

"Let me get you an Uber at least, it's pretty late. I don't feel comfortable with you being out alone at night."

She nodded—the ride-share called, the two of them waited outside under the golden glow of the streetlight, hands intertwined.

The car pulled up, a bright neon sign in the window showing its designation, and Sebastian gave the back of her hand a light kiss before he let go, watching her leave. She blew him a kiss from inside the car, and he could smell her on his clothes. The breeze cut through his button up, a slight bite to the September air. He was so close to everything he'd wanted, then she swept in and stole his pastry and a little piece of his sanity.

Somehow, in the space of a week and a half, she'd managed to completely bowl him over, and Sebastian had no way of knowing the kind of damage she could inflict as time went on. But judging from how much he enjoyed her company and how time with her seemed to pass by in the span of a few breaths, he knew he was in for far more than he could handle. His concern shifted from worrying about leading her on to panicking at how much he wanted her to stay.

Farren

Farren was a mess at school. It was starting to impact her work. Marginally, but still. She'd mixed up the names of two of the students, forgotten her phone charger, and had to be reminded twice about a field trip that day.

A call to Corinne was in order because Farren was two steps away from being totally lost for Sebastian, and it was definitely no bueno. She found herself daydreaming about him somewhere between graham crackers, finger painting, and running one of the students over to the bathroom before there could be another incident. They were sweet, chatty, and Farren knew she'd miss them when she left in October, after their regular teacher came back from her maternity leave. She really needed to get her head out of her ass and focus on the job at hand. The students deserved that much.

Six weeks would be just long enough for her to know their names, personalities, and for some parts of their personal lives to be divulged. Just long enough for them to trust her before she said goodbye, dusted the crumbies and stickiness from her clothes, and stepped into an older classroom where the attitudes were so much bigger, their hearts already more guarded.

Farren couldn't blame them. Wasn't she the same? Didn't she close herself off on purpose? Sebastian threatened that way of living and challenged her resolve. He genuinely listened to her, and the time they spent together seemed too fast and too little all at once.

She hadn't seen him since Monday night when they'd celebrated his opportunity; work picked up even more for him as the week carried on. This close to the end of September was hell week, at least it was the impression she got from him. They texted here and there, a phone call on Thursday night where they spoke about a bunch of nonsense for almost an hour until Sebastian fell asleep on the call by ten PM. Slowly, but surely, she found herself wanting more.

More time. More depth. More of Sebastian.

So, that call with Corinne had to happen, like now. Especially since she didn't want it to be a whole thing at game night later. Her friend picked up on the third ring.

"Hey, what's up?"

"I need to talk to you about Sebastian."

She heard a rustle, then a change in the clarity of the call, probably when Corinne changed it back from speaker.

"Is he coming tonight?" Her friend sounded a little too excited at the prospect.

"No, he's on deadline for some development stuff, so he's been working a lot. It should hopefully calm down by the end of September. Anyway, that's not what I'm calling about."

Farren plopped down onto her bed, staring up at the ceiling, phone pressed to her cheek as she gave a hefty sigh—not quite sure how to put into words what she was feeling and why it was such a bad thing.

"Spill."

She could always depend on Corinne not to beat around the bush.

"I like him—a lot. We went on a date this past weekend, and

then I went over to his place on Monday to celebrate his promotion. We text a little every day." Farren knew she tended toward rambling, so listed it out in the most clinical terms, trying to keep more emotion from tumbling out.

"Okay, and...?" Corinne asked.

"*And*? What do you mean, *AND*?"

"I mean, you make it sound like it's a problem. You've never called me freaking out about any of the others before. What's the deal with this guy in particular?" Corinne had a point; Farren was usually a little more level-headed about these sorts of things. Not that she didn't get excited, or turned on, or enjoy her time with other guys.

"He's just... different? I don't know. You've seen me in relationships, I'm breezy, mostly unaffected. I mean it's not like I don't feel strongly about them, or hurt when it's over. I..."

"You try to stay detached. It's not a news flash. I've known you coming up on five years, and I've never spoken with one of your family members. Heck, I don't even know half of their names. You have me listed as your emergency contact. You don't *do* commitment, Farren." Corinne sounded a little tired, her words sharper than Farren was expecting. She'd hoped her friend might be able to give her some advice, calm her nerves and get her back on track. Not shine a glaring light onto the heart of what was apparently wrong with her.

There was nothing bad about looking out for herself first, right? No one else did, so she'd better do it for herself. If it meant people were transitory in her life, she'd happily pay the price for independence.

Farren didn't know how to respond, sputtering before she fell into an uncomfortable silence.

"Look, I love you. I do. You're my best friend, you're vibrant and hilarious. Everyone loves being around you. But you're not serious. You don't respond to people being serious with you either. It's what makes you, you. If I need help with my taxes, I call Rebecca. If I need help planning a party or a game night, I call you because that's where your strength lies."

Right.

Right, it made sense.

She said as much to Corinne on the phone, trying not to let the statement hurt her. Corinne gave a little huff of frustration on the other end of the line.

"But what do I know? I'm up to my eyeballs with Alison and work, plus dealing with crap at home. Luis's mom is sick and might have to move in with us for a little bit. I'm swimming in 'serious,' and I envy you. I do. I wish I had your outlook on life, your ability to find joy in small things and move on to the bright and new. I've got blinders on to the bitter end out of pure stubbornness, you quit before it can get you down and follow what makes you happy. We kind of balance each other." Corinne's words soothed her a little, taking the edge off the sting. She wasn't wrong about Farren; when it was put like that, when she laid it all out, everything was true.

"I'm sorry, really I am. I'm here for you, you know that, right?" Farren offered, feeling ashamed she didn't know about all Corinne was dealing with.

"I know, thank you. I just think, if you're freaking out about Sebastian, maybe take a look at why. What is it about him that scares you? Is it that you guys are too different and you're forcing it into more than it has to be? Or is it because you're afraid of wanting him more than he wants you?" The words sunk like stones into Farren's stomach.

The little bit of insecurity she'd felt on their date slunk back in. Sebastian seemed too good for her. Traditionally good looking, successful and focused. Farren wasn't conventional, she was exuberant. She'd never been great at "keeping her eye on the prize," and she had no idea where her life was headed. On paper they didn't fit. Corinne was right; what did Farren have to offer but a fleeting good time? If things were allowed to progress between them, Sebastian would be the one tiring of her first.

Only, she couldn't bring herself to pull away. Where leaving had previously been easy—attachment flimsy and simple to break—things were a little different this time. This was so far outside of her "safe" zone, the area should be lined with blaring beeps and hazard warnings.

"He's... he's someone I'm afraid to want. Sebastian is put together. I've only ever dealt with assholes and disasters. He's neither. What if he hurts me? What if I'm not good enough for him?" The words were small, the first of her fears to be spoken aloud.

Farren spent so much of her childhood blending into the background, being forgotten, no care given besides whether she did the minimum to get through school and life. Her mom was too busy dealing with the three others that came before her, and then those after—including Lindsay with her health issues. A struggling child, one who was fragile took precedence over one who seemed to do perfectly fine on her own. It wasn't Farren's fault her parents felt guilt over Lindsay getting so sick before they noticed.

Countless hospital visits over the weeks ate at them all, first in worry then in guilt as the aftereffects of her illness became apparent. By the time Lindsay was hale and hearty again, Farren was deemed old enough to see to herself and had older siblings to make up the difference. By the time she'd left home, with little fanfare and a sense of relief, Farren stepped into being loud... being needed. On her own terms.

Sebastian didn't seem like the type of guy that needed any help. Sure, he was lonely. But so were thousands of other people. If they got down to it, if Farren stuck around, she worried she'd become dependent on him, and it would make it so much harder when the inevitable happened. He was a man of ambition, steadfast and determined. Farren was chaotic, incapable of making it to the finish line. What chance did they really have?

"What if he's exactly what you've been missing and you're just afraid to put yourself out there? I feel like I'd be quoting you to say 'live a little.' You never know, it could be wonderful." Corinne's voice was kind, the words settling over her and quieting the distress climbing up her throat.

"Thanks. I'll see you in a little bit?" Farren asked, trying to build up the energy to get up and ready. Between the work week and this constant emotional back-and-forth, she was kind of whooped.

"Yeah, see you there!"

Farren stayed in bed for a little bit, contemplating her next move. As if he could sense her thinking about him, Sebastian sent her a text message apologizing for not being able to make it to game night, again. She knew he wouldn't be joining, realized the demand of his job more as the week progressed and she got little bits and pieces from him. It was a little ridiculous. More than a little, if she was honest, but she respected how hard he worked and how much it seemed to mean to him. If she possessed even an inch of his drive, she wouldn't have an unfinished pipe dream on her coffee table and a hunger for something she could never satisfy.

It was strange, watching him spend so much time on something that left him with so little—no free time, no friends, just stress and deadlines. She didn't dare utter that out loud though.

She responded to his message, letting him know it was okay but that her friends were bummed they hadn't gotten a chance to meet him yet. She finished it off with an offer for him to come over to her place when he got some free time. Dangling an offer for a home-cooked meal and some more introductory games so he could be more confident by the time he actually made it to game night.

Farren didn't wait for his response; she got dressed for herself. These few instances of old insecurities inching their way into where they didn't belong made her that much more determined to get back to her true self. She wasn't going to let a man, no matter how cute or sweet, allow her to wander back down those roads and question her worth—physical or otherwise.

She pulled out one of her favorite tops, a cool-weather staple, copper with a caged cutout detail at the neckline. She paired it with painted-on black jeans and chunky velvet heels. The look was finished with a sharp cat eye and mascara. Too much for game night... for sure. Too much for Farren? Never.

The walk to the cafe was just what she needed. Crisp early fall floated on the breeze, teasing her hair and fluffing her curls. It snaked under the fabric of her clothes, the slightest yellow turn to the leaves. Her feet pinched a bit by the time she got there, her eyes watering slightly from the wind, but she felt good.

Her friends agreed, a few of them giving wolf whistles and cheers when they saw her walk in. Corinne came over to give her a hug with a suggestive eyebrow waggle.

"Sebastian change his mind?" she asked.

"Nope, I wanted to feel hot after dealing with kid boogers all week, so I dressed up." Farren shrugged, sliding into a chair, ready to dive into the games for the night. She was pleased to note Braxton decided to come back and was currently sitting super close to Cute Chris.

They'd decided on deception games for the night, so after some rounds of One Night Ultimate Werewolf and a pretty long game of Betrayal at The House on The Hill, Farren got up for some sustenance. Her mind flitted over the mechanics of each game, wondering at what made them so compelling in their own right.

Standing in line, ignoring the urge to check her phone and equally hoping for a message... she treated it like Schrodinger's text. Such a wreck in her own head, she didn't notice how close she'd gotten to the front of the line, or the large hand that reached out to rest on the side of her waist, a warm body leaning forward toward hers and a familiar velvet voice whispering in her ear.

"We've got to stop running into each other like this."

Sebastian.

Farren turned, looking up into his eyes, albeit a less severe angle than usual in these heels.

"What are you doing here?" she blurted before she could make the statement sound nicer. He didn't seem to mind, chuckling and pressing a kiss to her cheek. "I mean, I thought you couldn't make it tonight."

"I wasn't sure you guys would still be playing. It's later than I would have come in on a normal Friday. I didn't want to say yes and then disappoint you. I'd hoped, but if you weren't here, I was just going to grin and bear it, grab my croissant and head home."

It was Farren's turn to laugh, to shake her head at him.

"That damn croissant. I see your real motivation. Game night or not, you were coming in for it. Well, I hate to break it to you, but they've been sold out since before I got here. No croissant for either of us tonight." It was meant to sound sad, a little scolding, but none of it came through when Farren had the stupidest grin on her face.

"We'll both have to content ourselves with the company instead. I'm game if you are." When he said it, it sounded almost more like a question, as if he was worried she wouldn't want him there.

"Joke's on you. I'm getting a sandwich on a pretzel bun and a really gooey cinnamon roll. If you're content to survive on company alone, that's your prerogative." Farren stepped up to the cashier, surprised to see Sebastian following her, his body close by and almost crowding her. But she liked it.

Farren placed her order, Sebastian chiming in that he'd have the same, but a water instead of her chai latte. Before Farren could reach into her purse for her wallet, he'd already tapped his smartwatch against the receptacle sending an online payment, the card reader happily chirping the receipt of the money.

She started to argue, little more than a sputter passing her lips before he smiled at her, patient as can be, and asked her to introduce him to her friends.

They were on their best behavior—well, as good as this group could be. Most of them asked benign questions about his job, where he was from, and how he came to be here. All stuff she already knew. All the while, he rested his arm along the back of her chair like it was the most natural thing in the world.

Giddiness bloomed in her belly, nerves melting into excitement and, strangely, a sense of pride. Having him here, joining in on something she loved doing, looking at her like she was a goddess walking around the cafe. It was a heady thing.

Corinne was the one that ended up asking the first risqué question. "So, Sebastian, what's going on between you and my girl?"

Farren's stomach knotted into a stone, the chai now somehow bitter and gritty on her tongue.

"I'm not quite sure, Corinne. We haven't really discussed it, but from my side of things, I'm just happy to stick around and see where things go from here." It was said with tact, Sebastian looking at her as if he wanted her to clarify, his thumb tracing a circle into her shoulder.

"So, you guys are dating?" Corinne continued, and Farren turned away from Sebastian to give her friend a warning look. "What?" Corinne asked, acting oblivious. Farren tried to drive home the message with her eyes, raising her eyebrows to punctuate her point.

"We're all curious, Farren. You can't blame us for asking now he's actually here. He's an elusive office gremlin, so we have to strike while we have the chance, before he disappears into Cubicle World again."

"Hey!" Farren interjected just as Corinne chimed back in with, "No offense."

Sebastian laughed it off good-naturedly.

"No, I get it. My job has been kind of crazy lately. But yes, we've seen each other a few times, so I guess that counts as dating."

"Exclusively?" Corinne asked without skipping a beat.

"Corinne! None of your business, now drop it." Farren was getting more than a little mortified by her friend and the audacity on that side of the table. Sebastian shook with laughter beside her, the heat of him pressing against her side, and she let it wash over her to calm her ragged nerves.

"I think Farren and I should discuss it in private first. I'd hate to speak for her, but I know I'm not seeing anyone else," he said, planting a kiss on Farren's blazing cheek. "Now that it's sorted, I'd like to play a game with you all, since that's why I'm actually here." His fingertips left a trail of fire on the outside of her arm, a quick kiss burned into her temple.

The contact shot through her like an arrow, straight through sinew and flesh, keen and to the heart of her. Her insides did a flip, the slightest bit of dizziness reminding her she hadn't taken deep enough breaths since Corinne started this whole thing. Farren focused on slowing her breathing, trying to calm down the excitement that started and spread at his unspoken claim.

Luis pulled a hot pink box from his tote bag on the floor, unveiling the contents with a whoosh of cardboard against cardboard. He laid the drawing pad out in front of them, dispensing a marker to each before he jumped into the rules. Farren was already well-versed in the game.

"This is 'A Fake Artist Goes To New York.' Everyone will be aware of the image you're supposed to be drawing, except for one—the fake artist. Each person will get ten seconds to draw in one continuous line, and then it will have to be passed to the next person to continue the drawing. It's up to the fake artist to try and stay hidden while figuring out what the picture is. The rest will be trying to determine who the fake artist is. At the end of the game, the team will have to vote on who they think the fake artist is. If they're caught, the team wins. If the fake artist is not exposed and they can guess the image, they will win."

Luis wrote on the back of a dry erase card for each of them. One was marked with an "X," but only time would reveal who exactly was the culprit. Though as it went on, she had a sneaking suspicion.

It was cute watching Sebastian try to keep a straight face, not to give away his position. Farren tried her best not to peek at his card, wanting to give him the opportunity to win it on his own despite the sense of surety growing within her. He did surprisingly well, making it all the way to the end before he accidentally veered a little too far from what they were supposed to be drawing.

When the voting round came, everyone ended with their index finger pointed at Sebastian and his neck blushing pink.

"What the heck were you guys drawing?"

"A bathroom," Corinne answered, her tone more than a little smug.

"A bathroom? No way. How is any of this a bathroom? This

looks like a ladder!" Sebastian pointed toward one of the aspects of the drawing.

"It's supposed to be tile," Chris said, acting offended, and the group dissolved into eye rolls and giggles.

Things wound down pretty soon after. Corinne and Luis had to get home to relieve the babysitter. Farren tried not to smile too big when Braxton and Chris left together. Soon, it was just her packing up her bag of games and Sebastian waiting patiently. The cafe emptied out quite a bit, with staff members cleaning up around them.

Some of her breathless feeling returned, the prospect of more time with him thrilling and terrifying at the same time. "Live a little" echoed in her mind, courtesy of Corinne, and Farren had the question out before she could overthink it too much.

"Would you like to come over to my place and hang out?" It wasn't too bad, not too clumsy or frantic. Despite how she felt inside, the words came out reasonably casually.

"I'd love that." The smile was back in his voice, and he seemed so much more relaxed this evening compared to when they'd first met.

Their fingers intertwined as they walked back to her apartment; even in heels, she had a harder time keeping up with his long-legged gait. Autumn freshness sent goosebumps skittering over her skin, and Sebastian pulled her tight against his side, an arm around her shoulder. Her arm was around his waist, and they did the slightly awkward shuffle of trying to walk in tandem with another person.

When his embrace changed to a reassuring hand on her lower back as they ambled their way up her staircase, Farren knew she was in for a world of potential mistakes. She was granting him access into her world and mind, truly, by letting him see her safe space. She could excuse it as a regular effect of being physically attracted to someone—inviting them in for an escape in each other's bodies—but there was no guarantee of that even happening tonight. This was an invitation of a different sort, one she very rarely issued, and she only hoped she didn't end up disappointed. Again.

Sebastian

Her body was warm under his hand, superheated as if to remind him that he trod on dangerous territory and she'd consume him like a flame if he got too close. Farren walked in front of him along the narrow staircase. Her heels clicked against the stairs on the way up to her apartment. Sebastian watched her hips sway and wondered if her face was ruddy with emotion like his. She made him feel like a teenager, giddy and inexperienced, the whole world seemingly balanced on this precarious moment and what it precluded.

The lock clicked, knob turned, and wood rushed against wood as the door swung open. Her shoes clunked against the floor as she stepped out of them, and he followed suit. None of the overhead lights were on, but she'd left a strand of string lights on, framing the bay window overlooking the street. Little potted plants littered the wide sills, covered by diaphanous curtains which were mostly sheer, barely enough to provide privacy from those peering in.

A deep sectional was tucked into the wall, a television facing it, and books strewn all over the room. Some were on a shelf, some lived in little groupings on the coffee table or on the console housing the television. Her kitchen was a nook, a little window open to the living area, the light over the stove on and casting a warm glow.

Farren flicked on the overhead light for the living room and Sebastian was able to make out so much more. The old wooden floors of the entryway had deep grooves and scratches from years of use by probably dozens of past inhabitants. The walls were a modest beige, but she'd covered one up with a tapestry, a bold abstract landscape offering pops of blue and green. A plush rug covered the floor in the living space. Shoes were stacked, piled up near the door, as if Farren didn't bother putting any of them away, just rotating them to her pleasure, ready as she rushed out of the door.

It was clean, if cluttered, and so much homier than the space he inhabited. He could see her here, the aspects of her he'd noticed and held onto. They helped when his own anxiety and stress threatened him with sleepless nights, and a dark gnawing in his stomach. She fit here. It was a little loud, colors used in a way he never would have imagined could work, but did. Farren's space was comforting, and when he sunk down onto her couch at her urging, he couldn't hold back the pleased little groan that escaped him. The fabric swallowed him, and the tension he'd been holding in his back.

"Comfy, right?" she said.

He knew it was rhetorical. There was no need for confirmation when Sebastian was ready to pass out right there.

"Oh yeah. Where did you find this?" He patted the arm of the sectional he leaned against.

So fucking smooth.

Ugh.

"It was Corinne's; they only had it for a few months. Then, after Alison was born and they moved into a bigger house, they decided they wanted an upgrade to accommodate more people. So, it became mine." Farren shrugged. Sebastian wondered if she was the type of person who liked to collect things, and if he was one of them. He wasn't sure how he felt about it. It was conflicting, wanting to belong to someone like her and wanting to protect them both at the same time.

He tried to keep his distance when she sat down beside him, inspecting the contents of her coffee table and being puzzled by what he found there. Scraps of paper were folded into cards, a square of cardboard with black marker outlined what looked like a board.

"What's this?" he asked, lifting one of the little cards to read the content. "Romantic Comedy, +2 if you attach this to a romance query, +5 if it matches an agent's MSWL," Sebastian read aloud, shocked when Farren climbed over him and tried to pull it from his grasp.

"It's nothing," she muttered, grabbing at the hand he held above his head and away from her reaching fingers.

"Doesn't seem like nothing to me." It was meant to be teasing, would probably have been if she hadn't poked him in the ribs right then. He huffed a surprised breath and jerked from being tickled.

Farren's fingers yanked the piece of paper from his hand, gathering up the rest on the table and folding them within the cardboard like a taco. She rushed to her bedroom, placing it somewhere inside, emerging a moment later as she fixed her unruly hair.

She joined him on the couch as if nothing happened, but Sebastian wasn't ready to let it go.

"Farren?" It was tentative. The last thing he wanted to do was upset her, but his curiosity won out over everything else.

"Sebastian, please." She shook her head, cuddling up against him and flicked the television on, obviously trying to divert so he would drop it.

He peeled the plastic remote from her loose grip, placed it on the coffee table, and turned to face her.

"You can tell me." His hand cupped her cheek, thumb stroking the edge of her mouth where it was downturned.

"It's really nothing. Just an idea I've been kicking around forever that's never been completed. I tried tinkering with it again this week. It happens every couple of months, and it always ends the same way: with me disappointed and unable to see the way forward."

She sounded so dejected by it, all Sebastian wanted to do was appease her, reassure her she could do whatever she set her mind to. It was true, but also sometimes that required some help.

"Is it a board game?" he asked, his free hand reaching out to hold hers, the two of them facing each other on the couch.

"Technically? It's... supposed to be." Farren shrugged, shrinking under his gaze as her words spilled out.

She sounded unsure, and it was new for him. She'd always seemed so confident, so unfazed. It was stark to see her struggling with something openly; he'd thought her invincible, immune to the pitfalls he wrestled with constantly.

"But?" he urged, gentle, not wanting her to shut down if he dug too deep, the way he knew he probably would if he was in her position.

The words were a rushed huff, tumbling over each other as she tried to get them out as quickly as possible. "The mechanics aren't finished. I have the first round thought out. Players receive a manuscript idea at the start of the game, then slowly collect plot points and twists to beef it up. At the end of the round, they have to try to query in order to find an agent to represent their story. I'm not sure how to make it all work." Her brows were drawn down in concentration, and he knew this must be her "thinking" face.

"How so?" he asked.

"I can't decide if I should have the players take turns to play the agent, and the writers would have to pitch their story. But then I'm worried they'd all be vying for the same job or genre. Their stories might be too similar. I thought of maybe having multiple agent cards and players trying to amass enough tropes or the like to reach that agent's preferred wished-for story and collecting agents." Farren spoke, her hands punctuating some of her words, and Sebastian settled back against the couch to watch her.

She got more fired up the more she spoke.

"But that also wouldn't work because then people would be trying to get the most agents, whereas from what I've read about the publishing world, that wouldn't be how it went down. It's just a struggle to finalize the mechanics in a way befitting the theme."

"How long have you been working on this?" he asked, a little breathless by how beautiful she looked when talking about this thing she was so clearly passionate about.

"I've dabbled over the last year, nothing consistent." Farren chewed her bottom lip, the flesh caught between her teeth.

"I think it's a great idea! Have you tried having your friends play and give you feedback?"

Her eyes widened, a quick "No!" sputtering out before she backtracked a little on the intensity. "No, I haven't."

"Why not?" He was genuinely puzzled by this. They would be the best equipped to help her get it off the ground stage. Their shared experience playing games gave them an insight into what worked and what didn't... what was fun and what wasn't.

"What's with the third degree?" she asked, her voice edged with something very close to defensiveness.

"I'm only taking an interest. I'm sorry," Sebastian said, contrite, deflating a little at the harshness of how she responded.

It had been a rare insight into her and her interests. A line she didn't want him to cross, clearly.

Her face softened at his statement, and she leaned forward to press a kiss against his cheek.

"No, I'm sorry. It's... it's not something I've spoken to anyone about. Not even Corinne. I guess it's easier to work on it in secret because then at least when I fail, or quit, or lose interest... whichever happens first, no one is there to watch and judge." She shrugged as if it was no big deal, but he could tell from the tremble of her bottom lip she wasn't as unaffected as she pretended to be.

"When, not if?"

Her face seemed to crumple at his words, true vulnerability covering her expression for the first time since they'd met. It was a revelation to see these sides of her, the depth he'd been denied until now.

"I'm not like you, Sebastian. You're so focused. You set goals and you reach them. I'm not the most responsible person, nor do I have the staying power required for something like this. Publishing a game is a lot like publishing a book, only far more expensive because you need a workable version of it before you can even think about pitching a publisher." She looked so sad, so resigned already.

"And? That doesn't mean you can't do it. Doesn't mean you shouldn't. Farren, when you were talking about this, your face lit up in a way I've never seen. You care about this, I can tell. Why not give it a try?"

"I—" she broke off, and he could tell she was about to reiterate the points she'd just made.

"—Can do it. I can help you, if you'd like." The words were out before he could think about the repercussions, about the hours it probably required. She had a solid theme, an idea around some of the mechanics, the main issue being the win condition and how the game might be able to progress beyond the first round or set of goals.

"Sebastian, you don't—I know how much you have on your plate, and I'm not even sure this would ever be worth it, or if I'd be able to finish it with this idea block."

"I know, but things should calm down for me soon. If this is something you want, even if you're scared to fail, I think you should honor this dream." Like he'd done. Like when he'd stepped away from his family and everything he knew to pursue what he'd been chasing. *Or what you'd been running away from?* The thought was shoved aside, his focus returning to her.

If this was her dream, her goal... that made sense to Sebastian, and he wanted to help her see it through.

"Let me think about it, okay? I appreciate it, I just didn't expect this tonight." She chuckled at something she must have been thinking, and it made him wonder.

"What exactly did you expect tonight?" he asked, trying to keep any anticipation from his voice, not wanting to make her feel uncomfortable.

"Well, first off, you weren't supposed to be there. So, I expected to miss you—a little," she clarified, smiling. "And then you *were*, and I asked you back here and..."

"And?" He tried to ignore the piercing hope cutting through him at her statement, or the dark wanting that seemed to seethe in him at varying levels of intensity throughout the day.

"And we keep doing this dance. I'm not sure where this is headed. I'm sorry for Corinne by the way. I'm not sure how it was for you, but it was a little like middle school." They chuckled at the comparison and how close it rang to the truth.

"She's overly involved. She used to take it upon herself to try and pair me up. So, I apologize for how strong she came on, and if she made you say stuff you didn't mean or weren't ready for." Farren was getting flustered again, and Sebastian found he very much enjoyed it. Not that he didn't appreciate her humor, or the surety in how she carried herself. But this new side of her was even more adorable, the openness and fragility of what emerged between them too enticing for him to avoid any longer.

"I didn't say anything I didn't mean. Sure, we didn't get to have that discussion beforehand, and it might seem a little sudden. But I like you, Farren. I only hope you feel the same because I'm sort of out of my depth here." His own vulnerability was on display for her now. Sebastian felt more than a little exposed, unused to having people see deeper than the surface, new to them even wanting to.

Farren seemed to want to. She looked at him like his revelation struck something inside of her, a resounding chord echoing the noise in his own chest.

"I... I like you too. It would be a lie to say I didn't enjoy hearing you say those things in front of my friends. I'm only sorry we didn't have the moment to ourselves." Her statement was a little breathy, the huskiness of it doing something wildly inappropriate to his insides. His mind reached for the imagined sound of it wrapped around his name and followed by moans.

"We have it now," he responded, his own voice deep and faded around the edges, the heat that built within him escaping with his smoky tone.

They were alone together. The prospect never seemed as enticing as it did right then. Sebastian leaned over for a kiss, and Farren responded with an intensity he hadn't been expecting. His arms wrapped around her, and her hands threaded through his hair, holding him in place with the slightest bit of pressure. She was intoxicating, the scent of her surrounding him. Her hands gripped his biceps, and something tightened deep in his core.

When he finally managed to pull away for a gasping breath, running his hand through his own hair in agitation, a rapid surge of feelings swept through him. Farren's eyes were wide, pupils almost swallowing the color, lips parted and deliciously waiting for the next onslaught. She seemed to catch herself, consciousness returning in increments. She stood up from the sofa, resting her hand on the edge as if slightly off balance.

"I'll be back in a sec, would you like some water?" Her voice was barely above a whisper, her eyes trained on the kitchen.

"Please."

Though the thirst within him, the longing, was for nothing other than her.

Slow your roll. They'd had one date. *Officially, if you count them all as dates, then this is technically your fourth date.*

His mind was clearly not cooperating. She returned with two glasses of ice water, condensation dripping down the sides, the frosty touch of the glass a shock to his system. Sebastian gulped down a few mouthfuls, feeling the cold snake down his body, settling some of the heat that simmered between them.

He fought the urge to ask her what she wanted. To delve into her mind to see if it corresponded with the turmoil within him. It had been no time at all, taken barely anything for her to reduce him to a mess of a man, thoughts filled with her for the majority of the day. He wondered if she was immune, or if like with the game, there was something deeper hidden beneath her vibrant facade.

Farren saved him from wondering, at least providing a distraction, before it could overwhelm him. Sebastian's propensity for overthinking would do nothing but send him toward an obsessive loop of playing scenarios and conversations in his mind.

"I'm not quite sure what's going on here. I'm a little scared, to be honest. When I'm alone with you... heck, even when we're around other people, I can't seem to contain myself. I know you and I have very different ways of approaching things, so I'm trying to respect that." Her gaze seemed to roam everywhere but on him. It seemed like she was trying really hard to be reasonable.

"Different ways of approaching things?" The question fell dumbly from his lips.

"You seem like the sort of man that plans. You think things through. I tend to jump first, ask questions later. It's gotten me hurt in the past, and it's left me in some less-than-desirable situations. I'm trying not to jump. I'm trying to take things slow. If that's what you want?" Her words were soft, careful.

Nope. No way. No slow going.

"I appreciate that, and honestly, I think it's wise. Best we get to know each other first, so even if it doesn't work out the way we want, we're not in too deep." Easier to heal from a shallow cut. Easier to try and contain his feelings now than lose his head when his dick started controlling the narrative.

Sebastian was way out of his depth, and Farren deserved honesty. He just had to try to find the right words. Even though his mind was at odds with his heart and body. He had to be reasonable.

"I'm not going to pretend I have a lot of experience when it comes to relationships. I'm enjoying letting this unfold without thinking of all the ways this can twine or unravel," he said.

Such a fucking liar, you've already planned all the ways you want to watch her unravel.

"That doesn't mean I don't want you, I'm just... trying to do things a little differently this time. I've gotten intimate quickly in the past, and it's never ended well. But trust me when I say this is difficult. It's hard to back away when all I want is more of you." Farren's words seemed to pierce through him, one sentence at a time, until all he could think was how badly he wanted her then and there, the future be damned.

But she'd spoken about respecting his assumed boundaries

and wishes, so he had to do the same for her. There was no way he was going to risk her regretting him, or running from what was arguably the best thing to ever happen to him since moving here. Or at least the most alive he'd been in a long time.

Sebastian nodded, and she pressed a chaste kiss against his mouth.

"Okay, so how about as a distraction, you tell me more about game publishing and what you have in mind. Maybe it could shake something loose?" He hoped she wouldn't think he was overstepping.

She sagged in what he assumed was relief and headed back to where she'd hid her idea, spreading it out between them. Sebastian watched her as she talked, her hands telling as much of a story as her mouth did. He learned about gaming conventions where thousands descended on different cities to play test games, launch ideas, and discover brand new offerings. Companies displayed booths where you could buy not only tabletop games but also trading-card games, Magic: The Gathering (whatever the heck that was) and even merch.

Farren seemed so animated, her eyes bright as she spoke about how excited she was for the next con she planned to attend: PAX Unplugged. It wasn't until later in the year, but the date was Sharpie'd into her calendar in the kitchen. She often either went with friends or took the AMTRAK up to Philly. December was practically around the corner, and he hoped they'd still be within each other's orbit by then because he'd love to watch her in her element.

She didn't talk about teaching this way. Sure, she was still excited and enjoyed it or she wouldn't be doing it. But there was none of this deep-seated fire when she spoke about lesson plans or racing after unruly children. There was an air of exasperation around the substitute teaching. Sebastian wondered how much of her transitory nature was due to her actually enjoying it, or if she, like he, hid behind what she was comfortable in.

He couldn't say shit, not when he'd buried himself in work to ignore the crushing feeling of knowing his parents would rather he be like them than his own person. They'd always been so involved in each other, in picketing, in sustainable living... fair and righteous, but they didn't notice they had someone relying on them, living alongside them. Sebastian became independent from a young age, and it carried over since. When Ashley pulled the rug out from under him, ruined his chances and his trust, it only seemed to steer him deeper down this path.

He longed for a sense of security he'd convinced himself couldn't come from people, especially not when those closest to him had proven otherwise. Still, with Farren, it made him wonder. Was this side of her—the light and easygoing—a coping mechanism? A pretty cover over a cracked surface? Probably not. Sebastian might just be projecting his own damage onto her.

Later, when conversation wound down and they cuddled on the couch under one of her soft throw blankets, he dared to ask a probing question.

"Tell me something you've never told anyone else," he said, quickly interjecting when she opened her mouth as if to argue, "The game doesn't count because I stumbled upon that myself, it wasn't volunteered."

Farren's little huff was hilarious to him, and he laughed. "Fine, but only if you promise to reciprocate." It was a caveat he had no choice but to honor.

"I've never told a romantic partner I love them." It was said carefully, as if she worked hard to keep her tone bland.

There wasn't much he could say, especially given he hadn't either. Though Sebastian suspected her reasoning was different from his. He'd merely not dated much, most encounters not reaching a serious level because he kept himself apart, aloof. Sebastian knew she'd done a lot more for partners than he had—even moving states and cities for those she'd been involved with. Her keeping the sentiment to herself, whether she felt it or not, was deliberate.

"Because you haven't been in love or because you simply didn't want to tell them?" he asked before he could lose his resolve.

"I'm fairly certain I've experienced it, I just... I've never been brave enough."

It was Sebastian's turn to scoff. "You? Not brave?"

Her breath seemed to catch in her chest before she launched into the rest of her confession. "Okay, fine. I didn't want to give them power over me. I've spent my whole adult life trying to come into my own—something I'm still working on—and I was afraid if I gave into that... gave into them, I'd end up where I tried so hard to leave."

"What did you leave?" he asked, needing more. Sebastian wanted to draw as much from her as he would be allowed, eager for information, for intimacy and secrets, the depth he'd previously deprived himself of.

"My family. The traditional expectation of what my life should look like. They never took the time to see me outside of their mild-mannered child, a good little Catholic with a too-big body, and not as smart as some of my other siblings. The unspoken rule was I'd stay in New Hampshire, become a home-maker like my mom—not that there's anything wrong with that," she paused, sighing heavily, her heart racing against where they were pressed together. "But it wasn't what I wanted. I was tired of being invisible, ignored, forgotten in the fray. No one noticed me while I was there. I doubt they miss me much now." The words were bitter, her forehead pinched as she talked about her past.

Sebastian stroked the pad of his thumb against the crease between her eyes, trying to smooth out the worry and pain there.

"Farren, I'm sure they miss you very much. There's no way anyone could forget you. I know I haven't been able to keep you off my mind."

She answered him by leaning closer to kiss him, soft and sweet.

"How about you? What lies beneath that stoic surface?" she teased, the smile creeping back into her words, the pain of the past set aside for another day.

"My parents never wanted me."

She shifted out of his embrace, a little shocked from what he could gather, staring at him intently, waiting for him to expand on the statement.

"How?"

How could they? How did he know? Her question prodded at his own insecurities.

"I heard them one night when I was about ten years old. They were talking about how surprised they'd been when they found out about me. They hadn't been trying, assumed infertility early on in their relationship, and it suited them. So they never tried to find a way around it." It was his turn to try and breathe when a stone sat in the middle of his sternum, pushing out air quicker than he could take it all in.

"Apparently, they'd briefly considered abortion—which, you know, good for them and I'm glad they were able to have an open discussion about what would be best—but then the romantic notion of someone like them, a product of the deep love they had for each other, made them stick it out. They seemed disappointed that I was so unlike them. Quiet, studious. My mother mourned the lost years they would have liked to travel through, the difference they could have made if they were still in the Peace Corps or the like."

His hands were shaky as he ran them through his hair. He'd never mentioned any of this to anyone, not even his parents. At ten, he'd wanted nothing more than to confront them, his anger seething so hot inside him, it was a miracle he hadn't burst at the seams of his own skin.

"They've always been this impenetrable unit, the two of them orbiting each other, and me the asteroid trash on the periphery, burned when I got too close to their atmosphere. You talk about not being missed; I get that. I know that. I haven't spoken to them in months, and they haven't bothered to check-in. They don't know about my pitch opportunity and they don't care. They think it's ridiculous, capitalist, selfish." The vitriol behind his words, the aching loneliness left over from his childhood was out on display for her to see.

She looked at him with kindness and care. Not the pity he feared he'd see, or the self-loathing he himself felt at his inability to move past it. It defined every single one of his relationships as an adult. He'd never wanted to get too close because he didn't want to fall into that same pattern.

Heaven forbid he ever had a child because Sebastian was so convinced he'd mess them up. The detachment he'd grown up with would probably produce the opposite in him out of pure spite: an overbearing husband and father. Since he'd spent so much time being on the outside, it became a comfort, a familiarity difficult to shuck now, and got harder with each passing year.

"I don't have what you do: the bubbly personality, the unforgettable face and giving nature. I've seen you with your friends, I've heard you talk about your job. People need you, Farren. They love you. I cannot say the same about myself. It's my own doing. I've alienated myself, never letting myself get too close, scared of being like them... and now... scared of being like this forever."

Despair seemed to sit on him like a second skin, a heavy burden he forgot he carried until moments like this, when he pulled the curtain aside and revealed the coldness inside. A coldness melting under her gaze, the way something in him seemed to burn for only her.

"Sebastian." It was compassion, a caress. Her eyes shone with unshed tears as she contemplated what he'd said.

"I'm sorry. I've said way too much." He cleared his throat, moving to get up, to get away from those dark eyes that saw far too much and promised a reprieve from all he languished under. Sebastian moved from the hand she perched on his knee, rubbing soothing circles. He had to leave. A few steps and he'd be out the door. A few minutes until he could be free of this.

"Wait, please." The words stilled him, his feet planted to the scarred wooden floors, staring at the door with her at his back, this evening's game night an eon away.

"I'm sorry. I'm sorry they hurt you. They sound like shitty parents, and even though they loved you in the way they could, it doesn't mean it's enough. Trust me, I know. I understand. You're not alone." Fabric shuffled behind him, Farren's socked feet making soft footfalls as she stepped up to him.

She wound her arms under his, around his torso, planting a kiss in the center of his back. He lifted a hand to one of hers, stroking the outside of her fingers where they gripped his shirt, over the knuckles and encircling her wrist to pry her hand away.

"I guess we're both a little gun shy, huh?" he asked, turning in her embrace to look down at her. Sebastian tucked an errant curl behind her ear, stroking down the edge of her ear and to her neck, planting his hand in the mass of her hair.

His lips found hers, once. Twice. Building in intensity until they were both trembling in her living room. Sebastian rested his forehead against hers, their frantic breathing mingling. She held onto him, and he did the same. Hands roving over the generous give of her body, relishing the way she seemed to melt against him when he'd heaved her closer and closer still. Both of them shivered, and his breath came in little pants that were a clear testament to how affected he was.

"I should go, before this turns into something far harder to disentangle from." He softened the words with light kisses pressed to the freckles dotting the bridge of her nose and over her cheekbones.

"I'll miss you," she said, devastating him. Those few words gave him the validation he'd craved from his family for so many years.

"I'll miss you too, Farren."

Farren

Farren should have known it couldn't last. The bubble she found herself in, the tentative groove at work, her comfort with her friends and hobbies—the budding promise of something amazing with Sebastian and a renewed fire for her game idea... She had a propensity to self-sabotage, so it shouldn't come as a surprise that she was falling back into old habits, or manifesting negative energy with her own doubts.

The week started fine, and then she'd had a rough day at school. One of the children, a little boy who didn't want to say goodbye to his mom at drop-off, was tearful all day. When Farren tried to get him to engage in a group activity—he wailed that he wanted his mom and kicked her in the shin. Which *hurt*. Farren tried to cuss under her breath, really she did. How was she supposed to know the kid heard her? Or that he would repeat it immediately and loudly? And the other kids would follow suit?

Of course that was the class the assistant principal chose to observe.

Sebastian had back-to-back meetings, despite the fact it was practically October, so close she could taste it. Then as the week continued and they crossed the threshold from September— what was supposed to be the end of Sebastian's suspense period

—and he still didn't have time for her... Well, her mood only soured more.

Sebastian was trying. He was so incredibly sweet. But she wanted his midnights. She wanted to go out for dinner with him and not have him pass out halfway through. Farren felt guilty for him ignoring much-needed sleep when he sat bleary-eyed and stressed out of his mind. He apologized, explaining his position leading up for this big pitch meant researching not only the company but their competitors for this idea. He spoke to her about coding until midnight, and although the confidentiality around the project prevented him from saying too much—she got the impression this was a career-maker. By the weekend, he was grumpy, and tired, and Farren wished she could make it all go away.

Since their conversation last Friday, she'd been thinking about him constantly, how vulnerable he'd been, and the age-old hurt that seemed to linger so close under the surface, Farren was surprised she hadn't recognized it sooner.

So, even though she was miffed at not getting to see him as much as she would have liked, he more than made up for it by showing up some nights with bags of craft items from Michaels. Sebastian was bound and determined to help her realize her pipe dream, the vague idea she had for a game slowly shaping itself under their hands.

He laughed when she somehow found glitter he hadn't purchased, flicking some onto him. Sebastian joked he'd never get rid of it all; when he died one day, there'd still be at least one fleck of gleaming silver on his skin. Farren promised to kiss every inch to make sure they got it all before it came to that. It was worth it to watch him blush, his neck turning an endearing shade of pink.

Soon, she hoped. Soon, she would be able to do more than just ruffle his feathers and enjoy the shyness that was such an anomaly to her, from a distance. They'd have uninterrupted nights, maybe even time away. Farren was really starting to resent the double vibrations inching his phone across the coffee table and drawing his focus away from their time together.

She could tell exhausting himself at work and trying to fit moments in with her took its toll on him. They saw each other once a week for the first part of October. Fall snuck in, blasting the area with a chill that brought everyone excitement over pumpkin spice and sweaters. Gourds lined the steps in front of residential doors. Only for the weather to turn into days hovering in the mid-eighties. It was the kind of whiplash she'd learned to expect from the area.

By the time they hit the third week of the month, Farren was prickling with an agitation she couldn't explain. Maybe it was sexual frustration, maybe just plain-old, regular frustration.

She'd already snapped at Corinne on the phone when she made an innocent comment about Farren and her future, another one of those vague notions toward how unmoored she was, how nothing ever tethered or bothered her. When her friend made that comment, the one about how Farren was so fun and fancy free, it rankled stronger than she could ignore. Corinne talked about how she had so little at stake. Not knowing the work Farren put into the game, into maybe having a dream become a reality for once in her life.

It was a twinge of jealousy from Corinne's side, Farren assumed. Luis's mother moved in with them, and since then, Corinne had been walking a tightrope of anxiety and misery. Farren suggested a girl's day to smooth things over.

They walked the gleaming floors of the mall, somehow still clinging on to life despite the influence of online shopping. It felt stilted, though. Corinne was caught up in her stuff, and somewhere between the pretzel stand and the department store they headed toward, it irked Farren past the point of being able to listen to the tirade.

This shopping date was supposed to clear her mind and give Corinne a bit of a reprieve from her home situation. Instead, Corinne's complaining started to wear Farren down.

Corinne wished out loud she could walk away from it all, for a short time. Pick up and put things down on a whim. Not knowing that Farren wrestled with how badly she wanted Sebastian to stick around.

"It must be so nice not to have constant responsibility. No one follows you into the bathroom or criticizes your every move. Being alone has its perks. I wish I was free to care less, like you," Corinne said.

It was insulting. Sure, Farren's track record wasn't the best, but she was trying with Sebastian. They were putting as much time as they could into their relationship, plus he'd helped her with her idea. It was shaping into something tangible, on both counts. Sebastian knew her deeper than many of the men who passed through her life like ships in the night. Farren liked to think she'd been getting to know him.

They knew each other's favorite movie and least favorite food. Farren was astonished to find whenever he didn't take the Metro, Sebastian loved playing music in his car at an almost-excruciating volume as he scream-sang his frustrations out in traffic. And she'd been right; his voice was lovely, when it wasn't pitched as if he had to project to the back of a packed auditorium.

Sebastian found out she loved having her back tickled in bed, and her favorite place to fall asleep was the wide expanse of his chest with one of his strong, sure hands resting between her shoulder blades. The intimacy between them, without ever having sex, astonished her. It never felt like this before, so easy despite both of their misgivings impeding their progress.

Being with Sebastian was like breathing. Being the recipient of that hazel gaze, the way he feasted on her with just his eyes and left her a little dizzy, was the cruelest and most enticing slow burn she'd ever experienced. They'd come close a few times, one or both of them pulling away at the last moment, as if they knew as soon as that barrier was crossed, there would be no turning back for either of them.

At least that was how it felt to Farren.

So, she said as much to her friend. Pausing with her hand on a soft sweater she had her eye on, Farren rubbed the fabric between her thumb and forefinger to ground her.

"I resent you saying that. I'm putting in effort here. Sure, I wasn't the best girlfriend in the past and I tend to pull back from things before they can hurt me—which, for the record, I think is super valid." Farren knew she sounded defensive, but it just kept coming. It was no wonder she hadn't brought up her game idea, no wonder she wouldn't want to either. Her best friend didn't think she had it in her, and no matter what Sebastian said, there was a part of Farren that doubted her idea was good enough for the fuss that would follow.

"My job record is spotty, and my exes haven't been the best guys, but with Sebastian, it's different. We're taking it slow, we're talking about so much, what I have in mind for the future," she said, wanting to ease her budding hopes for the game into their conversation.

She hoped she could finally come clean to her friend, divulge something she'd been too insecure, too caught up in self-doubt to envision as a reality. Farren never told her friends because even though they may have been excited at the prospect, none of them believed she had the chutzpah to see it through to the end. With Sebastian's help and encouragement, she was *so close*.

Corinne stopped perusing through her rack to scoff at that

word–future–and Farren let go of the fabric in her hand to focus on her friend.

"What?" Farren asked.

"Don't act coy. Don't pretend you don't know exactly what I'm going to say. The number of times you've been on my couch crying about a guy, or not knowing where you were going with your life... You do this," she gestured around as if the 'this' she spoke of was tangible. Corinne threw a blouse over her arm to take to the dressing room and started walking as if she expected Farren to follow.

Which she did. Farren always did, terrified to get left behind by her friends the way she had with her family. If she kept herself useful, they would want her around. She didn't know how to respond, just stood outside the curtain, swapping out clothes for Corinne to try on as her friend carried on talking.

"You cycle through these flights of fancy. You try to get your life together, you start a new career, date a new man. You're convinced it will finally be the time you pull yourself together, nothing else has ever aligned like this."

Corinne pulled back the curtain and exited the dressing room, giving Farren the opportunity to try on her own selections. As she stood there, Corinne's words made her feel stripped barer than her state of undress and weighed down by more than the pile of clothes in her arms.

"You love animals, so being a dog walker is perfect. You're an aunt to multiple kids so substituting is perfect for you, even though we both know you've barely seen your nieces and nephews. Hiding out here, away from your family." Corinne's words were scathing and unexpected.

Logically, Farren knew a lot of this must be the added stress Corinne was under. Realistically, she wanted to assume some good intent behind her friend's words.

Emotionally, she was flogged, exposed and ashamed. She

kept her mouth shut so the tears that threatened wouldn't be as obvious. Farren yanked her clothing back on and hastily returned items back to their hangers, swooshing the curtain open to hang them back up.

"Corinne?" Farren asked, trying to keep the hurt from her voice and failing. Her throat was stuck in a vise, emotion crushing against her larynx.

"Just... no. I can't do this right now. I'm up to my ears with Luis and his mom. Alison is being a complete terror plus they're threatening the funding at the museum so my contract might not be renewed, and even if it is, it'll probably be a huge pay cut. I have serious problems, Farren. I'm a little tired of doing this with you every couple of months. Not everything is about you."

The words shut her right up, and all she could do was nod, tears obscuring her vision, the dark bob and glasses distorted. Corinne started to say something, reached out toward Farren, but she pulled away. Her feet carried her away from the hurt, turning around before the tears could fall and wondering if what Corinne said was true. Was Farren the drama? Did she inevitably make everything about herself due to her complete inability to fully let people in?

The afternoon only got worse with Sebastian telling her he was going to be late to game night, again. Farren told him not to bother, she had no desire to go now anyway, not after her fallout with Corinne. He offered to bring food over to her place, sensing something was off and still wanting to spend time with her.

Farren tried not to check her phone for the time every few minutes while waiting to hear back from him, her mind unable to slip into her usual escape of trashy reality TV or sweet British confectionery wrapped up in a kind-hearted competitive environment.

Around seven, she received a phone call, picking up without checking the caller ID, assuming it would be Sebastian to let her know he was either on his way or already at the door. At worst, he was calling to get her food order again because he might have forgotten it.

So, when her mom's soft but unmistakable New Hampshire accent bled through the phone in a very innocuous-sounding, "Hi, hon," Farren knew something was up. Within twenty minutes, she was in her bedroom, shoving cold-weather clothes into a suitcase, her hair a crazed mass around her head. Her curls were fluffy from the frenzied way she was trying to get ready for a late-night train that would take her up the coast and as far as Boston before she switched to a bus to get to her hometown.

Sebastian arrived during the craziness, Farren buzzing him in briefly before returning to the explosion of clothes on her bed. He entered the unlocked apartment, set the paper bag of takeout on the kitchen counter, and presumably followed the sound of her cussing as she tried and failed to shove the zippers together to close her suitcase. He took one look at the frenetic look in her eyes and stepped forward to wrap her up in his arms.

She wanted to disengage, to tell him she couldn't do this right now because too much was going on. Instead, the warmth of his embrace, the steadiness of his body cradling hers left her sagging against him in relief. Grateful, overwhelming emotion flooded through her at how safe she felt there, in that moment.

Farren explained in harried breaths and between sobs that her younger sister, Lindsay, had been in an accident with her husband; they should be okay, but it'd been a scare for the whole family. After those fraught days with Lindsay in the hospital as a child, it resonated within them deeply. With good reason. Back then, her fever hadn't abated for days, and she'd screamed in pain for the entire trip to the children's hospital. Who still got mumps? In this day and age. It cost Lindsay the hearing in one of her ears and so the guilt sat heavy on her parents.

Her mother didn't tell her about this week's car accident until the doctor gave the okay and sent them both home. Farren tried not to be upset by knowing she was probably the last to find out. They waited until the emergency passed to call her.

Lindsay was pregnant, and it was a rough few days, her mother said. Farren offered to come immediately. Donna urged her that it wasn't necessary, they understood she lived far away and didn't want to alarm her. Even though they didn't seem to want her there, even though it hurt to think about, Farren insisted. She couldn't deal with how far removed she was, how quickly something could have gone very wrong.

She bought the first ticket she could find to get her there soonest. The guilt at not being there to help, at not seeing them in so long ate at her. Her mother sighed, giving in to Farren's strong feelings. Part of her knew she'd be underfoot, in the same way as usual, but she wanted to see them all okay. Her sister's screams from back then seemed to ring in her ears, and all Farren wanted to do was take some of the pressure.

In his arms, she broke down completely, conflicted by what she was feeling. Abject terror at the prospect of almost losing a loved one, shame because it was the family member she'd grown up resenting, and she hadn't seen any of them in nearly a year.

Sebastian stroked her hair, peppering kisses against the crown of her head as she trembled, as she sobbed how helpless she felt. In a strange way, it came at an okay time. She'd just finished up her six weeks at the kindergarten job, not yet committing to a different placement. Technically, she had the time to go, finally. Only now there was someone she was leaving behind, who she would miss very much.

He whispered he'd miss her as well, and after her sobs

quieted to little gasps and they ate in front of the television, Farren asked him to stay. To hold her after what was proving to be the hardest day she'd had in a while. In the dark cocoon of her bedroom, she told him about her fight with Corinne, the self-doubt echoed back at her.

"You can do whatever you put your mind to. You've been working so hard on this game, and it's great! I want them all to play it to see how brilliant you are. I'm sorry she didn't even give you the chance to talk about it." The words were whispered encouragement against her temple as he held her under the covers.

He'd stripped down to his undershirt and boxers, Farren in her own fluffy pajamas given the chill enveloping her, her emotions overriding the heating she'd only just started turning on recently.

"How is it that you have so much faith in me when I have none?" she asked, a little broken.

"Because you're... you're the most alive person I've ever met. You're bright and creative and you make me lose myself in your eyes when they light up in excitement. The way you talk about the things you're passionate about—makes me wish I felt even an iota of that about my own professional endeavors." He sounded awed, a little put out by his perceived lacking.

"You're so driven though, and I don't have that. Even if I'm excited, or creative, it means nothing if I can't realize it. Or if I stop myself out of fear. You know what you want and you take it," Farren said, highlighting the juxtaposition of their personalities.

"Totally untrue. It might be when it comes to work, but personally, I'm terrified. This thing between us is like an ocean, fathomless in its depth, and I'm being flung around by the tide. I've never known anything like this, but no matter how much I want this, I can't escape the worry that when you leave here tonight, you might not come back." The words fell like pebbles into a pond, spreading out in circles, getting more and more devastating as they sunk in.

"Sebastian…"

"Your job isn't keeping you here, your friends are here, sure… but you're in the middle of a fight with Corinne. What do you have to lure you back here?" He stiffened beneath where she rested on his chest. His breathing was uneven and harsh.

"*You*. Numbnuts." She didn't mean to say it out loud. She barely stopped herself from uttering the other three words dancing on the tip of her tongue, spicy and heady. Farren couldn't bring herself to admit how much of a draw he was to her, how strongly she'd come to feel for him over the last six weeks.

Sebastian's chest shuddered beneath her head as he gave a shocked laugh, heart pounding under her ear. He wrapped his arms tighter around her and stroked a hand over her loose hair.

"I—" he started and stopped, unable to finish the thought, or perhaps like her, he was unable to voice how much he was weighed down by it.

"I'll be waiting for you," Sebastian said finally. The words wrapped her in a surety she rarely felt. When he kissed her, she knew he meant it. He tasted her, savored her skin. His lips sent shivers zinging through her body, and he danced around the boundaries they'd set which felt flimsier by the day. Sebastian slowed when she pushed lightly against his chest, afraid to get caught up in him when she felt so shaken.

His kisses turned sweet, and Farren was running out of reasons to keep things low-key. All she knew was, now was not a good time to give in to this. It wasn't right to have this be a way to get out of her own head. The last thing she wanted was for it to be purely physical, for her to use him.

They fell asleep twined together, almost impossible for her

to extract herself from when the alarm went off under her pillow. She left him sleeping in her bed, a spare key on the bedside table, and a note promising she'd be back as soon as she could. She rolled her bag behind her, a sense of trepidation filling her chest at what awaited her back home.

After hopping on the train and then the bus, Farren stood bleary-eyed outside the Circle K, unsure which of her family members would show to pick her up. She was pleased to note it was Toby, the younger brother she'd always been closest to. His truck rumbled down Main Street and sputtered to a stop where she waited.

"Hello, Dolly," Toby greeted, and to this day, Farren wasn't sure if the nickname referenced the musical she'd loved as a kid or Dolly Parton. Being a blonde with big boobs muddied the water.

"Hey, fart-face." It was the best she'd come up with as a child, an insult carried over to all her brothers, away from her mother's keen ear at least. "Can't believe you're engaged. Wasn't it just recently you got blackout drunk at your dorm and tried to jump off a roof with an umbrella, stripped down to your undies, convinced you were 'Mary-fucking-Poppins' after watching that Marvel movie?"

He cringed at the reminder, giving her the stink eye as he pulled out of the parking lot, the truck rocking slightly as they drove. "That was years ago, and you know it."

She did know, but it was fun to give him a hard time. It was difficult to shake the feeling he'd slipped away, or she had, sometime in the intervening years. Because the silence between them was not as comfortable as it was before. More than a few of the storefronts had changed, names she didn't recognize emblazoned on the front of buildings she'd frequented in her youth.

"How's Linds?" Farren asked. Her mom had given the barest information, filling the call with inane comments about how the neighbors recently repaved their driveway, and how Farren's dad threw out his back a few weeks ago trying to power-wash the outside of the house. Apparently, he slipped in some water and went down "like that time you belly-flopped in the Anderson's pool." All useless information.

"She's okay. They were worried for a bit she might have complications with the pregnancy, but they all pulled through. Just a head's up, mom's planning to throw a baby shower since you're going to be here. Usually, she'd wait a little bit longer, but she wasn't sure what you were doing this year for Thanksgiving and Christmas, so she figured she'd get it in while she could." Toby sounded gruff, a little put out.

His words were meant to hurt, burning through her like hot acid. "Toby, I'm sorry. I'm sorry I wasn't here for your engagement. And a lot of the other stuff." She couldn't even begin to list all the milestones she'd missed, the invitations that went unanswered until they didn't bother anymore. Graduations and other baby showers, birthdays and cookouts... all the living happening in between when she'd left and now. But it worked both ways. None of them came down to see her in five years, and she held onto that kernel.

"It's not me you have to say sorry to," was all he said. Farren wondered who she'd disappointed this time. It seemed to be a constant state of being for her.

The long driveway up to her parents' acreage was the same dirt road she'd driven over on her way to school, work, and the one unpleasant date she'd had with the Anderson boy of said pool fame. The trees that surrounded the land cast long shadows on the ground and reminded her this time of Sebastian's scent, not the other way around.

Her mother waited on the porch, a tired look on her face aging her beyond what Farren was ready for, the house looking somehow smaller than she remembered in her head. Its shutters had faded slightly, the old colonial style seeming shabbier than the last time she was up here. It could just have been that the yellowing siding and graying roof tiles were as old as she was.

Toby grabbed her bag from the back of the truck, giving their mother a kiss on the cheek on the way into the house and up the stairs. Donna folded Farren into a tight hug, her mother's warmth and familiar scent sending a keen ache of nostalgia and longing through her. It had been too long. Her mother said as much to her as she rubbed her arm and gestured for Farren to come inside.

Josh—the youngest of them all at nineteen—was the only one there besides Farren and Toby, and the only one still living at home. Everyone else moved out, settled into their own homes and lives nearby. Lindsay, eleven months younger than Farren, lived thirty minutes away with her husband Logan.

Josh had just launched into a whole tirade about the game he was playing in the family room, explaining to their mom for what Farren assumed was the umpteenth time he couldn't "pause" it to come and say hi to Farren because it was an online game moving in "real-time." Donna responded by turning the television off and placing a hand on her hip, daring him to say a word.

Farren's dad came up from the basement at the ruckus, his face folding into jolly wrinkles when he smiled at her and wrapped her up in a hug that smelled like sawdust and woodsmoke. He must have been loading up the stove downstairs. The New Hampshire air was much cooler than D.C., especially without the press of people and the urban heat island effect to help it.

"How long are you staying, Bug?" he asked, the nickname another one from her childhood, though this was far preferred. Jerry used to call her cuddle-bug because she hated getting up in the mornings as a young child, and he'd have to carry her downstairs to breakfast.

"Not sure yet, Dad. As long as you all need me." It was insufficient. Especially when she knew they didn't, in fact, need her.

"Well, the shower's on Sunday, so best stay 'til then or your mother will lump some of that good-ol' Catholic guilt your way." He said it with a slight eye roll, bumping his shoulder against hers in camaraderie, and her heart ached with how much she'd missed them without realizing.

As the years passed and she visited them less and less, she found when she came home, it was accompanied by a twinge inside that wouldn't let up. So many years she'd been swallowed by the crowd. It didn't occur to her that as they all left home, the sound of kids disappearing, her parents might actually notice the quiet where she used to be.

She settled into her old bedroom, the pink walls muted by age, the bedspread on the twin bed the same one she'd left behind all those years ago. Her mother had at least thought to take down her embarrassing posters and box up her knick-knacks into clear totes lining the inside of the closet.

The weekend passed how she'd expected, her siblings stopping by when they pleased without much fanfare or notice. They hugged her tightly, told her they'd missed her. As they all gathered in the basement—the largest room that could barely hold them when they were kids, let alone now that they had kids of their own—Farren got to meet some of her new nieces and nephews, the echoes of the faces she remembered from her youth.

"Hey, Chase, your kid's got your nose," she told her older brother, tickling the aforementioned gremlin as the kid tried to escape her clutches to race around the room again.

"Hate to break it to you, Farren. But we all have that freaking nose."

The room erupted into laughter, Farren's own tummy shaking with the chuckle, a freeing feeling being around people she didn't have to pretend in front of.

Then Lindsay came down the stairs with one hand poised over her belly, a nasty looking cut across her eyebrow and a black eye to match. Farren found all the animosity she'd carried toward her sister... All the jealousy she'd felt at the fact that Lindsay was thinner, prettier, got more attention from her parents and the teachers at school... It faded away into concern and a deep, dark dread sank in her chest at realizing she'd spent so much time angry at someone who hadn't done anything to hurt her. Someone she loved very much. Someone she'd almost lost.

Just for a moment, Farren was frozen, realizing everything she held onto was juvenile. The tar that stuck to her feet and made her want to do nothing but run was her own self-doubt and baggage. They did love her in their own way. But she was caught up in years-old hurt she'd done nothing to mend. It wasn't to say her pain wasn't valid or the life she'd known growing up was perfect, but in this moment—this moment they almost hadn't gotten the chance to have—it faded away for the time being.

She stood up on shaky legs, eyes blurred with unshed tears, and walked over to her sister, wrapping her up in a huge hug, careful not to squeeze too hard. When Lindsay wrapped her arms around Farren and she heard her sister sniff, all the tears welling in Farren's eyes trailed down her cheeks with a sob. They stood, slightly swaying, crying and laughing, and something in Farren's chest seemed to settle for a while.

A wild, caged thing she'd been neglecting for years, calm.

Sebastian

Who are you and what have you done with Sebastian Clark? His mind mocked him when he woke up that morning, twisted in Farren's watercolor bedspread and reaching for the spot where she'd been only hours before. His chest was strangely tight; not an unusual feeling for him physically, but the "why" of it all was so different. Sebastian missed her, wanted to wake up beside her and pull her closer, relishing the half an hour after waking where everything was fuzzy and soft.

He had no idea what he was going to do to fill his time without her. He'd worked late the night before and had very little to see to over the weekend. She'd left a note for him on the bedside table. Sebastian pored over the words, the sloping surety of her handwriting, etched bold and deep on the page.

Hey, sorry I dipped out while you were sleeping. I can't put into words how much it meant to me to have you here last night, holding me while it felt like everything was crashing down at once. You're so much more than I deserve and I hope you never figure that out.

Here's the spare key for you to lock up when you go, and so you can come up with take out next time without having to use the buzzer LOL

P. S. I miss you already

Sebastian traced his thumb over the last line, a hefty breath shaking out of his chest. This woman would be the death of him, he was sure. How she'd managed to worm her way so deep under his skin in such a short span of time was nothing short of incredible.

He checked his phone next, pleased she'd texted him to let him know she got there safely.

He responded with a selfie in her bed, trying not to feel embarrassed or weird about it. Wanting nothing more than to make her smile at how ridiculous he looked with his pillow hair and sleep still crusting the corners of his eyes. Sebastian finished it up with a message letting her know that just like her couch, her bed was far superior to the one waiting for him back at his apartment.

It was ages before she responded again. Sebastian slogged back over to his place to change and then finally took the time to go for a jog along the Mall. It was awe-inspiring. The scope of it was insane. Every building had something unique he couldn't wait to explore one day. There was no way he'd be able to run multiple loops around the whole thing without busting a lung. He made it from the Capitol building down to the WWII Memorial and back before taking time to sit in the grass somewhere between a couple of art museums and sink his hands into it. He'd almost convinced himself he wasn't waiting for her response when it finally came.

> Well, maybe if it's so much comfier, you should spend some more time in it 😏

God, this woman...

He leaned back onto the grass and stared up at the sky, blue interspersed with fluffy white clouds. Although the air held a chill, it helped him focus, especially when he was thinking about all the things he'd like to do to her in that bed.

Farren had a way of reaching into his torso and rearranging his insides. She left him off-balance, aching for more of her. Dangerous. Farren was fucking dangerous. It wouldn't do to dwell on thoughts of her, it would only get him into more trouble.

After his sweat cooled and his heart returned to its normal tempo, he ended up at the coffee shop for a bit before slinking back home, moping at the lack of her wherever he went.

How did he pass his time before? How had he kept himself sane in the absence of her?

That feeling carried over into the week, and he knew, he *knew* it was bad. Sebastian found himself checking his phone so much more often, distracted by her. She hadn't told him when she'd be back, but an idea bloomed at the back of his mind. A gift of sorts, something he could give her when she got back... or possibly later depending on how long it would take to organize and ship. By the end of the week, he was prickling with the urge to make it a reality.

Unfortunately, the people he could think of to help him weren't ones he was close with. He didn't want to piss Farren off by overstepping. Sebastian himself was peeved at Corinne given how she'd lashed out at Farren. And Farren, every kind and caring inch of her, excused her friend's behavior by explaining how difficult things were at home at the moment.

Sure, understandable, whatever. But still not okay. Not okay to rip into your best friend and not apologize. Sebastian waited on tenterhooks to hear how things were going with her family. From the bits she'd told him, he gathered she wasn't the closest with them. They'd done a number on her, same way his parents had to him, although maybe his were not as bad. She probably wouldn't say anything while she was still there. Sebastian would have to wait until she came back—if she came back—for her to tell him whether or not he had to make a very angry phone call to people he'd never met, who probably didn't even know who the hell he was. So, he searched for a diversion.

Sebastian sat at his desk during the weekday, his chair squeaking every time he rotated it slightly, bored out of his mind. The research for the pitch was complete, he'd written up his proposal, and all he could do now was wait. Best to fill the time with something productive because staring at the stupid gray walls was too dull to handle. He pulled up the site with Farren's gift and worked on that instead.

Sebastian didn't notice Andrew was behind him until far too late, his browser still open on the freaking gift he'd just placed an order for, and he was too slow on closing the window.

"Can you see me before the end of day, please?" Andrew asked, though it was less a request and more a notice he'd get reamed out before leaving.

Fucking great. This is what happens when you let a woman get into your head.

His thoughts were less than gracious. By the time he stepped into Andrew's office later that day, his irritation had grown. It grated like a burr under his clothes, chafing more and more until he felt red and raw. Andrew sat in his executive chair, desk gleaming mahogany with no knickknacks out. The same as Sebastian's in a way, only more intimidating. The air smelled like furniture polish, starched shirts, and dread.

"Close the door," Andrew instructed, and the click of the wooden door shutting out the rest of the office was strangely final. His project manager gestured for him to take a seat across from him.

"Ian, I'm going to cut to the chase." He gave a small sigh, pushing his glasses higher up onto his nose. "You're slacking."

The words jolted through Sebastian, his nostrils flaring as his breathing sped up imperceptibly.

"Excuse me?" he asked, unsure he'd heard it correctly.

"You've been distracted at work, cutting out early whenever you can. The volume of what you were completing last month has decreased. But now you're also spending time and work resources on things that have absolutely nothing to do with your job. That's just unacceptable."

The volume was different last month because you threatened the renewal of the contract if we didn't put in overtime hours, you stupid prick. How could he say that? How could he let any of it leave his mouth?

Andrew pushed a paper across his desk, a wall of black text capped off at the bottom with a line and the date.

"I'm going to have to ask you to sign this warning, Ian. Online shopping during work hours... it's just not okay. I know you know that."

The muscle under Sebastian's eye twitched, his jaw so tightly clenched, it was a wonder he didn't crack a tooth. What could he say when he was blindsided?

"I gave you extra responsibility to see how effective you'd be in a higher position, and I hate to say it but you're not meeting expectations. I should have given the opportunity to Keith instead. He expressed interest." The threat hung there, a glistening knife ready to drop.

"With all due respect, sir. I've been doing my best, staying late more often than not, taking work home. The hours I put in last month were well over what is stipulated in my contract." Sebastian tried to keep his aggression from his voice, working to maintain an even tone and unclench his fists where they rested on his thighs.

"I don't want to hear excuses, Ian. If you need so much extra time to do your job, then maybe that's not a good sign either. Your peers don't seem to be having the same problem. I'm going to have to ask Rachel to step up and do the pitch on her own. There's just not enough time to get Keith up to speed."

The workload is not the same as mine! They're working on one contract; I'm doing my regular work plus preparing for a whole new app idea. It's nearly double!

He grit his teeth, bitter bile coating the back of his tongue. Rage, white-hot and feral, ran up and down his muscles like electricity. One wrong move, and something would get destroyed. The table in front of him, his fist, his career.

"I'm sorry," he managed, even though he wasn't. Not even a little. "I'll do better." It tasted like vomit, the words acerbic and nauseating in his mouth.

"I hope so. I hate that I'm the one to take this away from you. The bigwigs have to be kept happy, and if it's not happening, then my hands are tied." Andrew shrugged a little, leaning back in his chair. "You seem like a good guy, Ian. I don't want you to lose your job. I'm only trying to help you out here."

Sure. Fucking-A. Helping, my ass!

Sebastian nodded, rising from the chair and giving Andrew what he hoped looked like a smile, or something similar. Internally, he was screaming, ready to rail, aching to shove his monitor from the desk or chuck the keyboard at the sterile gray walls closing in on him more and more each day.

Just suck it up. This is what you wanted, remember? Got to focus on this over other stuff. It's okay.

But it wasn't. Not really. This time, the lie was precisely that, and no amount of cajoling or minimizing what he was feeling made a difference. Sebastian was exhausted. The time and effort, hell just the mental energy that went into trying to get ahead, wore him down. He was concerned that soon, he wouldn't be able to brush it off anymore. Eventually, he'd reach a breaking point, and Sebastian wasn't sure what that might look like.

He gathered his things together, aching to leave and so ready for the weekend. Sebastian slung his laptop bag over his shoulder, only to be faced with Rachel when he turned around. The last fucking person he wanted to see right now. She leaned against the wall, lithe and poised, watching him carefully. He'd never paid her much heed. She was competition, but beyond that, she'd done little to warrant his attention.

"Hey." It was friendly, sort of. Her black hair was pulled back into a low knot, still impeccable after a whole workday, the cut of her suit severe.

Sebastian gave a pathetic little wave in response, walking by her, toward the door, hoping she'd leave him the fuck alone so he could sink into anger and loneliness in the comfort of his own home.

Her arm shot out as he passed her, sharp fingernails gripping his sleeve and slowing his progress. It was strangely aggressive given he didn't know the first thing about her on a personal level, and they were definitely not "touchy" with each other. Sebastian's mind was suddenly cast back to his first meeting with Farren and how he'd reached out for her in much the same way, only there was no electricity at this touch.

"Did you need anything?" Sebastian tried to keep his voice even, stop the fatigue and annoyance from leaking out. Her hand dropped to her side, useless, and something behind her eyes seemed to be stirring.

"Come and have a drink with me. I know Andrew's been giving you a hard time, and you look like you could use it." It was almost convincing, and for a moment, Sebastian actually wanted to believe she cared. His mouth tingled with the denial he knew he should give, but something inside, a gentle nudging gave him pause. She'd already won. Perhaps this was his chance to actually make a friend. He didn't have any work friends, nothing to fill his time with outside of these miserable cubicles and Farren.

"Okay, one drink," he agreed, following her lead as she strode with purpose, down the elevator and out onto the congested sidewalk. A few trees, most dotted with orange and red, started to drop swirling leaves to the ground. Sebastian couldn't shake the whirring in his mind, made even worse by the nearby din of a bar growing louder as she swung the door open and stepped inside.

"Rooftop okay?" she shouted over the cacophonous sounds of happy hour, already headed in that direction. Sebastian nodded and followed, strung along by the thread of his own mind telling him this was good. This was what he needed, right? He was tired of feeling like a void, lost and gnawingly empty.

The noise petered out once they'd climbed the stairs and reached the outdoors again, twilight setting the early evening sky ablaze. A row of lights lined the periphery of the space, smooth music pulsing over the speakers, too soft to make out the words but enough to feel the bass in his chest. She strolled up to the bar, comfortable and sure, the opposite of where Sebastian was at right now.

It occurred to him this situation could be misconstrued. He wasn't loud about his relationship status. Neither he nor Farren thought to bring up the whole "social media official" thing, since they rarely used it. Perhaps Rachel got the wrong impression.

She placed an order for a dirty martini, while Sebastian went with his usual Moscow Mule, a creature of habit right down to the core. Minutes later, chilled drinks in hand, she claimed a table nearby, and the discomfort in Sebastian's stomach grew. Then his foot-in-mouth disease surfaced, predictably.

"I'm seeing someone." He cringed at how panicked it sounded. *Breathe, dumbass!*

Rachel scoffed at him, rolling her eyes in what he could only assume was disbelief at how stupid he was.

"You're not my type. And anyway, that's your damn problem, Ian." She punctuated the statement with a tip of her glass in his direction before taking a swig. "Stop overthinking things. You have too much shit going on inside that brain of yours. There's always this wounded puppy expression on your face." Rachel shook her head with a disgusted sound.

"Even in the meeting where Andrew gave you the opportunity to pitch, you still had that damn look on your face. Long-suffering and a little shocked. If you don't want to be there, if you don't plan on putting in a good showing, then you need to step aside for those of us who do."

Sebastian took a gulp of his own drink, alcohol and ice burning on the way down, and he sputtered out his response.

"What the hell do you mean? I put in the work! I've already been pushed aside to make room for you." He was still smarting from his meeting with Andrew and the precarious edge he dangled over. She looked slightly taken aback, shaking her head. For the umpteenth time that week, Sebastian wished Farren was there.

"I'm not talking about working sixty-hour weeks and being Andrew's pack horse. I don't know what happened in your meeting with him, but this is news to me." A thin dark brow raised, and Sebastian understood why she'd gotten to where she was. She paid attention; she wasn't afraid to speak her mind. In a male-dominated field, she made sure to leave her mark. Even now, one look was enough to silence him.

"It's about networking, it's about looking like a model employee—someone who embodies the company values, approachable and smart." She finished the swig of her drink and set the glass down on the table, no coaster. "You do the work, you go home, then work some more. They pile it on because they know you won't complain. They give you this extra shit with a shiny label on it. And you shut up about it, and you look miserable."

It hurt to hear. His chest cracked under the truth behind what she said. Sebastian's whole thing was keeping his head down, getting work done, hoping it would speak for itself. Wishing he could redeem himself for how badly things ended at his last job. His plan was always to go back to the grindstone, regardless of how he felt daily. But maybe it was eroding too much of him away in the process.

"You have to sell it. You need to have confidence and grit. I don't think you have that in you, Ian."

What could he say when she was right? What could he say when his boss had effectively told him the same?

"What would you have me do, Rachel? If you're so convinced of my ineptitude, why don't you complain about me to Andrew. He seems about ready to kick me to the curb for good." Just like Ohio. The bitterness from earlier welled inside him, rising with the leftover anger he'd tried to smother and which flared back to life under her scrutiny.

"Because I play by the rules, or at least I try to. I don't plan on sabotaging or screwing my way to the top. The same way you want people to view you based on merit..." She shrugged, her gesture at sympathizing not lost on him, so different from Ashley, he felt a little ashamed for judging her. "Only I know I bring more to the table than you do." So much confidence, brash almost.

"Then why invite me out for a drink, when you've already won, when you know how badly I wanted this and how hard I was working on it?"

"You looked like you were about to lose your shit. It was either a drink or a fistfight, and I could only provide one of those. Seriously though, you're difficult as hell to read most of the time, and you keep to yourself. It's hard to believe you even want to be there. Until right now, your ambition seemed like spinelessness. If you want this, really want it, then you're going to have to show some backbone." She leaned forward as if getting ready to tell him a secret. "Fight for it!"

"Why are you giving me advice? I know you want the exact same thing I do, and you're closer to it than I am. Why not keep your mouth shut and let me falter? You're taking the lead on the pitch now." It didn't make sense. He wouldn't do it if he was in her position. It wouldn't even occur to him.

Rachel and Keith were blips on his radar at best. This was the longest conversation he'd had with either of them outside of work, and even on company time, it was minimal.

"I'm not a total bitch. Plus, I can't stand Keith, and if I'm going to give a dumb man a pep talk, it might as well be you." Her smile was small, barely a quirk up on one side, but he found himself returning it. "I'm still not giving up though. Don't get comfortable because I was kind of nice to you. The project manager job is going to be mine; I just want to make sure it's a fair fight."

"Whatever you say. We'll see who makes it to the finish line." It felt bold to say, and Sebastian wasn't ashamed to admit he'd borrowed some of Farren's spunk for his response.

They chatted about some bland stuff as he finished off his drink, TV shows they were watching, the tiniest bit of office gossip—apparently Keith signed up for ballroom dance lessons outside of work, and one of the secretaries saw him there. Rachel made it sound like a potential meet-cute but couldn't confirm or deny a relationship. Although it was meant to be teasing, a light ribbing of a fellow-employee, Sebastian found himself thinking *good for him*. At least he'd found something to keep him happy outside of the pressing demands they bowed under.

Sebastian left her with a wave, asking if she'd be okay to get home, and Rachel assured him she had a long night to go before she was ready to leave.

He mulled it over as the train bumped along on his commute home, again when he walked by the coffee shop and saw some of the gamers enjoying their weekly meetup. What would it be like to have something like that? Somewhere he could be himself and do something purely for the enjoyment of it all?

When his phone rang later that night and Farren's voice was choked with tears, it all faded into background noise. She was in a car, and she was on her way home. Wouldn't arrive until early morning, but Sebastian offered to wait up for her.

"I just want to sink into my own bed to forget this whole trip even happened!"

"I'm here, tell me what you need, and I'll do it." He had no idea what was going on. Last time they'd spoken, she'd been a little bored in her small town but good otherwise.

She sniffed on the other end of the line, seeming to take a break to mull it over. "Can you wait for me at my place?"

Of course, of course he could. Sebastian agreed, already shoving clothes into an overnight bag and drawing the strap across his body. He grabbed his keyring and held tight to the spare key she'd given him a week before, the notches digging red marks into his palm.

He had no idea how her week devolved into this, but he knew one thing: whoever hurt her—whatever happened out in New Hampshire—there was going to be hell to pay.

Farren

Baby showers always made Farren feel older than she was, or imagined she was anyway. They were a blatant reminder of her life moving at a different pace, a parallel plane but removed from the people she knew back home. In the city, being unmarried and child-free in your late twenties wasn't unusual. Rural New Hampshire, in a family of devout Catholics? Less commonplace.

Sunday came, and the family was shoved into the too-small basement once again after mandatory Mass, but this time, her sister sported a sash labeling her "mommy-to-be" and the Sam's Club blue cupcakes her dad drove half an hour each way to pick up, sitting on a folding card table. Farren sent her dad a list of gifts and her credit card so she wouldn't show up empty-handed. Streamers draped from the white drop ceiling tiles and the chatter around Farren almost made up for the lack of city sounds she'd grown so used to.

Lindsay's husband Logan was close by always, a hand on her hip, cradling her belly as he whispered into her ear and they giggled. Farren was struck with a fit of strange jealousy she'd never felt, which made no sense. She hadn't changed her mind about what she wanted; children were a lovely mirage on the horizon but something she could do with or without. It could have been the setting, her and Josh the only unclaimed ones in the room, leaving her adrift.

Children raced about, and at least one of them had some baby-blue frosting on the corners of their mouth, indulging a little earlier than they were supposed to. Lindsay sat in a dining room chair, ripping into wrapping paper and cooing over each gift. Mom brought down a big laundry basket, wide and low, to fold and set clothes into. Since it was just family, there was no need to carefully separate the items to remember for "thank you" cards. Maybe the coziness, the feeling they all had of someone to reach out to, someone to whisper to or scold was what left her feeling lonelier than ever.

Even though Farren was with her family, she fell back into her niche, the little hole she'd carved out for herself to disappear into, the invisibility that formed so much of her early life. She kept to herself, the high of seeing her sister okay fading back into the bruised feeling she felt when they'd neglected to inform her of what was going on. Or every other thing that happened when she'd been growing up. She wasn't sure if mentioning it would help at all, or if it might just drive a deeper wedge between them. Either way, today wasn't the day for it.

They finished the shower out with some fun, themed games and dinner, each sibling dipping out around a different time for bedtimes or nap times and the like. Farren trekked up to her tiny childhood bedroom, texted Sebastian she'd been thinking about him and wished him luck with the week ahead, then buried herself under her overbright 2000s covers.

Farren hid out in Wakefield for a few more days, helping her parents, meeting up with people she knew from school who stayed or came back to start their own families. It was brutal. She felt like no one wanted her there—so caught up in lives she was no longer involved in. Farren's siblings were all settled, with no time to catch up or hang out.

She felt nervous and insecure about her place in life, stuck back in the town where she tried and failed to learn how to parallel park. A few days after she'd arrived, she reached a boiling point, the feelings that calmed with relief now back with raging force. She sat at dinner that afternoon, her leg bouncing under the farmhouse table, her mother admonishing her for doing it. Unused to eating dinner before four in the afternoon and feeling more than a little scrubbed raw. All the vibrancy, all the energy she surrounded herself with in D.C. was gone. It left her feeling like she didn't know who the hell she was supposed to be. No more distractions, just the ebb and flow of self-doubt and fear.

It was just them, the tick-tick of the wall clock punctuating the silence in between bites. Her mother's ugly crocheted table-cloth tickled her skin through her leggings. Afternoon sunlight lit the trees outside on fire, and it should have been pretty. She should have been awed, but all Farren could focus on was the anxiety of sitting there in her feelings and not being able to hold back anymore.

"Farren Ruth Davis, you better stop that!" Donna tried to look and sound stern, but it just came out a little tired.

"Or what, Mom? I'm leaving soon anyway and then you won't have to deal with it anymore." She shoved a forkful of green beans into her mouth, the squishy vegetables no match for her aggressive chewing.

"What's gotten into you? We didn't ask you to come up here, and now you walk around moody all week. If you don't want to be here, don't threaten me with leaving. You're grown, you do as you please."

"Exactly. You didn't ask me. You didn't even bother to tell me Lindsay was in an accident until days later! Then you had the nerve to tell me more about your bird feeder and the goddamned neighbor than my own sister. I'm not a stranger. I'm not an acquaintance. This was my home too. You're my family too." Her voice cracked on the last two sentences, the feeling of being an outcast in a space that was supposed to be safe too much to contain.

Her dad set down his silverware, giving her the look, the one that told her she was on thin ice. Especially since she'd dared to blaspheme in front of her mother.

"Well, maybe if you came home more than once a year, you might be more involved!" Her mother's voice bordered on shrill, face pinched as if she were fighting hard to rein it back in.

"Are you telling me I should be sorry for that? Is that what Toby meant when he said it's not him I should apologize to?"

It wasn't as if her mother could speak for Toby and whatever he'd vaguely referred to, but she leaned into the sentiment regardless.

"Now that you mention it, yes. Yes, an apology would be nice."

"Yeah, it sure would. So, whenever you're ready, I'll be waiting for yours. You're quick to give me crap for not coming up more than once a year, but when have you ever come down to see me?" Farren rose from her seat, gathering up her plate, silverware and dirty napkin, and stomped to the kitchen. She hoped they heard the loud clank of the dishes hitting the bottom of the sink. Farren knew this was an overreaction, but the scab she thought mended opened right back up being home. She'd tried to heal, tried to grow as a person away from here. It was scary how quickly it felt like it was negated.

Farren wanted support, she wanted attention. She wanted Sebastian.

Her father murmured something, probably telling Josh to stay put, and Farren heard her mother enter the kitchen behind her, breath harsh and hard.

"What are you talking about? What do I have to apologize

for? You know I can't fly with my DVT." Donna's incredulous tone raised the room's temperature to scorching, and although Farren knew she should try to hold back, let it go... she couldn't. Not this time. There were buses. Trains. If any one of them wanted to spend time with her on her terms, they could have.

"What is my favorite meal?" The questions started and poured out of her relentlessly. "What's my favorite color? Who was my first kiss?" She turned away from the sink, taking a step closer to her mother with each question. Anger flooded her, anger at being forgotten and overlooked. No one considered her unless they had to.

It was no wonder she was lonely, no wonder she'd sought out crappy boyfriends in the past. She'd just been happy to be the center of someone's world, even if it was only a little while. Even if it was only for as long as Farren could stand it without panicking.

"Which classes did I fail in school because you weren't able to help me with my homework and Mikey was drowning in SAT prep and couldn't do it? Did you know I have hypothyroidism? Did you know it took me until I was living in D.C. to get a diagnosis and treatment because nobody noticed I was exhausted all the time or cared enough to get me to a doctor? Everyone just assumed I was lazy!" Her voice rose in volume, hysteria bubbling up and choking all maturity from her. This was little Farren, teenaged Farren that could have done with so much more, the one who'd needed her mom. Current Farren was well past that need.

"Where were you when I was sobbing my face off on the side of the road because Ryan-Fucking-Anderson called me fat and disgusting on our date because I wouldn't blow him, then kicked me out of his car to walk home in the dark, hmm?" Gross, heaving sobs clawed their way up Farren's chest, tears streaking down her face.

"What wisdom did you have to impart on me when I left home? What well-wishes? All you said was 'see you soon, hon' as if I was going to the store!"

Donna was crying now as well, silent tears which seemed almost worse than Farren's in their solemnity. Her curly hair, so like Farren's but strawberry tinted—those Irish genes coming through strong—seemed much whiter than Farren ever noticed before. Shot through with age and stress, her body was small and slight under Farren's onslaught.

"Where was the phone call when my sister was in the emergency room because some drunk asshole ran her off the road? It feels like I'm unimportant, like I'm too much work. You all seem okay with just letting me float along and not knowing what's going on in my life."

Her heart broke, all the cracks that accumulated over the years overwhelmed under the weight of continued harm and neglect, pain and silence weakening her resolve.

"I get it. You had seven kids to look after, a husband, a home. It just bothers me sometimes, that I don't know you and you don't know me and I have all this love for you but it hurts me. It hurts me to know how low down on the list I am—I've always been." Farren deflated, her piece said, adrenaline fading after whatever the fuck this was. A way to purge the hurt she carried for so long? An arrow released from a bow that just stored and stored energy, poised for the kill?

Donna was shaking, ashen. Farren's father stood in the doorway watching them both with wide eyes and deep brackets beside his mouth.

"Hon, that's... that's not true." Jerry stepped into the kitchen, taking Donna's shaking shoulders into his hands and trying to stroke soothing circles into the knotted muscles there.

"It is, though," Donna whispered from behind them. "I let my family down, time and time again. I was overwhelmed, I didn't know how to ask the right people for help, so it fell to you all."

It should have felt validating, should have been what Farren wanted, but somehow her chest was just hollow. The words came too late to be a balm on her spirit. Especially when there was no genuine apology there. "I did the best I could. I'm sorry you couldn't see it," her mother sniffed, defensiveness back after the brief crack in the wall between them.

Farren felt herself wanting to respond, wanting to lash out at how her mother couldn't even take ownership for her part in things without making an excuse or turning it around on Farren.

Her dad stepped between them, sensing it might kick off again at any second.

"We love you, we love you so much," Jerry said and Donna nodded, her fingers pressed to her mouth to hold back a sob.

"I love you too." *But that doesn't make any of it okay. That doesn't make me okay.*

Her father gave her a small smile, the spackle trying to repair the rift between her and her mother. Farren felt herself being pulled into a hug, her dad wrapping her up and patting her back. His words were clunky in her brain, not really permeating the fog of demons she'd unleashed to wreak havoc on her childhood home. She pulled back, stepping away from them, trying to hold her tattered remains in place until later.

"I think I'm going to head back down the road. My boyfriend's been under a lot of pressure from work, and I need to get ready for my next placement."

Her statement felt too detached, her eyes unseeing, just focused on getting back home, back to safety.

"You have a boyfriend?" her mom asked, piping up with a hopefulness that cut through her teary tone.

"Yeah, Sebastian. It's still sort of new, but he's really kind. And serious. He's basically the opposite of me in so many ways.

Only child. Brooding grump." How could she quantify the feelings, the moments she had with him? How could she boil it down to two sentences and have it make any kind of sense?

The kitchen felt small, too small for her body and her feelings, and so outdated. Her mother's ancient KitchenAid mixer sat under its floral cover. A dish towel with the same pattern hung off the handle of the oven. A corner of the linoleum had started to chip off near the back door. Nothing in here seemed to have changed.

"Well, hopefully, we get to meet him. Maybe at the holidays?" Her tone was quiet, wistful, and Farren wanted to respond to the bid, wanted it to all be fine and normal. But she wasn't sure how soon she'd be back when being here just felt like one giant bruise.

"I'll let you both know. Either way, I think it best I leave. Sorry for blowing up at you, and for not being around as much. I guess it kind of felt like it didn't matter if I was here or not, when there were plenty of others to fill the space." Farren gave a halfhearted shrug before she turned to head up the stairs, only vaguely aware of her parents saying, "It mattered."

As quickly as she'd packed a week ago, she shoved her stuff back into the bag now. No train ticket, no bus ticket. Farren would have to rent a car to drive the eight and a half hours back home. Her dad gave her a ride over to the Enterprise in Rochester before it closed at five, heavy silence infecting the air around them. She held it together, finished the registration and brushed her dad off when he urged her to wait a day, just for a train ticket.

She couldn't take it, couldn't bear to when she felt like she was held together with tape and glue, and a stiff wind would take her out. Her thanks were stilted, her hug a little too tight. When she was on the road, New Hampshire firmly behind her and into Massachusetts—one state closer to sanity—Farren called Sebastian. He promised to be there when she got home. His assurance was enough to see her through the rest of the drive. When night fell and she passed in and out of cities, lights coming and going, Farren understood why they said you can't go home again.

Because she wasn't the same. The girl that left was long gone, with scars and scrapes to show for her years, and so much growth. Letting her feelings out, airing what she'd dragged along with her was arduous but somehow, she knew it was like letting go of something cutting off your circulation: the blood rushed back in painfully, but you didn't lose the limb. Now, without as much childhood baggage cutting into who she was, perhaps she'd have the strength for more.

Sebastian was asleep in her bed when she arrived a little after one AM, exhausted and so, *so* happy to see him snuggled up and holding onto her pillow.

"Hey," she whispered, hating having to wake him, but that pillow was a requirement for a good night's sleep.

Sebastian stirred, slowly coming to consciousness and then sitting upright with a gasp, looking around the room as if he'd forgotten where he was. Farren rubbed her hand against his arm, trying to soothe him.

"It's me," Farren whispered.

"What time is it?" He flopped back against the pillows.

"It's late. I'll be in bed in a moment, just need to change clothes. I wanted to let you know I was here and tell you to stop hogging my pillow!" A tired chuckle was all she could manage, but he obeyed, fluffing the pillow back up and returning it to its rightful spot. She undressed and redressed in the dark, relying on muscle memory to see her through. When she slunk under the covers, he pulled her tight against his body and branded a kiss into the side of her neck.

"Missed you," he mumbled, arm wrapping around her waist,

tugging her back closer to his front, and for the first time in a week, Farren relaxed. Exhaustion dragged her into blissful oblivion, and somewhere between sleep and waking, she knew for sure she loved him.

It almost slipped out that morning, when she stumbled into her kitchen to notice he'd taken the time to tidy and get her a few groceries after her week away. Sebastian stood by the stove, the extractor fan whirring loudly as he cussed under his breath, trying to keep the bacon smoke from setting off the fire alarm. His brown hair stuck up all angles, pajama pants slung low on his hips, and she wished for a moment he'd been shirtless. Just that tiny, shameless part of her that wanted to jump his bones. They kept dancing around it, Farren worried it might not happen at this rate. Things held steady between them, the emotional side of things growing, both of them holding back on the physical.

After another less-whisper-more-growl expletive from his mouth, Farren couldn't hold her giggle in anymore. He looked over his shoulder at her, devastating her with a smile before he schooled his face into something a little more serious.

"You're supposed to be in bed, and I'm supposed to be bringing this into your room as a nice surprise," he scolded, no ire behind the words.

"Blame it on the smell. Besides, you weren't in there with me. For a moment, I worried I'd dreamed you."

"Yeah, that's me. Man of your dreams." His lopsided grin and saucy wink had them both dissolving into laughter, and she rewarded his joke with tiny kisses peppered all over his face. It got carried away a little too quickly, the undercurrent of hurt and anger left over from her family bleeding into the kiss, making it rougher than usual.

Sebastian took it in stride, one arm wrapping around her body, the other hand cupping the side of her neck. He pressed her firmly up against the wall, and her heart thundered in her chest as he devoured. Vaguely, she remembered food was cooking nearby, but they didn't pull apart until the smoke from the spitting bacon set off the fire alarm.

Farren helped him finish up breakfast, popping some bread in the toaster, both a little breathless. She tickled Sebastian's side as she reached past him to get plates and glasses, trying to shift the mood from its intensity.

Breakfast and the rest of the day together—spent catching up and even some time toward the game that became a bonding point for them—was one of the best she had in a while. They'd finally figured out a win condition that made sense, and Sebastian took the time to start a little document with the rules. His experience with pitching ideas helped her iron out the presentation portion of the game. It was beginning to look like something real. Watching her dream take shape and working on it with someone who believed in her went a long way to soothing the hurt she'd carried back with her. Slowly, she filled him in about what happened with her family, the feelings of unworthiness echoing into adulthood.

Sebastian listened without interruption, kissing her knuckles when she fisted her hands in anger, agonized by how they'd left things.

"And then they had the gall to say they hope they get to meet you soon, maybe the holidays. Without even asking if you'd be with your family, or if you were religious, or if we were even at that point. Besides, I don't know about your work schedule and everything." Farren scoffed at their assumption, their blind belief she'd even come, let alone bring someone. Sebastian's face dropped into an expression she could not decipher, but she knew it couldn't be good.

"Yeah, so about that—" he started, and her stomach dropped.

Before she could ask him about it, assure him how she felt had nothing to do with him, her phone rang.

Had it been her parents, or maybe even Corinne, she wouldn't have bothered. But Cute Chris's name flashed across the screen, screaming pop music blaring from the speaker. He usually didn't call without a reason.

"Can I get this?"

Sebastian nodded, and she answered, putting it on speaker, keeping her fingers crossed that Chris didn't say anything inappropriate. Though on second thought, she probably shouldn't have, just to be safe.

"Hey! You've been MIA lately!" It was said without malice, not accusing or mean.

"Yeah, there's been a lot going on. I ended up going to New Hampshire last Friday, and I've been there all week. So I missed the last two sessions, sorry!"

"No worries, we all just assumed you were off somewhere with lover-boy, folded in half like a taco or something."

"Hi Chris," Sebastian chimed in, and Farren knew her face was flaming, could only hope Chris felt a smidgen of the embarrassment she did.

"Girl! You could have given me a warning!" He sounded fake-scandalized, eliciting laughter from both of them.

"But this was more fun," Sebastian said, and Farren felt the hole she was digging, the one where she planned to bury her feelings, get even deeper. They hadn't talked about this, and she wasn't sure she was ready to have him totally upend her life.

"Listen, do you guys have plans for next Saturday, Halloween?"

Farren looked over at Sebastian, both of them shrugging. It hadn't come up, at least not until now. So much else took precedence.

"Nope, we're free. What did you have in mind?"

I t turned out Braxton's family had a considerable property somewhere in Maryland, and Braxton lived in the old farmhouse that bordered their family's land. Their relationship with Cute Chris grew steadily, every week blooming into something deeper, Braxton's own relationship with the group members turning to friendship by the time Halloween approached.

Usually, the group joined one of the various Halloween parties around the city, or hosted a smaller get-together at one of their houses, games broken up with some booze and music. This time, however, Chris convinced Braxton to host a large party out on their land. Outside of helping Braxton host, Chris also took it upon himself to assign a costume theme to the guests, complete with a virtual drawing-of-straws so there'd be no arguing over costume assignments. Farren thought it was overkill, but on the other hand, she also loved dressing up, so she wasn't going to complain too loudly.

The real cold snap finally arrived, and the leaves reflected the change, not only in weather but in her relationship with Sebastian. Things progressed slowly, painstakingly. Both of them held back for one inane reason or another, his work getting in the way more than once. Her unexpected trip up north and her stubborn fear of being hurt now that she knew her feelings did little to help their progress. But after the last time she'd seen him, how close she'd gotten to uttering words she could never take back... it was time to dive in, to lose herself in him at least once before she fucked it all up and he went running. One last hurrah before she had to get back to work, a fourth-grade placement up near Columbia Heights, starting Monday.

Sebastian would be picking her up a little after five, and they'd drive to Braxton's acreage.

Farren pulled a stocking cap over her unruly curls, trying her best to control them so she could slip the brunette wig over it. She lined her eyes with a dark cat-eye, her lips shiny with the drying liquid-lipstick that promised not to rub off, even with kissing—or other activities. It would probably be too cold for the costume she found, but alcohol would hopefully help numb the chill.

They'd drawn their characters from a random generator and entered them into the Google doc. It was "supposed" to be random, but somehow, Chris managed to get Dionysus... which was a little too on brand. Farren was assigned Nike, goddess of victory. Chris helped her procure the items she needed for her outfit: the carefully draped cream gown, the gold-leafed head-piece, and a pair of golden wings he'd scored from a place he used to work for—a local theater company going out of busi-ness. Those would have to wait in the backseat of the car, or they'd never make it there safely.

Sebastian drew Ares, god of war. It seemed a little out of character for him; when she'd asked him what he wished he'd gotten, he joked that he'd wanted Morpheus so he could be the man of her dreams, again. Farren tried her best not to eye roll at the joke and the call back to the weekend before, a giddiness sweeping through her at the sweet sentiment.

She planned on a long coat over the outfit, not keen to ruin the reveal at the party and wanting to be sure she had something to keep her warm over there if it should prove too brisk for drinks to soothe. Her toes would have to suffer regardless; the gladiator sandals they'd found in the clearance section of Target were leftover from summer and no match for the evening chill.

He arrived a little early, while she was still fastening her shoes in the front hallway, and for the third time since she'd handed it over, she was glad she'd given him a key, hearing the lock click midway through a buckle. It would have been a bitch to try and buzz him in while struggling with these fastenings.

"Wait a second!" she yelled, pressing her butt against the door to stop him from coming in. He laughed at her ridiculousness, but she was able to bundle up just in time, preserving the full effect for the party.

Sebastian opted for a bomber jacket to cover his costume, the war helmet obscuring most of his face, a golden breastplate stretched across his torso over the tunic making him look like a freaking snack. Farren couldn't stop the giggle that slipped past her lips at the sight of his lower half, a skirt made of leather and golden armor swishing around his muscled thighs.

"You're wearing a skirt." Another laugh burst through her.

"It's a Pteruges." Sebastian defended, folding his arms. "It's traditional."

Farren could hear the pout in his voice even if she couldn't quite see it through his Corinthian helmet, and it took everything in her not to snort in amusement.

She gathered her purse, wrapping her long coat around her even tighter, grabbing the massive wings covered in a black plastic bag. It was unwieldy, and soon, Sebastian took the wings, both of them shuffling downstairs looking frankly ridiculous.

Wings and helmet safely in the backseat, he entered the location into his GPS. As the faint glow of the city crossed over the planes of his face, Farren realized he'd shaved and gotten a haircut for tonight. A Saturday away from work well spent, apparently. He looked devastating.

The murky full moon partially hid behind diaphanous clouds, and the further they got from the city, the spookier it felt. The black off of the highway combined with moonbeams and wrapped them in shadow, and Farren considered all the things she wanted to do with him in the dark.

"You excited for tonight?" His words pulled her out of her inappropriate thoughts.

"Yeah, you?" she asked, her breath hitching a little when his hand found the slit in her dress, warm palm spread over her thigh.

"A little anxious, I haven't been to a party—a real one, since my college days."

She gave a nervous laugh, throat unbelievably dry, when his fingers danced over her skin. "It'll probably be the same, just as much booze but maybe a little more nerdiness? It'll be great, and at worst, you can just stick to my side all night." It was supposed to be reassuring.

His hand tightened on her leg, and something shot up her core. "I'm counting on that."

The drive wasn't too long, though getting in and out of the city was a hassle at almost any part of the day, especially the beltway. Still, they made it to the outskirts of Poolesville with little fuss, and just a little too much heat. Farren wasn't sure she'd need the alcohol to warm her up when Sebastian's hand on her thigh was enough to set her ablaze.

They made their way over the uneven ground, dry grass crunching under their feet, and the full moon, ominously yellow, hung low in the sky but rising slowly. From afar, they heard the pulsing beat of music, barely contained by the old farmhouse surrounded by acres of dark woodland. The house seemed to sag a little, the porch dipping in spots, one or two shutters dangling slightly off-kilter.

The porch creaked as they stepped onto it. The windows steamed at the edges from the heat being generated inside. It smelled like dust from the drying corn husks around the property, and surrounding her was the cologne she'd noticed on him the first night they met. Sebastian pulled his helmet over his face again and handed Farren her wings. Once she was ready, he knocked, and Cute Chris opened the door.

A crown on his head made of flowers and grapes, a glass of wine fittingly in his hand, he welcomed them both with a bright smile and a hug. Braxton joined Chris soon after, shyly greeting them, gesturing to a random room on the ground level where all the coats lived for the night. Chris coaxed Sebastian out of his coat, urging him to get a drink for himself and Farren. Chris stole her away around the corner. Her friend giggled as they escaped to the room, wings in tow, Chris draining the last of his drink. The double bed was barely visible under the variety of coats piled on the bed like a giant lump.

"Farren... Farren," he tutted. "Please tell me you sampled that fine specimen!" It was practically a stage whisper, though the music covered most of it.

"Not yet." She sighed. "But soon."

"Tonight! You both look fucking banging, don't waste this chance to jump his bones."

Chris helped her out of her coat, tossing it onto the mound. He fastened the wings to her shoulders and gave her a once-over before he winked in approval. Neither of them noticed Corinne entering the room with her and Luis's coats until she cleared her throat. Her dark hair was covered with a blonde wig, braided with strands of wheat. She must have thought they were trying to figure out who she was because she gave a little nervous chuckle and said "Demeter." Corinne gestured to the hair and the earthy tones of her dress.

"Nike," Farren pointed to her own wings and olive branch crown. Her stomach felt like it was in knots at seeing Corinne for the first time since their fight and subsequent radio silence.

"Dionysus!" Chris exclaimed, and all three of them giggled at his excitement. "Okay, so I'll tell you guys this, and you can pass it along to your men. Drinks are out in the dining room along with some finger foods. The signature drink for tonight is Ambrosia, of course! And we have a phone set up in the bathroom with my TikTok on it."

Farren and Corinne shared a look, both unsure why it was relevant.

"We're going to be playing a game of who we think is going to turn out the drunkest tonight. So, when you go into the bathroom, you're encouraged to film a little snippet of who you expect will win that particular competition, and we'll stitch them all together!"

She wanted to turn to Corinne, share another look or an eye roll. But something inside still smarted at their last interaction and the way her friend dug into the aspects of her life she was insecure about.

"Sounds good. I'm going to go find Sebastian." Farren left the bedroom without meeting Corinne's gaze, intent on escape and the security she felt in his presence.

The dining room was empty. Chairs had been pushed up against the walls of the room so people could gather around the table freely. In front of them was a veritable cornucopia of food and drink. A feast fit for gods. The next room was the living room, and she finally found who she'd been looking for.

Sebastian waited beside the fireplace in the room, a smoky crackle near his bare legs. He leaned a forearm on the mantle, her drink up on the edge nearby. He'd poured her a generous glug of the golden liquid into the goblets Braxton set up in the dining room, marking a tab with her name and smoothing it onto her glass with some scotch tape.

He stared into the flames, looking pensive and fucking hot. Something about his outfit and the primal vibe of the fire in the hearth transported her mind back to a past she'd never experienced. Mismatched couches, floor cushions, and velvet chairs were arranged in a circle around the coffee table with a half-played game forgotten there.

Farren couldn't stop the smile that spread across her face when he felt her watching him, turning to face her, and noticed her—in full regalia. His eyes burned with their intensity, and he looked like he wanted to devour her. She closed the distance between them, rewarding him with a searing kiss. Farren pulled away to take a swig from the cup on the mantle, her name in his handwriting marked in Sharpie.

Apple cider and bubbly sparkling wine burst over her tongue, the remnants of cinnamon and nutmeg warming the back of her throat. It seemed that "Ambrosia" tasted suspiciously like caramel apple mimosas.

His dumbfounded expression gave way to a sly smile of his own, a dimple she'd never been able to see under his beard carved deep into his left cheek. Without his jacket, the sleeveless tunic showed off his toned arms, looking every inch the warrior god he was supposed to embody.

She didn't notice Braxton was beside him, or that the room was littered with the rest of her friends. Farren only had eyes for him, so when his hand wrapped around hers on the glass and he gave her a grateful kiss that wandered a little too close to a certain spot near her ear... she understood they were in for a world of trouble tonight. Somehow, she knew before the sun rose, before the world could intrude and force them apart again, she was going to take her chance. Farren only hoped he'd be ready when the time came.

Sebastian

Sebastian forgot how to swallow, how to breathe, how to function at all. He'd been drudging along the whole work week, and every second paid off because it was one second closer to this moment—looking upon a golden goddess.

She'd understood the assignment.

Farren Davis looked every inch as divine as she was supposed to be. She sashayed toward him (a term she'd exposed him to through an episode of Drag Race,) eyes dark, skin even creamier against the brunette wig. Her dress fluttered as she walked, a thick and luscious thigh exposed by a slit up one side, and wings that were worthy of a Victoria's Secret model. To say Sebastian was thankful for the drink he'd gotten was an understatement. His mouth had gone dry.

Braxton's place was so warm and welcoming. The floor looked rough, patched over the years, some parts of the wood sagging and creaking. The walls were a dusty shade of green, and Braxton's furniture was a mishmash of styles that somehow worked together in their eccentricity. When he complimented them, Braxton informed Sebastian with a chuckle that most of it was repurposed from Goodwill or upcycled from local pieces. All the while Sebastian watched Farren move around the room after their searing kiss, interacting with her friends and checking in with him occasionally.

She laughed with her whole body, head thrown back, the wig making her look like a stranger and the person he adored all at once. They danced around each other, especially when the night was young and everyone was still mostly sober. The group got in a few rounds of party games, which devolved into drinking games, and Sebastian realized his body couldn't handle alcohol as well as it used to. College never felt further away.

He excused himself to the bathroom, splashing water on his face, a little disoriented at the lack of beard he was so used to. Briefly, he remembered he was meant to be filming himself as part of Chris's request.

"Hi, uh. It's Sebastian... Ares." He shrugged, remembering too late he was supposed to use his character's name. "And I think Chr—Dionysus is going to be the drunkest tonight."

It was awkward, stilted, the alcohol clearly not erasing the shitty parts of his personality yet, like the social anxiety and his inability to relax. After a few deep breaths, he rejoined the party, music overtaking the games and conversation.

A plethora of tipsy or full-out-drunk gods and goddesses were grouped together in the living room, swaying to the pulsing rhythm that washed over them from the speakers. Farren wasn't among them, so he wandered over to the dining room, intent on grabbing some food or water to stave off the swirling feeling that came from imbibing.

Corinne stood, or leaned rather, against the wall in the dining room with a handful of nuts and a glazed expression on her face, straightening up when she noticed him and walking over with what Sebastian could only assume was purpose. Her small but surprisingly sharp finger poked him in the shoulder, where the armor didn't cover and couldn't protect him from the prodding.

"You." She slurred slightly. "You better not be an asshole to my friend. If you hurt her..." She pointed a shaky finger at his face.

"Corinne, I think you're a little out of it. Why don't I help you find Luis?"

"Why don't I tell you how it is? Hmmm? She's my best friend, and I will protect her. Got it?" She seemed so serious, trying hard to be stern but her minute swaying detracted from the overall effectiveness of the threat.

"Okay, Corinne. I got it. You should probably try to reach out to her when you're sober, and apologize for tearing into her. I know you hurt her, plus she had some family shit go down as well in the interim. She shouldn't have to come to you first." Sebastian didn't mean for his voice to sound so harsh, but he found he didn't really care once it came out.

She blinked up at him from behind her glasses, his words sinking in slowly, comprehension crossing her face. "I... I didn't mean to hurt her."

"Maybe you didn't. I'm just letting you know where she's at right now. She needs you, and what you said really upset her."

"What?" Her mouth went slack with shock, something in her eyes cutting through the alcohol-haze. "She said that... Oh god. I have to find her. I've been so stubborn and stupid, caught up in my own shit." Corinne seemed like she was talking more to herself than to him, and before he could get another word in, she darted from the room to find her friend.

Sebastian felt out of his depth, a stranger at a party full of friends, and he kind of hated how much he relied on Farren, especially in this situation. Even without words, just having her pressed against his side with his hand resting on her hip, she grounded him. He craved that surety, the soft give of her body under his hand.

He'd been trying his best to stay level-headed, to let her lead, but the way she looked tonight and the gazes she kept sneaking his way... Sebastian wasn't sure how much longer he'd be able to hold back. He'd wanted her since day one, and as the weeks passed, his desire only seemed to grow. Sebastian hadn't been this gone for anyone since Ashley, and even then, it never felt like this. Farren was a new phenomenon and a risky one at that. One with the ability to send him to his knees.

He poured himself another drink against his better judgment, letting the alcohol warm his chest and cloud his brain, sobriety looking less appealing in the face of his feelings. When she came up to him some time later, he felt blissfully relieved of the thoughts churning within him.

"Hey, stranger," she said over the music, lifting onto her toes to plant a kiss against his mouth, her lips tasting like sugar and cinnamon.

Sebastian set his glass down on the dining table beside him, gathering her up in both his arms and pulling her flush against his body. He hated how the breastplate deprived him of the feel of her soft chest against his, but the little moan that got caught at the back of her throat was worth it.

"You look so fucking good. I don't think I've gotten a chance to tell you yet tonight." He rasped it into her ear, control fraying with increasing speed.

"The feeling is mutual. I've been having a hard time paying attention to much else."

She initiated another kiss, her hands cupping his cheeks and her mouth slanting over his in a way that let him know there was no chaste intention behind it. She left him breathless, pulling away briefly, and he mourned the loss of contact.

"Thank you," she said between kisses.

"For?" He wanted to take credit, but he had no idea what she could be thanking him for.

"Corinne. She told me you talked to her and she came over to apologize. She was lashing out because she felt out of control. I was the one caught in the crossfire. We had a nice little chat about what's been going on. And about you. There might have been a mention of you being protective and intimidating."

"Me? She came on fairly strong herself. I was worried she was going to poke a hole into my shoulder." It still smarted slightly.

"Yeah, she was checking in to see how things were going between us. Obviously, the answer was 'well.'" Farren smiled, brazen and teasing, her dark eyes sparkling with humor and a little bit of intoxication. Sebastian smiled against where her hands still cupped his cheeks, sinking down to sample more of her.

He backed her away from the table, walking them over to the wall and pressing up against her. His lips burned a trail down the side of her neck, and she gripped his hair in her hand, pulling his head back in a way that had something tightening deep in his stomach. They had the room to themselves for now, others finishing up the game in the living room, a few messing around outside playing a drunken version of hide-and-seek in the woods.

"We shouldn't do this here." Her voice was breathy, disappointed.

Sebastian pulled away, trying to gather his wits, but she grabbed his breastplate and tugged him toward her.

"I said not here. I didn't say not at all." One last heated kiss, and she threaded her fingers through his, leading him away from the common areas and potential prying eyes. The first door they found was the kitchen, dark and uninhabited but not the most conducive. A rough-hewn door to the backyard wasn't his pick either.

Farren found another door off the kitchen, white and unobtrusive. Both of them were astonished to find a day room, just a step down from where they stood. Light and breezy curtains covered the windows encircling the room, bathing the space in a silvery glow from the moon, a beam slicing through the gaps in the fabric and casting long fingers of light that seemed to reach toward them.

She didn't hesitate, stepping into the room and urging him to join her. He had the presence of mind to check the door, locking it from the inside so this private moment could stay theirs.

"I've been waiting for this for so long. I've been carrying a freaking condom in my wallet for weeks." His words were harsh, unable to keep his cool any longer. She answered by kissing him deeply before stepping back to undo her shoes.

A daybed was tucked up into a corner, a few other chairs and a sofa finishing out the room. Farren pulled him toward the bed, already yanking on the hard chest plate, and he pulled away briefly to relieve himself of the barrier, tossing the condom on the bed. His Pteruges joined the growing pile on the ground, leaving him only in his boxer briefs and the tunic.

He leaned forward, trying to lace his fingers through her hair, a frustrated growl coming up from his throat when the wig got in the way. It was Farren's turn to rid herself of cumbersome accoutrement, wig and wings draped across one of the chairs.

"I need you," he pleaded, hands gripping her waist and his cock straining, aching for her.

"I've thought about this for so long," she answered, and they stretched out onto the bed, his body poised over hers, her leg out of the slit and wrapped around his waist. Sebastian's hand roamed, under the fabric and over the curve of her hip, pulling back in surprise when he realized she didn't have any underwear on.

"Just for you," she said, and it fucking devastated him.

Sebastian nipped at her neck, a small bite at her ear lobe, and she rewarded him with a soft moan. Her nails tried to find purchase on his back, fabric in the way. She made a little dissatisfied noise in the back of her throat.

"I know. I want to touch all of you too but there's no time. Need to be in you right now." He pulled his boxer briefs down his legs and fumbled for the condom on the bed.

"Fine. But I will have you totally naked soon. Quick, before anyone finds us." Farren didn't have to say it twice.

Sebastian hissed as the fabric rubbed against his engorged head, frantic for her and the promise of her body. He moved between her knees, his large hand working the material up her leg until they were both free of the dress, and he could slide back down the bed between her thighs to taste her.

The fucking beautiful gasp she gave when his lips pressed to the inside of her generous thigh was only surpassed by her hand gripping his hair. Her back arched up when his kiss found her sweet heat. She was there, wet and hot already.

"Please."

He wasn't sure if it was her or him that asked, knew only it was what tipped him over from hungry to starved. Sebastian rose, sheathing the condom over his hardness and lifted himself, held his body poised over hers and so close, he wanted nothing more than to sink into oblivion.

"You ready for me, sweetheart?" he asked, trying to keep her in the forefront of his mind, wanting her to enjoy this just as much as he did.

"Yeah—" Her fingers lifted the tunic, hand skating over his tensed abdomen, wrapping around where he waited, heavy and hard. It was Sebastian's turn to teeter on that edge, hissing in a breath at her small hand wrapped around him, pumping a few times before she lined him up and he pushed into her with a groan.

Her mouth fell open, hands digging into his ass as he slowly stretched her, enjoying every inch before he bottomed out, and Sebastian could have sworn he'd died and gone to heaven. Not that he'd ever been particularly religious or concerned with the afterlife. But here, with her heat wrapped around him, her hands laying waste to the parts of his body she could reach—it felt like being burned by the sun, consumed by the divine fire of her body.

The throbbing beat of music carried on, the fall night around them swathing them in darkness, secrecy, and moonlight that only highlighted the ecstasy on her face. Farren wasn't shy about expressing herself. There were one or two times when he hit a spot she seemed to particularly enjoy, and Sebastian had to place his lips against her mouth to swallow the moans.

They chased that high. Sweat collected on his body, muscles burning in the most exquisite way, but Sebastian was determined to watch her fall apart beneath him first. He could tell she was straining for it, and he grunted into her ear, telling her to touch herself.

Her hand snaked between them, dancing over herself and her pleasure seemed to build, her cunt fluttering around him as she climbed ever higher.

"You're taking me so well, Farren. *God*, you feel exquisite."

His words urged her on, her fingers increasing with speed, her eyes screwed shut, and little mewls escaping her mouth, unintelligible words falling from her lips.

"I can't wait to watch you come. I can't wait to feel you milk my cock." Sebastian leaned forward, searing her neck with a bruising kiss before rasping into her ear. "I can't wait to come inside you, make you mine."

She fell apart beneath him on a scream he swallowed with

his mouth, feeling her grip him, her body writhing beneath his as he followed her over the peak, dragging his lips across her jaw. She whispered something, her voice unable to cut through the din of his orgasm. Sebastian grunted his own satisfaction into the salty skin of her neck, her pulse thunderous beneath his mouth.

"Beautiful. So fucking beautiful," he rasped.

They savored those few stolen moments, somewhere outside of Poolesville, in the sunroom with the hunter's moon shining down on them. Sebastian nipped and kissed at her skin as he pulled out, sucking a hickey into the inside of her thigh, proof to himself and her that this had happened. It was so much more than just a fantasy.

She helped him dress, hands lingering on his body as she fastened the skirt and breastplate back onto his body. Sebastian kissed her shoulders where the wings had left indentations. She carried the wings and her wig back to the coat room, his own fallen goddess, depositing them on the bed beside her coat and giving him one more intoxicating kiss before she left the room. They rejoined the party, Farren's lipstick long gone and her eye makeup slightly smudged. No one noticed; no one was sober enough to.

They joined her friends, dancing to the punishing beat undercut by the dark cry of the singer. It felt almost ritualistic, that feeling only increasing when they headed outside to start a bonfire. Flames crackled, licking up into the sky, embers arcing from the orange heat and scorching little patches of ground at their feet. Sebastian held her from behind, warding her against the cold so she could soak in the heat of the fire. She sipped another one of those Halloween drinks, her mouth apple-tart when he kissed her again. He cut himself off, switching to water so he could drive them home safely.

By the time midnight came and went, some people starting

to leave, he was sober. Cold. He gathered up their coats, wrapping a very sleepy Farren up into hers, then putting on his own. They thanked their hosts, exchanging hugs and happy thanks for a wonderful party. Sebastian wondered if anyone noticed him blushing when he thought about just how wonderful it really was.

The drive back to his place was quiet, Farren half asleep, slouched against the window. He should have told her about the demotion, Ashley, and the situation in Ohio before the party. Should have told her when she got home from her family, or before that on the phone. He'd been carrying this strange feeling of fear, resentment, and worry. Best to just push it down for now, until he knew what to say to her. The last thing he wanted to do was lash out, even if his brain told him he wanted to. Mostly to Andrew, but the worry that Farren might get caught in the mess sat uneasily in his stomach.

Sebastian let the mindless prattle of one of the nighttime radio hosts keep him awake enough to drive, and he was astonished when he looked up to find himself at home. Even following the GPS, he'd done most of it on autopilot.

He woke Farren from where she'd fallen asleep, and she gave him an adorable pout as she stepped out of the car, following him up the stairs. Sebastian let them in, turning on the kitchen light and then his bedroom light. She didn't wait for instructions. Farren rid herself of her dress, the fabric pooling at her feet, and her bra was next. The view of her voluptuous naked body walking past him toward the ensuite bathroom left him hard and aching for her again.

She shut the door, the sound of rushing water the only thing he could hear, and she emerged from the bathroom a few minutes later, her face bare and her eyes tired. They slunk into bed, Sebastian holding onto her tightly as sleep claimed her.

His mind and body however were far more awake, his brain

teasing him with the aftermath of their stolen time. Her panting had bordered on sobs, unintelligible words falling from her lips, her body trembling beneath his. Sebastian had gotten drunk on her, kissing every part of her he could reach, and it wasn't until now that he finally realized what she'd been saying when they both fell apart.

I love you.

And fuck if it didn't scare the hell out of him. The night bled away, lightening with a new day and little to no sleep for him. Though that wasn't unusual.

Sebastian fought against asking her about it the second she woke up, when she groaned against the intruding sunlight, burrowing under the pillows to prolong sleep a little bit longer. It seethed under his skin, slithering, and every second he spent in bed with her was one step closer to him saying the wrong thing.

He must have misheard her. Perhaps the culprit was the corner of his mind where he kept his secret wishes. Maybe he'd conjured it on Halloween night, like a spell broken with daylight. Sebastian made it all up, right?

The soft pat of his feet pacing the living room floor was broken up with the occasional sigh. Sebastian ran his fingertips against his mouth, trying to imagine what it would taste like to speak those same words.

She emerged wearing one of his shirts while he was fretting, and he imagined he looked in a state. His hair was probably sticking up on all ends from running his hands through it. A T-shirt, boxer briefs, and bare feet completed the look.

"How did you sleep?" he asked.

"Ugh... hungover. Do you have any Tylenol?"

Farren staggered over, rubbing the sleep from her eyes, the tiny bit of leftover eye makeup she hadn't quite washed off streaking black under her lashes. She gave him a quick kiss on the mouth before she continued her mission for hangover relief.

Sebastian wouldn't have cared that she knew where his glasses were and helped herself to some water, chugging it down as if she was parched. He wouldn't even have noticed. But then she'd said those words last night in the heat of the moment. Three words paired with others like "future" and "forever" filled his belly with a snaking dread. He felt like he was faltering. He still hadn't found the right words to tell her about work and wasn't ready for the conversation that would follow. The one where he would hurt her. The one where he stepped back to fix his fuck up because he couldn't handle his career being derailed again. Her revelation at the party did nothing but make him panic.

"Yeah, counter to the left of the fridge, top drawer," he answered.

Farren struggled with the childproof lid for a minute, a slight growl escaping her, but then she pried it open. Tablets shook against the plastic container as she coaxed some out, dropping two into her palm and straight into her mouth. She chased them with another big glug of water before setting everything back to rights. Pills in the drawer, glass in the top rack of the dishwasher.

Too comfortable. Too close.

"We didn't discuss plans today. Would you hate me if I wanted to go home? I have a placement starting tomorrow, and I have done zero preparation. I hope you don't mind," she said, seeming worried about how he'd react. Little did she know that space was exactly what he needed. Of course, he wouldn't mind. Not this time. Not when she tied his insides up in a knot.

"Sure, let me give you a ride."

She changed back into her party dress, holding all her items to her chest as they walked the steps down. Farren didn't talk much on the drive over, eyes a little bloodshot, circles a testament to her tiredness.

He parked the car against the curb outside her building, the engine stalling to a stop and going quiet. They sat there for a moment, neither of them saying anything, and then they both seemed to jump to attention at the same time.

"Thank you so—"

"Last night was—"

Tension was broken with laughter, Sebastian gesturing for her to go first.

"Thank you for everything. I had a really good time with you last night." Her cheeks were flaming, no makeup to hide the blush that swept under her skin.

"Last night was phenomenal, Farren. I... I don't have words."

When he tried to help her out, offering to walk her up, she shook her head with a small smile. She assured him she would be fine and she didn't want to put him out. Farren leaned over, poking her head in through the open car window to give him a sweet kiss.

"I'll see you around?" she asked.

"For sure."

Sebastian watched her leave, conflict battling within him at how badly he hated to say goodbye, even temporarily... and how scary it was to think about asking her to stay.

The week that followed was similar to those before, the ones before Farren happened at least. Work—too many hours of it— too much bullshit. He was still tinkering with the app and the pitch, in secret, and doing an awful job of it in his distraction. He hoped if he got it ready, he could get himself back into Andrew's good graces and his career back on track.

Farren and Sebastian exchanged some texts, and a phone call around midweek. She was a little frazzled, tired. Her new placement was more challenging, with far more kids to see to who were less cute than the kindergarteners she'd told him about. Now that Halloween was over, reality crept back in.

Sebastian said nothing when she expressed how drained she felt. How could he when that was his default setting at work? He just tutted in sympathy and let her vent. If she talked, he wouldn't have to say anything. If she spoke, he wouldn't have to admit he'd gotten demoted and that it was so close to what he'd run from, the thought of having to do it again was too much to comprehend. He'd buried it behind her talking about her family and prepping for the Halloween party, throwing himself into getting ready for it. But there was nowhere to hide now, no matter how badly he wished the demotion hadn't happened or how much he wanted that pitch.

He felt sick at the prospect of telling her, thinking of how she'd reacted to the opportunity in the first place, how proud she'd been. Letting her down, letting himself down... he just couldn't face it. So, when the conversation turned to him, and she asked him about his week, about work, he mumbled something about coding and SOPs.

The box with her gift lay unopened on his coffee table, mocking him every time he sat down to watch television. Sebastian wanted so badly to give it to her, to see her. Yet.

Yet those words were carved into his skin, and no matter how much he tried, he couldn't forget them. Farren said nothing. Not that Sunday after Halloween or the rest of the week, either. She issued the weekly invitation to game night, and he gave the usual "I'll have to see if I can make it. Work." Yeah right.

Work is not going well and you barely seem to care. If she means so much to you, you'd have told her by now, come clean about why you're such an untrusting, workaholic asshole. You're delaying the inevitable.

The voice in his head wasn't wrong, but it wasn't entirely correct either. She meant too much to him, and it scared him. It enraged him to have fallen under the pressure, and soon, he'd have to make a choice. Was he willing to let another woman derail his future? Heartburn he hadn't dealt with in a while corroded his windpipe. Sebastian tried to harden himself to the hope shimmering under the surface.

And felt lonelier than he had in a long time.

Farren

arren wracked her brain, rummaging through the memories of Halloween night to figure out if she'd done what she thought she did. It was hazy, the recollection bathed in moonlight and apple cider alcohol. She was pretty sure, though. She said the words she'd been trying to keep back for so long despite herself.

Sebastian either didn't hear her or was content to pretend he hadn't, though she couldn't entirely fight the feeling something was off. Was he just stringing her along? Did he ignore what she said because he was scared of the pressure those words added? Farren had yet to reconcile how she felt. It bubbled under the surface for weeks. Apparently, all it took to boil over was alcohol and the hottest sex she'd had in years. Fuck.

They texted less than before, but he wasn't actively avoiding her. At least, she hoped not. She issued her standard invitation for the Friday game night. Farren was strangely excited to go. She'd missed it. Between her family and her only-recent-reconciliation after her tiff with Corinne... She needed a sense of normalcy. He gave her the same spiel as usual, and the unease within her stomach spread.

This was why she didn't do this. This disgusting doubt and worry with the slightest hint of impending heartbreak. This was why she ended things first and ran. It was protection. No one else was going to look out for her best interests. It fell to her. She may have made a massive miscalculation in thinking Sebastian was in her best interest. Even though she did love him. Maybe this was one of those disasters again, the ones she attracted without trying. The ones that eroded her.

Dread followed her through the week, growing larger and larger. By the time Friday came and went without seeing Sebastian, she knew she was well and truly fucked. She whispered brokenly to Corinne about her drunken mishap and the fear of what it caused. Corinne tried to reassure her that she was over-thinking things, reading into it too much.

The cafe felt weird to her tonight, claustrophobic in a way it had never been. Chairs scraped too loudly against the wooden floors. The heat was turned up far too high, and a droplet of sweat trickled down the back of her neck. The scents of the food were too sharp, too sweet. Her nerves made everything feel off. Farren felt like she was waiting for something to go horribly wrong. Even the prospect of a cute game like Calico wasn't enough to calm her nerves.

"He's totally gone for you. You should have seen how he looked at you at the party." Corinne bumped her shoulder against Farren's as they placed tiles to create the coziest quilt.

Farren scoffed and bumped her back. "The only one who was gone was you. How did you pack so much alcohol into such a little body?" she tried to joke. *Deflect. Deflect, and maybe she won't give you false hope.*

"That's beside the point. I mean it. His eyes were on you all night," Corinne said, not taking the bait.

"Yeah, long enough for us to have sex and for him to start ghosting me." The words were bitter, sitting on her tongue, and she couldn't swallow them away.

"Wait... you guys—at the party?" Her friend stage-whispered, and Farren shook her head brusquely. She gave Corinne the look. The *you're-a-moron-shut-up* look. It almost worked. Almost. But Corinne lifted her eyebrow suggestively, and Farren's doubts flooded past the humor. "What if he ends up hurting me? I'm not built for this."

"Weren't you the one telling me just how different this is? Have some faith, Farren. Surely the risk will pay off, right? If it could mean forever, isn't it worth a tiny bit of doubt and fear?" Corinne was right. Farren hated when she was right because she tended to toss *I-told-you-so*'s around.

This was what Farren wanted. It may not be all she wanted in life. She may still have been trying to figure the rest out. But this piece of it, this surprise of a man, was top of the list at this point.

"You're right. I need to go see him. No use both of us burying our heads in the sand." Farren's apprehension would have to wait.

"Atta girl!" Corinne pumped her up, practically shoving the game they'd just finished into a bag and urging Farren toward the door. "Go get him."

The walk was chilly and dark, daylight savings stealing the last bit of summer and drowning the city in ink by six. Farren gathered her coat around her snugly, tucking her hands under her armpits to keep warmer. The trees were getting barer after an icy week, leaves crunching under her boots with each step. Should have brought a scarf. Should have called for a rideshare. Should never have lost her heart in the first place.

By the time she was outside his apartment, the cold wind stung her face to slight numbness, and all she felt when she rang the doorbell was trepidation.

"Yeah?" he asked through the intercom.

"It's Farren." Silence. Just a beat too long.

The lock buzzed open, and her boots clicked up toward his front door. Sebastian's door swung in, and his bulk blocked the doorway. Annoyingly, he was even better looking despite the sweats, or perhaps because of them. He looked disheveled when she saw him. His hair stuck up in multiple directions as if he'd been running his hand through it. Gone was the clean-shaven face from Halloween, the early makings of a beard shadowing his jaw and cheeks.

"Hi," she said. Unable to gather the courage for more.

"Hey. I wasn't expecting you." He mainly seemed surprised, not wholly dissatisfied with seeing her there.

"Yeah, sorry. I should have texted." Her statement was met with that little tucked-in smile people give to strangers on the street when they don't want to look rude, but there's been eye contact.

Why? Why was this so goddamned awkward? Being with Sebastian had been so easy once they got going. Farren wholly lost herself in him and how he made her feel. But at this moment, less than three feet apart, it felt distant somehow.

He still stood in the doorway, making no move to touch her or invite her in. Farren felt like she was about to fucking vomit right there on his welcome mat. Sebastian seemed to remember himself as the silence between them stretched on just too long.

"Come in," he said finally.

Farren followed him in, surprised to see the place looking messy. Every time she'd been here before, he had it pristine. Though again, it could just have been because he'd been prepared. He'd known she was going to be there. Still, it didn't seem like him.

He gestured for her to sit on the couch, folding up the blanket he must have been lying under before she interrupted his evening.

"I'm sorry. I shouldn't have come without notice." Caught between the living room and the door, Farren's eyes darted toward the exit, the ember of hope Corinne coaxed to life waning under his lukewarm reception. She moved toward leaving, surprised when his hand wrapped around her wrist.

"No, wait. I just... You caught me off guard, that's all." His eyes were shadowed, and she realized just how worn down he looked. The brackets next to his mouth sagged down a little, unhappy lines etched into his face. She thought of the dimple she'd seen on Halloween, wished it was etched into his cheek instead of the signs of stress and exhaustion.

"What's going on? You've been quiet all week. Is everything okay?" she asked, looking him dead in the eye.

He gave a small sigh. "I'm fine. It's just been a challenging few days." Farren could have sworn she heard him mutter "few months" under his breath.

"Do you want to talk about it?" She stepped closer to him, yearning for the heat coming off of his body, so close she could feel the whispers of it.

"No... No." He shoved his hand through his hair and shook his head as if the words weren't enough for her to get the picture.

"Is there anything I can do to help?" Farren wanted to erase his anxiety and ease whatever was bothering him.

"No." His answer was abrupt, and Farren just felt unmoored. Something was very wrong here, and she must have made a huge mistake coming here unannounced. Her fear bloomed, manifesting as anger in its freneticism.

"Well, what do you want? You don't want me to leave, but you don't want to talk to me? You don't have time to see me, but you're gripping my arm as if you're worried I'm going to bolt from the room. What is it? What do you want, Sebastian?" It came out more hostile than she'd intended, her insecurity tearing a hole through the reasonable tone she'd wanted to use.

Sebastian dropped her arm as if she'd burned him, stalking away from her, and she realized for the first time just how tall he was. Farren was large. She took up a lot of space. It was what it was. She'd never felt small her whole life. But seeing how far one step took him away from her, how distant one stride was for him...

"I'd rather not do this now." His tone was deadpan, something in his face shutting down at her questioning.

"Do what?" Probably not the best idea to try to pull more out of him, but she was hurting and wanted answers. She needed them. So that later, when she inevitably obsessed over what had gone wrong, she didn't have to wonder about her part in it.

"I don't want to fight. I don't want to make this a whole thing. It's been a lot, and I just need a second to avoid dealing with this." He sounded defeated, his voice thick with fatigue, his frown leaving indents between his eyebrows.

"Is it work? Is it me?" Farren hated how small her voice sounded, how she'd let herself care this much about it and was too far gone to pull back now.

"It's everything. It's the fact that no matter how hard I work, how many hours I put in, and how much I sacrifice my time... One misstep is enough to derail it all. One mistake related to you." He paced before her, gesturing toward her when he mentioned the mistake.

"Sebastian, what happened?" she asked, trying to keep the question careful, gentle, and kind.

"I got demoted, kicked off of the pitch I worked so hard on, around the time you were over visiting your family."

His words dropped like stones in her stomach. "Oh. Oh, I'm so sorry. I know how much it meant to you and how hard you worked for it."

"You have no idea. It's been months of grinding, scraping, fighting for progress, and it was gone just like that." He snapped his fingers. "Everything I've been working for since Ohio, and it was gone in an instant. Again. I'm not sure I can do it much longer. The hours, the stress. I put in so much of myself, and for what?" His pacing ceased as his voice rose, his face twisting in anger.

"What do you mean 'again?' I'm confused. I'm sorry. It sucks. I just don't get how this is my fault or why you're upset with me." Farren's stomach lurched with worry. This was it. This was the shoe drop. She was sure of it.

"My whole life got blown up in Ohio, so I had to leave. I had to prove myself and start over at this new company. I put in months and months of work. I aimed to redeem myself and my ideas and display my skills. All of it is gone. I have nothing to show for it." He gesticulated with his arms as if his feelings were too big for mere words, and his body had to express some of it as well.

"I don't think that's true. If you explain, if you keep at it, you'll get to where you want to be. I'm sorry things didn't go your way back in Ohio, but it can be different here." Farren tried to soothe, tried to get a grasp on what he was saying and what he wasn't. Something happened beyond just work.

"*Didn't go my way*," he whispered, then scoffed. "My ex and I were working on proposals. We worked at the same company, and were both trying to sell an app. All we had to do was pitch. More fool me because she pitched my own fucking idea before I got the chance, and when I went in to do my pitch, I was fired for 'stealing' her proposal. My career was over; my reputation in Ohio was ruined because I trusted someone and let them in. Now it's happening again because of you. Because you swept in and disrupted my life. It seems like nothing is normal anymore!"

Anger swelled within her at his reaction, disbelief because his "normal" wasn't healthy. The hours he put in, the hard work wearing him down couldn't be "normal," and hearing him call it that pissed her off.

"Whoa, okay. *No.* I had no part in what happened in the past.

I'm sorry you were hurt and your trust was broken. But this job you're chasing isn't a cure-all, and you don't need to prove shit to them or your ex. You know they treated you like crap long before I came around. We're both grown adults. You could have said at any time you weren't in this anymore. I'm not responsible for your feelings." Her chest ached with rage and the urge to lash out. It was that or run. Farren took a step away from him, closer to the door to escape. "There's two of us involved here," she reminded him.

"Exactly. Involved. Somehow within a short amount of time, it's become *involved*. I have a key to your place. I'm getting demoted for buying you a gift, and you're telling me you love me. What am I supposed to do with all that? I'm not good at this. I'm not ready for this." He yanked his hands through his hair, then rubbed a fist against his breastbone as if it pained him. Sebastian's face twisted in a way that hurt to look at. Her chest stuttered at his words. It ached upon finding out he knew... he'd *known* and didn't acknowledge it. Sebastian pretended he was clueless. Worse, he didn't say it back, *that* was the most painful part.

"This wasn't part of the plan, and now I'm fucking it all up because my goals were set in stone long before you." He went back to pacing, though it felt more like prowling within the small space of his living area.

Once again, Farren felt like she was the second choice, first with her family and now with him. It made her want to throw up right there on his floor. Maybe it would force him to stop pacing.

"You hit me with those words, and all I can focus on is no matter which way this goes, I'll be losing something important."

Somehow the word "gift" permeated through the emotional fuzz around her brain.

"What gift? I have no idea what you're talking about." Her confusion gave him pause.

Sebastian stormed past her toward his bedroom, emerging with a wrapped box, complete with a bow on top.

"This. This fucking thing practically cost me everything I've worked toward. Everything important to me." He held it out for her to take, but she stepped back. She didn't want it. Not if it came with so much resentment. Not much of a gift in that case.

"I didn't ask you to do anything for me." Farren's voice was shaky, her eyes welling with tears. She felt her insides shriveling up the longer this conversation continued, the more the pain within her seemed to sink deep.

"Yeah, well. You didn't ask for a gift, I got it anyway. I didn't ask you to love me, and you did it anyway." There it was. The consequences of her opening up to someone for the first time. For real. It hurt far more than she expected. Maybe later, she'd be able to recall how the mention of her loving him looked like it terrified him, but she didn't care right then.

"I didn't exactly plan it. Maybe I was just dickmatized. I don't know. But right now, at this moment, with you throwing everything up in my face, making me out to be like your asshole ex, saying I'm just a roadblock in your life... I'm starting to wonder why I ever thought I loved you in the first place." She hissed it out between clenched teeth, tears streaming hot trails over her flushed cheeks. "I thought this was different. I thought I was done wasting my time and messing around in something aimless, going nowhere."

He seemed to grow somehow—becoming more intimidating —with his chest heaving and his hair messy. Farren had never seen that expression on his face, the misery, the scowl a mockery of the smile she so loved.

"Ha! That's rich, considering I had to coax you into even *trying* to show up for yourself with that game idea you haven't bothered to tell your friends about. Do you really think subbing is going to get you anywhere? It's a dead-end job. I'm losing my dream trying to encourage yours." He stepped closer to her, his index finger pointed at her chest, punctuating what she could only assume was an accusation. "I believe in you! I want the best for you, and it feels like it's for nothing. You have no ambition, no drive. No matter how much I try to tell you your idea is worthy, you seem determined to diminish it so you don't have to deal with the idea of failure."

Failure. The word pelted her, relentless in its heft. All her life, she'd felt not good enough, not smart enough, not worthy. Protecting herself was all she had. How dare he throw that in her face? How dare he preach about failure when his whole career goal was just to spite someone else?

"Well, at least I have heart! You're all ambition, working yourself into the ground for a job where you're nothing but a number on a spreadsheet. You're doing it to prove what, exactly? You're better than your ex? That spite will get you to the top of a company sucking the life out of you? Nobody there gives a shit about you. Instead of putting time and energy into something that's going to benefit you, that could actually be good for you..." Farren gestured between the two of them, between what could have been theirs. "You're choosing to hide behind your fear, behind your stupid ego. I know this ex and your parents probably fucked up how you see relationships, but come on."

"Come *on*? Come on, what? I told you I couldn't do this tonight. I'm scrubbed raw. Everything is twisted up and wrong. We're yelling at each other! I still feel like I've been tossed in the washing machine and wrung out to dry. I can't do this. I feel like I'm being pulled apart. I want to be free of this pain. This is too much. I am not okay right now, and this isn't helping." Farren felt his unspoken: *you* aren't helping.

Sebastian's eyes glistened with tears, and Farren sat in the aftermath of the pressure they'd both been carrying exploding between them. He wasn't wrong. She was scared of failure, of being hurt. But so was he. He pulled away to retreat back to what he knew, what was safe, even though it added no joy to his life. Protecting himself the same way she was trying to.

"That still doesn't make it okay to be hurtful and mean or to make it out like I'm the bad guy here." When all she'd ever done was care about him and try to pull him out of his dour shell.

"I never said that. Not once did I say that!" His voice was doing this funny thing, dry and hoarse and tight. She wondered if he'd let the glistening tears fall or if he would hold onto them with his tight-fisted control.

"No, I'm not a bad person, just the wrong kind. You don't want a serious relationship, but you want to give me crap for not being a serious person. You're scared and stuck in the past. You don't even know what the hell you want," Farren scoffed, backing away toward the door and tightening her coat around her body to ward off a chill that had nothing to do with the temperature in the room.

"Sorry, Sebastian, but I don't see how those things add up. If you don't want to be in this anymore, just say so. Better to know now before I do something stupid like introduce you to my friends and tell my family about you. Before I sleep with you and stupidly think it means something!" Farren's voice cracked as she shouted, and she turned so he wouldn't see her cry, walking away while she still kept some sense of composure. Her hand wrapped around the doorknob.

"It did mean something!" he said back, and she stilled for a moment. Waiting.

But nothing else came, and inside her chest, she felt something shutter.

"Not enough, evidently. Good luck, Sebastian. I hope your

big 'fuck you' moment is worth it. I hope you find happiness. Or success. Whichever one you decide is most important."

The door clicked shut behind her. Farren made it down the stairs and onto the sidewalk before new hot tears obscuring her vision started to streak down over her cheeks. Cold cut through her clothing as she walked home, not caring, not bothering to call a rideshare. It was the loneliest walk of her life, and Farren never wanted to feel like that again. Ever.

Sebastian

A good night's sleep was relative. Sebastian was never a particularly restful man, but that night, he stayed up until dawn crept through the cracks around his curtains. His bed felt overly large, the room emptier than it'd ever been. Which was strange; she'd only spent the night here once. Her scent shouldn't be embedded in his mind. His hand shouldn't be reaching for her on the other side of the bed. Something in his chest collapsed, and it seemed like nothing would alleviate it no matter how slow he tried to breathe or how carefully he focused on the air stretching his ribcage.

It was the right thing. He wasn't wrong in being afraid, in wanting to avoid their blow-up in the first place, was he? In wanting to focus on what he'd come here to do. They weren't well suited. Though at this point, Sebastian wondered if anyone would be a good fit... or if he should bother being with anyone. Maybe the thing with Ashley fucked him up more than he realized until now.

It was fine. It would be fine. Farren would go on with her life, content with how it was. He would focus forward like he always did. Like he'd done when they fired him in Ohio. He had some tough decisions to make. On to the next project. The next pitch.

And miss out on all the living in between?

It was an annoying thought. A traitorous thought. It sounded so much like Farren, like something she would've said. Succeeding at work, in his field, was all he'd ever wanted, even before Ashley. He'd put in so much time—

Is that really it, or is it just sunk cost fallacy at this point?

He couldn't tell anymore.

It was too late. He packed away the box—Farren's so-called dream—still wrapped, in his hall closet to forget about.

It had only been a few months since they'd met. He'd go back to normal, and everything would be behind him. They were into November, so close to the new year and a fresh start. He could get back into Andrew's good graces. The pitch was a non-starter, but maybe he could prove he deserved the more significant project manager promotion when it became available. Not much time, but not impossible.

Okay. Yeah. He just needed to refocus. Get back in the game.

Work proved miserable. Sebastian forced himself to perform. His phone stayed silent and that little pep talk he'd had with himself—the one where he was so convinced he'd been right—its impact faded with each passing day the gnawing within didn't subside.

He missed her. And it pissed him off.

Sebastian was supposed to be beyond this. He couldn't love her, right? It was only ever meant to be casual, fun. Nothing more.

Even though you shared things with her you'd never told anyone else? Even though she made each day feel a little more vibrant?

Still, Andrew mistook his general quiet contemplation around the office for work ethic, so that was a relief. Rachel gave him a puzzled look, tried to strike up a conversation with him and offered another drink after work, but he declined. No use for frivolity, no time to waste.

Instead, he went home after working late, cooked himself a

meal, scrubbed the apartment, and exercised until he was too tired to move in the hope of getting some sleep.

On Thursday night, he got an unexpected call that made his breath catch in his chest, only for his stomach to shrivel up when he saw the caller ID. The name made him want to open up his blinds to check if it was a full moon or something. There it was: Ambrose Clark, plain as day.

"Hey, Dad."

"Hey, Bash! How've you been?" His dad sounded grittier, older than he remembered. Something in his voice sounded weary and made Sebastian concerned.

"Been doing okay. Just work and stuff. What's up with you?" It was stiff. It almost felt scripted with the words not flowing out as they should. Too many suppressed sentences stuck in between the ones he said out loud.

"Just 'Live, Laugh, Loving' it up! Your mom says hi," his dad joked, and Sebastian could hear her shouted greeting in the background, enough to put a slight smile on his face.

"Are you calling for any particular reason?" Sebastian asked, hating how brusque it sounded, unable to manage much else. Conversation had been limited for him that week. He was surprised his voice didn't sound strange from disuse.

"Thought I'd check in on you. It's been radio silence for the last few weeks."

A few months more like. The last time he'd bothered to call them was his mom's birthday. He tried not to dwell on the guilt pushing up his throat at the realization.

"Yeah, sorry about that. I'm working toward a promotion, and we just came off the crush of needing to meet targets before the end of our suspense date. So, I'm a little bushed. What's new with you?"

"We got a new alpaca!"

Oh my god. What now? Sebastian started pacing in the

apartment, socked feet gliding over the smooth wood floors making it easier on the turns when he ran out of room.

"Our neighbor got arrested, and they had a ton of animals—domestic and exotic—on property. We agreed to take on the chickens and his alpaca. So, that was one less thing for the authorities to deal with." It was so blasé, as if arrests including South American animals were no big deal in rural Ohio. He wondered how they were even allowed to keep the alpaca. Chickens were one matter but—never mind. He didn't want to know.

"Why the hell did he get arrested?" Sebastian could feel a headache sneaking in, his temples pinched and a sharpness behind his eyes which made him want to crawl into bed and sleep for two days straight.

"The property doubled as a weed farm. It was kind of ridiculous." His dad scoffed. "But that's what you get when you're dumb enough to sell to a cop."

Sebastian had to physically fight to keep himself from rolling his eyes, or reacting out loud, his real opinion of no use to this conversation.

"Well, at least you got an alpaca out of it!"

"And a huge bag of weed before Jerry was arrested! So, we're good for a while until we can find another provider."

Provider, like it was through fucking health insurance or something. Sometimes it was crazy to think how parents like his produced such a strait-laced, uptight asshole.

"That's definitely something. How's Mom doing?" Subject change. Hopefully, they could get the pleasantries out of the way, and this could be over quicker. There was a crash in the background, some shouting, and he could have sworn he heard animal noises.

"She's dealing with the chickens. One snuck into the house wreaking havoc at the moment, but she's good otherwise. There was a bit of a health issue a few weeks ago, but the doctor gave the all-clear." His father said it calmly like they were catching up on football scores or discussing the weather. Not that either of them ever cared a lick for sports. Sebastian stilled, the staccato cadence of his feet on the floor quiet, the silence in the room like a vacuum.

"What kind of health issue? Why didn't you guys call me?" His voice was more frantic than he would have liked, but then again, it seemed justified.

"It was good. It turned out to be benign. We didn't want to bother you. You're so busy. We handled it."

"Turned out to be... You guys thought it was *cancer*?" Sebastian's voice rose, the anger from work, failure, and Farren mingling with worry and helplessness.

Fuck. He was such a bad son. Such an awful person. Who has a cancer scare and doesn't bother to call? Did they really think him so uncaring? The thought of his mother, sick, withering... the emotions he'd been suppressing for a week welled up, and rage rose to the surface.

"It was just a small tumor on her thyroid. They cut it out, and they're keeping an eye on her, but it shouldn't resurface or spread. She's feeling much better. You know, they do that as an outpatient procedure now. It's really not a big deal. As I said, we handled it." His dad sounded like he was getting irritated as well, his casual tone slipping into something a bit harsher.

"Of course you did. Of course you handled it on your own. That's how you've done it for as long as I've known you both. The two of you against the world." The words were scathing, the front he'd tried to maintain in tatters on the ground. Now probably wasn't the time to process childhood trauma, but the thought of his mom being sick—potentially so ill they went to go see a specialist—and neither of them bothered to call...

"Yes, it is us against the world, always has been." His dad

sighed on the line, a slight rustling on the other end like his father might have started pacing as well, or potentially put him on speaker. "I don't know what you're getting at?"

Of course, he didn't. His dad didn't think beyond what was right in front of his face. Sebastian should be used to it, should be immune to it. But the pressure of the past few weeks wore him down, especially this last one. The lack of calm that Farren provided ate into him and infuriated him. He didn't want to need her. He didn't want to miss how she made him feel. He was supposed to be stronger than that.

"Always the two of you. No room for me. No consideration. Maybe I would have wanted to know, to help. Did that ever occur to you? Have you considered I would have liked to be involved in your lives and had you in mine?" The words were daggers, thrown without care or target, just plain chaos. There was a pause, a slight sniff on the other end of the line.

"You've never..." his dad took a shuddering breath. "You were always busy with school, then college, then work." His father stumbled over, trying to explain himself, the words stopping and starting as he apparently gathered his thoughts. "We had nothing in common with you. We thought you'd just like to be left alone to chase whatever you had your eye on. Your mother and I... you've always been a bit perplexing to us." His father must have been close to tears given how strained his voice sounded. It tore at Sebastian, guilt and release, things coming to a head finally with them so many miles apart. Just the tinny sound of his father's voice in his ear to keep him tethered to this moment.

"I filled my time with that because it was all I had. I could never get into your tight-knit unit. I always felt like an afterthought. A mistake." Sebastian was getting choked up himself, hand shaking where it gripped the plastic of his phone, briefly thinking he might crack it in his grasp.

"Oh. Oh no. Sebastian..." He heard a sniff, then more shuffling as the phone was passed from his dad to his mom.

"Sweet boy. We love you. I hope you know that." She tried to soothe, too little too late. His hurt made it almost impossible to climb down the peak of anger he found himself at. It was easier to lash out at them than face the fact he'd fucked up big time and a lot of it was his choice.

"I love you too, but sometimes that's not enough. Sometimes it takes more than that. I know I wasn't what you wanted, and I don't know how to force these parts of my life together. I don't know how to be the son you wished I'd been." Sebastian was whispering around the knot in his throat by the end of it.

"We might not always understand you, but we've always loved you. What's bringing all this on? You've never said any of this before." No, there'd been plenty left unsaid over the years, at home, at work.

Sebastian reached a point where silence carved him down to his last nerve.

"I've—I met someone, and it's been scary. When I left Ohio, it was with a bruised heart and ego. I avoided getting too attached to anyone here because I didn't want to get hurt or left, or so caught up that I lost myself and what I wanted." He took a deep breath, trying to verbalize what he'd barely begun to understand. "I'm out of my depth and realizing how much crap I've dragged along with me. I'm getting in my own way as a result."

"Bash, what happened?" His mother's voice was so kind, gentle and sincere.

"I fucked up. I think I fucked up big time, and I have no idea how to fix it or if I should even try." He walked over to the couch (inferior to Farren's and another reminder of his mistake,) sinking down onto the pillows with the phone cradled against his face. They'd always been better at talking about feelings than he was. Perhaps now that would come in handy.

"Tell me about her. I'm assuming it's 'her,' but it would be fine if it wasn't," she said, and Sebastian huffed out a strangled laugh.

"Yes. Her name is Farren. She's... bubbly, spontaneous. Kind of my antithesis and at first, I thought that was a bad thing, but now I'm not so sure. I felt gut-punched when she left, and I still can't catch my breath." Admitting it out loud seemed to cement his feelings.

He did miss her. A lot. Even the bits that annoyed him. Though not really. He'd been reaching for something— anything—to justify pulling away from her. Giving into his fear.

"She's really into board games. She's a substitute teacher, but she's been developing her own game on the side, and it's terrific. She just... she was too scared to go for it, and I—well, you know how closed off I can be. I was mean to her. I insulted her because I was hurt and lashing out. I ended up pushing her away in the process."

"Did you all have a fight?" This time, it was his dad asking, too curious for his own good, not content to let Mom drive the conversation.

"Yeah, a big one. We—uh—we both said some unkind things. I may have said she had no drive and her job was a dead end because she was too scared to do anything with her life. She accused me of being heartless, only focused on work and petty revenge."

She wasn't wrong. Even though it rubbed him the wrong way to admit.

"And you haven't spoken since?" his mom asked.

"No. I haven't reached out because I was being stubborn. I thought it was better it happened now before things got messier and we got even more hurt. She... it just wasn't a good fit." Sebastian closed his eyes, the statement he'd been consoling himself with since she left sounding weaker and weaker the more he said it.

Not a good fit. Not suited. Too different.

"But she hasn't reached out either. So, it's over." The words felt so final spoken out loud, and a hot tear streaked down the side of his face. Sebastian shut his eyes, forcing no others to fall.

"Do you love her? Does she make you happy?" his dad asked, and Sebastian realized this was probably the longest conversation they had in years.

"She made me very happy. I just..."

"Just what? Just don't know if you love her?"

"Yes. No. I don't know. How do you even know what love is?" It sounded so dumb saying it out loud. His idea of it was so skewed, selfish, and consuming from the example he'd had with his parents. Was that love? The kind to lock everything else out, the kind that could hurt others? It was a weapon in Ashley's hands. A means to an end, a blindfold to her duplicity. Was that love?

"If all you want is to wake up next to them every morning and hold them while you fall asleep at night. If their voice alone can calm your heart and they make you laugh until your belly hurts. If the thought of losing them makes you feel physically sick and all you want to do is spend time with them... that's love."

Well, shit.

His silence must have been confirmation enough for them because his mother giggled, and he pictured her elbowing his dad in the ribs, both sharing a conspiratorial smile.

"I was so stupid. I wounded her, badly. I didn't tell her how I felt." That was all he said, not wanting to say those words aloud. Not wanting the first time he said them to be to someone else.

"That's part of it. It happens. You've got to decide just how much she means to you. Are you willing to lose her forever over one fight? Or are you going to go for it and try to make it right?"

He hated when they made sense. Loved and hated that Farren brought them closer, at least in this. It felt... nice. Natural. Like a family.

"What if she doesn't want me back?" His voice was small, doubt crushing his diaphragm.

He heard his mom tut and wished they were closer because, although he wouldn't admit it, he could really do with a hug.

"That's a risk you've got to take, kiddo." His mom hadn't called him that since he left home, and the throwback was a little emotionally overwhelming.

"I'm glad you're okay, Mom. Please. *Please* keep me updated. I know I can get quiet and stuck in my head, but I love you guys, and I do care." He felt like a little kid, the thought of his parents older, the idea of losing them terrifying despite their distant relationship.

"We love you too, hon. You keep us updated as well! I hope to meet your Farren soon," she said, and Sebastian's heart seemed to stutter at the words: your Farren.

"I hope so too. I'll—uh—I'll check in soon."

"See ya, kiddo."

The line clicked, and the call ended.

Sebastian stared at his phone for maybe two breaths before he tried calling her number. Two seconds to decide he wanted her in his life for real. Two seconds to acknowledge what a stupid asshole he'd been. The rest of the time was spent building up the courage to say what was on his mind.

It rang.

And rang.

Then finally.

"Hi, you've reached Farren! I'm sorry I missed your call. Please feel free to text me if it's urgent. Have a great day!"

When he tried it again, it was more of the same. The third time he called, it didn't even ring, cutting straight to the voice-mail message, and Sebastian realized it wasn't just as simple as acknowledging his feelings or saying sorry. He'd hurt her and would do what it took to prove himself and his love for her. No matter what.

Farren

Farren hated feeling like a cliche. Stupid girl crying on the way home, sobbing on the couch. Sniffling all fucking weekend. She'd refrained from the stereotypical tub of ice cream because there was none in the freezer, and he'd kind of ruined the allure of the coffee shop's pastries. Farren didn't even call Corinne until Sunday night, and although her friend offered to come over with a bottle of wine, it was a school night, so she declined. Despite what Sebastian thought, she did take her job seriously. Even if it wasn't one with a ladder to climb, even if it wasn't a "career."

So what if it wasn't typical? She wasn't typical.

Farren returned to school, throwing herself into the task of shaping young minds, even if just for a few days. If she could be a safe place, a kind smile to a kid... If she could make them feel seen and important, it was enough for her. Farren wanted to be the person she never had and so sorely needed. It wasn't so much giving up on a dream. Dreams were fun and sweet distractions from real-world hurts. She was putting aside one goal for something more realistic, more grounded.

Time passed like it inevitably did, marked by darkened days and cold leaking into her apartment through the bad seal around old windows and under the door frames. Time marched on, punctuated by messages from Sebastian that she deleted before she could read them. She was done with men that did nothing but hurt her. Farren was tired of feeling like she wasn't good enough and like saying her feelings out loud were wrong. Dating would not be on her radar, not for a long while.

Loneliness was an old friend, one with sharp elbows that dug into her skin as it settled beside her. Nights with her friends alleviated some of the ache. Corinne must have prepped them because no one mentioned Farren's puffy eyes or how she seemed to lose more often than usual. She stayed longer, the group dwindling until it was just her, Corinne, Luis, and Chris. Chris pulled out Planet, the big blue box a welcome distraction from her dark apartment and his lingering scent on the other side of the bed.

This was Farren's first chance to play it, and she was eager to try it out given how tactile the game was. They held their planets in their hands, each with a specific ecological goal in mind, collecting animals to inhibit their worlds as the pieces dwindled with each round. Pentagons of nature slotted perfectly into each of the twelve spaces on her orb, held in place by magnets. By the end, they each had a unique earth.

Farren's was mostly made up of ice, interspersed with azure oceans and a few vibrant forests. She rolled the planet between her hands, loving the game's interactive nature and how singular it felt. It made her think of her own idea, little cutouts housed in an old box, gathering dust since the last time she worked on it with Sebastian.

The game would benefit from being more than just a board game. Perhaps there was a way they could elevate it. Maybe it might work in another format as—

No.

There was no "they," and there was no use tinkering.

She didn't win Planet either, but it was a fun way to lose. It barely felt like a failure when she held the proof of her efforts cradled in her grasp, like a god. Farren thanked her friends and wrapped herself in her coat and scarf, ready to retreat again.

Corinne wouldn't be deterred, and Farren should have expected it. There was no way her friend would let her get away with saying nothing. She could only dodge so many calls and change the subject so many times. Corinne was stubborn, like a freaking ankle-biter of a dog in a tug-of-war.

"You and me. Wine. Either at your place or a bar, but it's happening. I won't take no for an answer." She stood in front of Farren, the door to the outside chill a few feet away.

"Corinne, please. I'm tired." *Bone-tired. Too tired to pretend anymore.*

"It's Friday. No work tomorrow. No more avoiding me. We're doing this, so either pick or I'll pick for you." It should have been intimidating, but Corinne was freaking tiny. Still, Farren relented.

"Bar. I haven't cleaned." She grabbed her purse from the table, slinging it over her shoulder and waiting for her friend to collect herself.

"You know I don't care about that. You've been dealing with a lot." Corinne patted her arm, and Farren knew she was telling the truth, but it still didn't matter.

"I care. But whatever. Let's go get that drink." *So I can get you off my back.*

Luis kissed Corinne on the way out, headed toward their car, their daughter waiting back home with his mother. A short walk later, Corinne and Farren, freezing their butts off, made their way into an Irish-themed bar, pub, whatever. It was decked out in green and white like a leprechaun spewed over the mahogany wood interiors, and it was deemed a "mood." The aesthetic was rounded out with a large Irish flag hanging over the bar.

Farren did her little hop up onto the bar stool, the wood top sticky from spilled drinks. Corinne joined her and ordered them each a glass of red. At this point Farren would have preferred shots. The same result, only much quicker and without the stupid wine-headache she got about two glasses in. Apparently, it was a reaction to the tannin or something.

"Spill."

Farren resisted the urge to roll her eyes, instead taking a sip of the dry red wine, letting its bitterness coat the back of her throat before she spoke.

"We fought. It didn't go well. End of story." End of relationship.

Understatement of the century. You both fucked up there, and the pieces are still scattered on the ground.

"What were you fighting about?" Corinne leaned closer, trying to be heard over the bad cover band singing U2 in the other room with the small, elevated stage.

"We seemed to have differing views on things. I wanted love, he wanted to focus on his job. At least I found out pretty early on." Farren felt herself tucking her lips into a taut line, ignoring the uncomfortable stretch of her breath around her heartache.

"Farren—" Corinne warned, knowing there was more to the story. Farren turned toward her friend, leaning into her hair to talk over the music and avoid eye contact at the same time.

"He blamed me for his demotion, basically alluded to the fact that I was just like his ex who derailed his career. Said I was directionless and wasting my life. I told him he was heartless and so married to the idea of his job, he was missing out on something real." Farren sat back and shrugged, pretending it didn't hurt her.

Repeating it sucked. The words she'd been ruminating on, obsessing over, were at least somewhat in the open now. She didn't repeat the words taunting her at night when she struggled to sleep.

Those insidious inner statements about her not being

serious or driven or good enough. They chased her, unrelenting. Because they weren't wrong. She *was* silly, she enjoyed goofing off and enjoying what each day brought rather than planning for the future. Farren wasn't settled in her job, in her future. All of it was fluid, where Sebastian was rigid. His ideas had been cemented long before her, and his needs were beyond what she could provide.

How could she stop loving him—turn off the flow of her feelings to make him feel more comfortable? Farren wasn't a liar. She couldn't put it aside and do so convincingly. Sebastian wasn't ready. He might never be. But she'd come too far to turn back now. It was hypocritical of him to damn her for this, then turn around and berate her lack of career commitment.

Farren could commit when necessary; she'd wanted to try and go there with him. There'd barely been time to navigate the intense feelings he evoked. Now he was gone. All those feelings floated around, tangled in a mess of agony and anger at how things turned out. He was the one running away this time.

"What a dick. Honestly. You're like the best thing that's happened to him. He needs you to shake up his life a little. Such an uptight ass." Corinne held her glass out for Farren to clink her own against. She did, halfheartedly.

"It's not my problem anymore. He made it clear where his priorities lie, and they weren't with me."

Even though we'd only known each other a few months, and he'd worked on this for years between his old job and this one. Farren could do this. She could brush it off. She tried to get comfortable on the bar chair, but the seat was hard and unyielding.

"Where do you go from here?" Corinne's question was gentle, and Farren appreciated that she wasn't trying to insert her own ideas into the situation. She didn't need a spiel about being better off without him or forgiving and forgetting.

Farren needed time.

So much shifted for her. She needed to process through it, work through her own plans and ideas and decide where she was headed. She couldn't keep waiting for life to happen to her.

"I'm not sure, to be honest. I have all these bits and pieces floating around in my brain. One part thinks I should go to college to get a teaching degree so I'm not flitting between temporary placements. One part of me worries I only want it to spite him, to prove I can be serious about a career." *And then I'd be just as bad as he is.*

Farren's sigh was long and loaded, exhausted from the lack of sleep and answers. The largest of all that picked away at the scar tissue inside her: *Why didn't he love me? Why wasn't I good enough?*

"Farren, you and I both know a career isn't what defines you. Think about what's attracting you to teach in the first place. If it's to impart knowledge to children and guide them through learning, then, of course, you should pursue it." Corinne said it so kindly, her face open with hope, her eyes sparkling with alcohol and excitement.

Somehow that option didn't feel like it. Not quite. Not far off, but not a proper fit.

"I think it's more about feeling helpful, about being a support system for schools and kids. I swoop in and prove myself useful, and then I get to extricate myself before it becomes too hard." The words twisted inside her, the echo of Sebastian being too scared to be all in. They may have been different in big ways, but they were very much the same when it came down to it.

"But is that what you want or where you're comfortable?" Corinne asked and ordered another round for them.

Huh.

She had no ready response. No immediate words came to her lips even though she parted them slightly to answer.

"I'm not quite sure. It's hard to pin down. I just know I want to bring people joy and make a difference in the process." It was all she'd ever wanted. It was part of why she'd tried to design a board game in the first place. Games had given her a safe space to be herself despite life's turns. Games brought enjoyment and escape.

"So then take time to figure that out," Corinne said as if it closed the discussion. Problem solved. Next.

The bartender deposited two more glasses in front of her friend.

"I'm surprised you're not grilling me on Sebastian more..." Surprised and relieved, the wound was still very much open.

"You're hurting. I don't want to add to it. I just wanted to check in with you. We've been worried. Sebastian—he's not my focus. You are. If you want to talk about him, we will. If you want to get rip-roaringly drunk and curse his name from a rooftop, we can also do that. I'm here for you." Corinne pushed one of the drinks toward Farren, and she lifted the glass to take a swig, the alcohol burning down her throat.

"I just—I really wanted it. More than anything I've let myself want before. I shared parts of myself with him I usually keep guarded. Having Sebastian dismiss that, dismiss me... it just felt like I was back home and a kid again. I vowed I'd never let myself feel desperate again, aching for someone who didn't prioritize me." Tears pricked her eyes for the umpteenth time that week, and Farren was surprised she could still produce them after the deluge she'd cried.

"I'm so sorry. I want to kick him in the shin. Like really, really hard. The kind of kick that breaks the skin and leaves a purple knob." Corinne's face was twisted with mock fury, but the determination was there.

She said it so seriously, and Farren couldn't help the half-laugh-half-sob coming from her mouth at the thought of her short and small friend getting into a physical altercation with anyone, least of all Sebastian.

"If I need that, I know who to call. I appreciate it, Corinne. Really. I've been struggling this week, and this helped. A lot." Farren reached out her hand, squeezing the top of her friend's in gratitude, pulling back to swipe at the moisture escaping her eyes.

"He's been calling. Texting." It was as good as a whisper in such a noisy room.

"What did he say?" Corinne leaned forward, eager for more information. Farren wanted to scoff at her friend. Despite her earlier sentiment, she was nosy as fuck.

"I don't know. I've been deleting them." Farren took another swig of her drink, trying to avoid saying any more.

She could feel Corinne's pointed stare and focused instead on finishing off her glass of wine.

"Farren," Corinne said. Low and warning.

"I don't want to be that girl who has nothing else going on so she gets lost in a relationship. I don't want him to be right about me and feel like I'm pointless... stagnant." Stuck, like he was, even though he couldn't see it.

"Well, what can we do about it?" Her friend's words settled inside of her, the thoughts of her purpose swirling inside her brain.

What could she do if she was unburdened by pressure and expectation?

"I want to find my thing, something all my own that's meaningful. I struggled for so long, feeling alone. It wasn't until I met you guys and joined the game group that I felt like something could actually be worthwhile." *That I felt like I could make a home for myself here.*

Corinne's eyes got misty, and she held out her glass for Farren to clink hers against.

"I make a difference at school. I know I do. But what if it's not enough? What if there are other people like me: kids struggling alone with no outlet or escape from crappy home situations or mental health struggles?"

The shape of it was there. Farren could feel it just out of reach. She strained for it, fingertips reaching for an elusive idea. So close and yet an ocean away all at once.

"I can see how much this means to you, how passionate you are about helping people. That's one of your defining traits. You're so kind, Farren. Nicer than most of us deserve, especially me. I know you can do it. Whatever it is you decide to go for." Corinne leaned into Farren, giving her a sideways hug and leaving Farren feeling like a vice tightened around her voice box.

"Am I being stupid? Hubristic?" The words were quiet coming out of Farren's mouth, wondering whether what she wanted was actually good or if she only sought it out for surface reasons.

"What? No! Where is this coming from?" Corinne asked.

"I don't know. I feel like I tend to get swept away in stuff, hyper-fixating. I know a lot of it is my interests warring with my fear, and it's been difficult coming to terms with it. My jobs have barely been enough to cover bills, if I get caught up in something new... I'm just worried this is a passing phase. I'll end up right back where I started: flaky and reaching for something else. With people thinking I'm lazy or I give up too easily," Farren felt tears prick the corners of her eyes.

It was hard not to internalize what she'd considered a character flaw for years, even with an official diagnosis telling her the fatigue she'd fought for so long wasn't laziness; it was difficult to relinquish those old thought patterns of worthlessness. It seemed easier to act unaffected, to move along with the tide. People expected that from her, and eventually, she manifested it.

It was time she claimed her own identity. Farren was more than what people saw on the surface.

"I think you know what you want, on a soul-deep level. I'm not talking about jobs and relationships. Those things are fluid. I'm talking about the kind of person you are. If you want to be of service, figure out a way to make that work for now. It doesn't have to be perfect. It doesn't have to be a lifelong legacy. Fleeting things can have just as much merit." Corinne sounded very sage for someone two large glasses of wine deep.

Her friend brought up a good point, and Farren tucked away the thought that resonated with the mention of momentary things having merit. She knew what she had with Sebastian was real; even if they never saw each other again, it remained true. She learned from him. His drive worked alongside his passion. His belief in her bolstered her to try, put effort into what was important, even if it was just for a little while. She learned she was capable of love, the real kind. It meant something. It represented hope for the future despite the splintered state of her heart.

"I just wish I could smush all the parts of me together to make a cohesive whole," Farren mused.

"So, why don't you?" Corinne asked.

"What do you mean?" Could it be that simple? Could she have been so blind to the possibilities all along in trying to be one specific thing?

"You know what you're passionate about. Why not pull from all aspects of your life for the most authentic chance at something?" Corinne's words were biblical in their impact.

The ocean parted, the waves held at bay by her words, threading together into an idea.

"Yes." Farren felt her brain on fire. Games brought her joy and community. Gaming gave her a place to belong, one of her own, one that made her think about dreaming and plans and creation. What if someone else could find what she had, could find themselves in that safe space?

"You have a weird expression on your face." Corinne looked a little concerned, and Farren could only assume she appeared slightly crazed.

"A game club for kids." The words seemed so simple. The solution and rightness of it seemed silly. How had it taken her this long to find the answer?

"A game club for kids," Corinne repeated, slightly breathless as she tasted the idea on her tongue.

"A game club! I know it's silly. I know it's not a soup kitchen or clothing drive. I know it's not social work and therapy, but... it could still help, it could still mean something." *My ideas could mean something. I could make a difference.*

"I think it's a great idea!" Her friend beamed up at her, and Farren felt her own answering smile spreading across her face.

"It's me. It's what I can do and what I want to do. I'll keep subbing, obviously, because I enjoy it and I need to pay bills. But I could reach out to the coffee shop or maybe a rec center in my neighborhood and see what I can do. This could be a chance for kids to let go, to learn, and make friends. I'd provide a safe space, at least for a little while." Farren's brain raced with the logistics of it, of how to realize what was just a wisp of a thing right now.

"*We.* If you need it, I'm happy to help. This is big. I'm so proud of you!" Corinne looked like she was on the verge of tears, and Farren knew her friend was definitely well on the way to getting drunk. Farren truly felt how much changed in the last few months, even just between her and Corinne.

She'd let go of things that hurt her. She'd fallen in love and probably just found her purpose.

Not that her dream of game design was silly or wrong or something she would give up on, but this was meaningful and could make a difference for people other than herself.

"I love you. Thank you!" Farren gave up on the side hug idea and gave her friend a massive squeeze, feeling despair lifting off of her for the first time in a while.

Part of her wondered if Sebastian would've felt the same pride Corinne mentioned. It was a thought she pushed into the recesses of her brain. This wasn't about him and his feelings. It was about Farren, about her coming into her own. She had to do this for herself. She had to find her way. Maybe there'd be another chance with someone else later down the line. *Maybe with him*, her traitorous brain threw out. Either way, she needed this.

Farren wanted to prove to herself she could do it, and she would.

The friends sat at the bar for hours, plans and ideas scribbled onto the napkins that littered the bar top. Slightly sticky, not wholly formed, but it was the start of something, and Farren knew she'd found the thing that set her soul on fire.

Sebastian

Sebastian was fucking sick of himself after two weeks with only his thoughts to keep him occupied. The grind that kept him on track for so long wore him down to bones scraping along the rails, a runaway train with no end in sight. Farren ignored every one of his attempts to reach out, and he couldn't really blame her. He'd attacked her character.

She hadn't exactly been kind herself, but Sebastian held plenty of the blame.

She took up so much of his brain space. Sebastian hated that he could barely bring himself to care about sitting at a cubicle for hours on end when it felt like someone scooped out his chest, leaving him hollow. After he declined drinks multiple times, Rachel eventually wore him down to have a coffee with her before work.

"Why do you even care?" he'd asked when she loomed over his desk the afternoon before, looking put-together while he ran a hand through his hair and wondered when the last time he'd showered had been.

"You're on my team. Plus, I don't have many friends at the company. I know you don't either. It doesn't have to be anything other than feeling like a human being outside of work," she'd responded.

So, he agreed. They found themselves at some swanky coffee

place that covered everything from drip and pour-over to French press and siphon methods. It smelled like roasted beans; the sleek look of the shop was so different from the one where the game nights were hosted. The scent was too sharp, too focused, with none of the sweet notes from the pastries to cut through the acridity. Sebastian sat in an uncomfortable plastic chair, all swooshes and artistic angles, not built for practicality. This was not the sort of place people brought their laptops to or hung around all day.

The floor was glistening tile, the mug he held was clear glass. Rachel had no problem ordering. Then again, she seemed like she was always in control, at ease. He'd opted for the least complicated thing he could find and contented himself with burning the tip of his tongue and having the bitterness of it coat his throat.

They talked, and she urged him to open up, clearly seeing something was up. Andrew might not have noticed a dip in his productivity, but she did. He tried and failed to deflect, and it slipped out about Farren, about how horribly things went between them. How royally he'd stuffed it up. Rachel listened as he laid out how stupid he'd been, how much he regretted what he'd said, especially now when he couldn't apologize. No wonder it seemed like he had one foot out of the door at work.

"I don't blame you. Being a contractor is a soul-sucking endeavor. Especially if your reasons for being in it are flimsy. We're just there to keep the government happy. If I hadn't already put so much time into this freaking company, I probably would've found something else by now." Rachel nailed it exactly.

"Sunk-cost fallacy. I've thought about that as well. I've wondered whether I want to keep doing this, if I'm still trying to prove a point or if it's just all I know how to do." The mug was scalding in his hands, caffeine slowly injecting his body with energy. Insomnia was his constant companion, and the only thing that could even start to cut through the haze was coffee.

"Why did you get into this? Don't get me wrong, you're pretty good at your job, but it's no one's passion to sit in a tiny cubicle for nine hours a day," she said, and it felt good to talk about it, to finally think about how he'd gotten here.

"I can barely remember at this point. Teachers encouraged me, so I felt seen. Professors recommended career paths. It just seemed to stick. The line from where I was to where they pointed seemed so clear... uncomplicated. And then my ex screwed me over, stole my app idea, and I was fired in the blow-up afterward. It put a chip on my shoulder, gave me something to focus on besides the betrayal. So, I started working, and I haven't stopped. It was easy to let myself go to those places when I could justify it was to prove my worth, show I was better than her and the job that let me go." How much of his life was his own agency?

Sebastian had gotten swept up in defying his parents, in carving out his place and having it be meaningful. He'd lost his way in trying to prove he belonged in this world, grasping for his footing after Ashley ripped the rug out from under him. Even with Farren... It felt like he'd lost himself a little in her, his attention shifting quickly toward one so bright and stunning where he was a solar lantern at best—practical when needed but not something to marvel at. Sebastian wanted to be more than just a name on an office door.

He wanted Farren. Needed her almost. But he didn't want to be the same person he was when she left his apartment that night. Sebastian had some evaluating—some growing—to do. A niggling part of him knew it would probably mean quitting his job. The thought wasn't as scary as he'd feared once. The uncertainty of an unmarked path loomed ahead, but the freedom of it was exhilarating. Perhaps for the first time in his life, he could try and see where he truly belonged, not just where he performed best under pressure.

Rachel listened to him talk about the future he was afraid to admit he wanted, one with Farren, where he could breathe and try something new... possibly multiple somethings. It seemed a little blasphemous, entertaining the idea of starting over when he felt so close to getting what he'd worked for. But he knew the acid eating up his throat and the sleepless nights, and the general dread he woke up with every day weren't the best he could do.

He deserved better.

Farren showed him that.

And he only hoped he could find it and his way back to her.

"Well, even though it's not a real plan in any way, it seems like your mind is close to being made up?" Rachel lifted her mug for him to tap his against.

"I have no idea what the fuck I'm going to do."

He had savings. Even with a giant maw of uncertainty ahead, he would probably be able to hold off on finding something for a while. Sebastian was one man on a pretty big salary, hadn't upgraded his car in years, and didn't live beyond his means. He'd planned to accumulate his savings to comfortably put money down on a house, but maybe it could be a lifeline to him now.

"You're going to march back into the office and quit before you work yourself to death. Then you're going to get your girl back." Rachel said it so bluntly, everything black and white when she opened her mouth. She made it sound so simple. It kind of pissed him off how concise and effective she could be. Or maybe she was just really good at reading people and knowing when to push.

"She's avoiding me. I think it's over for real."

"She's probably got her own shit to work through, same as

you. If you really want it to work out with her, you can show her how important she is, and how much of an idiot you were." Rachel rolled her eyes at him, and he felt himself chuckle for the first time in ages.

"What do I do?" As usual, he was lost under the anxiety of not wanting to fuck up again.

"Jesus, dude. Do I have to do everything for you? You really need to work on deciding things for yourself. She loves you, right?" It wasn't so much a question as an accusation. Rachel's index finger pointed at him, eyebrows raised in challenge.

"Yes?" At one point. Whether Farren still did, remained to be seen.

"And you love her?"

"Yes, but I fucked that up. I was too scared to tell her," Sebastian sighed; admitting it was getting easier as time passed.

"Words hurt, words scar. She's not going to believe a placating voicemail. Action. You have to show up. You have to prove it. You know her and what's important to her. You'll figure it out." Rachel nodded, drained her coffee, and stood, waiting for him to get his butt in gear.

Apparently, this conversation was over.

He followed her to the office, the sharp clip of her short boots brokering no argument. When she gave him that look outside the office, the one that said she wasn't going to accept any bullshit, he knew it was now or never.

Sebastian had long passed the threshold of being reasonable when it came to being a cog in the government wheel. He didn't become a software developer for this. He was tired of them not giving a shit about him, of him not caring about himself and sacrificing good things for the sake of their circus. It was high time he took charge of his own life.

He walked up to Andrew's office, knocking twice and stepping inside as soon as he heard what sounded like vague acknowledgment.

"Ian. What's going on?" he asked. Sebastian shut the door behind him.

His fists clenched and unclenched, his mouth impossibly dry, tongue sticking to the roof of his mouth. But he thought of how miserable he was, even before meeting and losing Farren, how lost... Sebastian thought of all the life he'd missed out on. He thought of Rachel and her fucking stern look.

"I quit."

It slipped out. No preamble. No warm-up.

"Excuse me?" Andrew drew back in shock, eyes wide, and Sebastian watched as his boss's brain tried to catch up to what he'd heard.

"You heard me." He had no idea where the confidence came from. But now that the words were out there, relief came and embraced him.

"Okay, whoa. Is this because of another offer? Because we can match it." Andrew rose from his seat, not quite crossing the barrier of the desk between them. Clearly, the gesture was supposed to mean something.

"No. It's not about another offer or promotion. It's about me and how I'm not happy here." Because he wasn't; he was ashamed of how long it took him to see it.

It was the absolute truth. This job gave Sebastian something to do, a misguided sense of purpose, but it never brought him joy.

"Look, we can talk about this. A raise? You're a good worker, Ian. I'd hate to lose you." Andrew threaded his fingers together as he tried to negotiate something long gone.

"It's not business. It's personal. I appreciate your wanting to make it work, but I am not interested in remaining here. I'll have my desk cleared out within the hour." Sebastian didn't even care that all the "fuck you" speeches he'd practiced never materialized. Freedom was within reach, and pettiness seemed like an obstacle.

"An hour? No notice?" Andrew gaped at him, looking a little like a catfish.

"The District is at-will," Sebastian said and shrugged before he turned, pausing with his hand on the door handle.

"There's paperwork! Offloading procedures..." Andrew sputtered, his face turning red.

"I'll sign whatever I have to, relinquish whatever devices or files you need, but I'm leaving today, and I'm not coming back." He didn't wait for a response, just let the door shut behind him, walking toward the mailroom to get a paper box for his meager belongings.

Rachel gave him a thumbs up when she passed by his cubicle later that morning, and he stopped her briefly, smiling for real for the first time since his fight with Farren, thanking her for supporting him through it. His colleagues stared as he packed up his desk. Keith seemed slightly too happy about his potential departure, but Sebastian no longer cared.

He was out of there by noon. Badge turned in, admin privileges revoked, arms wrapped around a cardboard box holding the last almost-year of his life, and the sinking realization there was precious little to show for it. His ride home on the Metro was filled with quiet introspection, his mind jumping wildly between knowing this was the right thing to do and wondering if he would regret it.

Sebastian was filled with energy at the prospect of quitting—of closing down such a toxic and draining chapter of his life. But the adrenaline faded somewhere between Smithsonian and his stop at Potomac Avenue. When he got back to his apartment, he was shrouded in the feeling of *what now?*

Almost two weeks passed since he'd last seen Farren, and he

grew despondent at the prospect of them leaving things the way they had. If he could just have the chance to apologize, at least...

Sebastian didn't like the idea of showing up at game night; he didn't want to make her feel uncomfortable or cause a scene in front of her friends.

Friends...

Corinne.

Corinne could help him. Possibly. Maybe. If he groveled enough.

He was sure Farren told her everything by now, and after Corinne's warning to him at the Halloween party, he wasn't in her good graces. This was his only shot, though, and he wasn't ready to just let it go. All his years drudging up the corporate ladder forged a sort of stubbornness and tenacity. It was time to put it to work. He was ready to fight for what was important to him.

Sebastian did the only thing he could think of to reach out: social media.

Neither he nor Farren made a move to officially block each other on Facebook or Instagram. Corinne followed him after that game night when he'd joined in and surprised Farren.

Drafting up a message took longer and required more bolstering than quitting his job had, and after an hour, he still couldn't find the right words so he just sent the ones he had.

> I need your help. I messed up big time with Farren, and she's not taking any of my calls or responding to any of my messages. This is a long shot, and you probably hate my guts, but I really want the chance to apologize.

It wasn't flowery, it wasn't perfect. Sebastian could only hope Corinne would be a little receptive. She did make him sweat, though. About two hours after she read the message, he received a response.

Why should I?

She made a good point. There was only one good answer.

Because I love her. And I was an idiot.

The little icon showed her typing, then stopping, then typing again. Finally, after ages, her message popped up and injected Sebastian with hope.

What did you have in mind?

The ideas floated around his head, a dozen different scenarios discounted before they fully formed. This had to be meaningful. He wanted it to be singular to Farren. Sebastian's mind floated back to when she first talked to him about game design and spaces where gaming was celebrated.

Do you know if she's going to be at PAX Unplugged?

His eyes settled on the closet door and the wrapped box that lived there since the last time she was here, when everything changed.

I'll make it happen. What's the plan?

Operation Win Farren Back was officially a go.

Farren

December was right around the corner, and everywhere she looked was transformed. Inflatable Santas dotted the few lawns littered around the neighborhood. Others, like her, in apartments posted huge snowflakes or the like against windows. She even went as far as to put up her little Charlie Brown tree in her living room, its multicolored lights deceptively cheerful despite her dour mood.

Having somewhere to channel her energy... to focus, dream, and build helped distract Farren reasonably well. Work took up a bunch of her day, and she found herself more grateful for it than not. Although Thanksgiving break had given her the opportunity to head home, Farren still felt too raw to face her family. Especially with the reminder that she'd have to head up there alone. So, she sent her love and regards, promised to try and make a plan for Christmas, and carefully set her emotions aside.

Having something to channel her energy into took the edge off of the gnawing in her chest. First, she cleaned her apartment. She even went so far as to wipe down the top of the ceiling fan blades and felt pretty proud of herself.

Laundry came next. Farren found this fantastic account on TikTok that did laundry stripping. She spent at least a few hours with Borax, detergent, and hot water in her bathtub, pulling the impurities out of her blankets and watching the dirty water pour down the drain. Part of her wished it was as easy to cleanse herself of how she was feeling, but no dice.

She'd approached a few places about possibly being venues in her area to host the game club, including one of the schools nearby, but they weren't too keen on her using their resources. The room could go to any number of actual school clubs, and since Farren didn't teach there, she had no one to vouch for her, no clout. None of the venues she found so far seemed to fit the bill perfectly.

Restaurants or coffee shops with space wanted guarantees they'd be making money off the people occupying their tables, which—fair enough, but it cut her prospective list in half. Others wanted to charge high fees for the use of their spaces and to have Farren pay for liability insurance. While she was willing to pay—happy to—if it secured a space, she still had rent and other bills to think about. Was this idea doomed before it even got off the ground?

Corinne was a freaking rock through it all. Farren was so glad they'd been able to make up, even though some of what Corinne said during their fight came up occasionally. Farren did want to be dependable. Even if she wasn't inherently serious. She wanted to be someone people could turn to and know it was meaningful.

Her heart ached at night when all her distractions faded. In bed alone, she thought about whether she was being stupid, whether she should just pick up when he called. But the calls came less and less until, eventually, they didn't come at all. And she grieved, berated her own stupidity when it happened.

Farren felt so childish and silly for letting the hurt from his judgment and rejection get in the way of what she wanted. It felt like a stupid hill to die on. But she couldn't bring herself to reach out. She didn't want to put herself out there again, only for it to end the same way. At some point, she'd have to speak to him. Sebastian had a key to her apartment, and the end had come, but as usual, Farren seemed to lack the follow-through ability.

You can't ghost the guy you love. Her traitorous thoughts taunted her when she missed him most.

Well, she was going to try and get over him. Soon. At some point. Eventually.

In the meantime, she'd research more venues, think up lists of games that could be played, and consider how the heck to market the idea to schools and groups to draw people in.

Her phone rang, blasting through her do-not-disturb and sounding her Christmas ringtone, falsely cheerful. Farren's heart definitely didn't sink when she saw it was Corinne instead of Sebastian.

"Hey, what's up?" she asked.

"Are you going to PAX this year?" Corinne was her abrupt self; at this point, Farren was used to no pleasantries.

"I wasn't planning on it. Why?" Crowds didn't sound appealing, neither did having to be "on" for so long. Even though she enjoyed it, her mind strayed to Sebastian far too often.

"I think it's a good idea."

"Why is that?" Farren asked, trying not to sound exasperated.

"Because..." she dragged it out. "Luis's mom is going to watch Alison, and I think it would be a great way to get a feel for new games coming out. Specifically new kids' games. You could watch them being played and see what works and doesn't. Research for your endeavor."

Fuck. She had Farren there.

"I don't know. I'm not really feeling up to it." Maybe if Farren kept at it, Corinne would drop it.

"Do you want to accomplish this goal or not? I know you're still bummed about what happened with Sebastian, but I think this will be a great opportunity for you. Get out of the house for a bit. Spend time doing what you love with the people that love you," Corinne said, and Farren's resolve folded. She was right.

"Fine. You twisted my arm. Though I'm not sure I can get a ticket this close to it." Farren also needed to check her bank account to ensure she had enough play money left over after paying bills. Usually, she got the early bird tickets with the discount, but this year was such a crazy time, it totally slipped her mind.

"Already taken care of." Corinne's voice sounded smug, and she kind of wanted to be mad at her friend's assumption. Mostly, she was glad to have someone to pester her, to care.

"What about a hotel? I haven't had any time to plan." Farren's panic grew, accumulating under her ribcage.

"It's okay. We've got it all covered, Farren. All you have to do is show up and have fun. Can you do that?" Corinne made it sound like a challenge, and Farren had always been a sucker for a challenge.

"Okay, well... guess we're going to Philly!" Farren wasn't all the way enthused, but she wasn't going to bring Corinne down as well.

Her friend gave a little cheer, and Farren felt herself smile for real for the first time in a while.

Sebastian

The crush of people overwhelmed him, and the assault on his senses left Sebastian feeling uneasy. The convention center teemed with all sorts. Perfume mixed sickeningly with cologne and body odor. Every step made his lanyard swing, the strap irritating the back of his neck. Corinne hadn't mentioned this. It would be impossible to find her here. He should have expected it; in the back of his mind, he understood what a convention was like. He went to one or two for work.

But PAX Unplugged was unlike anything he'd ever experienced. It compounded as he walked from his hotel room to the convention center, and lines of people on sidewalks converged, filing into the building like ants returning to the hill en masse. Sebastian wished he'd prepared better. Mentally... physically. His long-sleeve T-shirt was already uncomfortably toasty given the warmth in the building and the sheer amount of body heat being given off at any time.

Giant banners were up along with arrows and floor numbers. Room numbers were listed for panels, more for gameplay. They'd set up a whole floor just for shopping. Sebastian felt silly for his comment so long ago, scoffing at this. Gaming wasn't frivolous. Freeing some room up for joy wasn't a waste of time.

The scale was impressive, the passion of the people around him so much more than he'd ever dared to allow himself. The colors and sounds gave the space a spirited air. A pulsing song played on the sound system, drowned out by too many people talking at once, feet shuffling against the floor.

The backpack felt extra heavy on his back, her game like a cinder block reminding him of the stakes. No pressure. All he needed to do was win back the woman he loved... prove to her how much he believed in her, and hopefully not piss her off entirely in the process.

Corinne was hesitant to divulge any information about her friend. But Sebastian explained his feelings, his mistake—the gift he never got to give her. They played the game, and he could see the pride on her face, both of them sharing a smile at how amazing Farren was. Both wanted to see her succeed and believed she could make it happen if she just saw her worth and the worth of what she created. He had no idea how, but Corinne managed to pull it together. She "knew people," apparently.

This is going to blow up in our face.

No. No. This was going to work.

His initial plan was to try and pitch the game on her behalf to a publisher, sparing her potential hurt and disappointment—but he knew she wouldn't appreciate him bulldozing his way through the work she'd put in. Besides, he wanted to be there to support her in going after her dream. She needed to believe in herself enough to try, even if it didn't work out.

The slot was at three PM. Sebastian had two hours to try and find her in this growing crowd. Two hours to convince her she could do this. Two hours to think of a better way to say what kept running through his mind.

He tried texting her again.

> Farren. Please. Just give me a chance to apologize.

No response.

It made sense after Corinne explained how Farren felt, how she internalized what he'd said and how much he'd hurt her. Sebastian understood not opening up, protecting yourself. She'd gone against her nature for him, and he rewarded her with nothing but derision. Farren put up a good front, a strong one, after pretending for so long nothing bothered her.

It still pissed him off knowing how neglected she'd been by her family, how she sought out affection because of it. The shell she surrounded herself with was far more fragile than she let on. He'd dismissed her, just like her family did. Corinne made so many things clear for him. Her parents ignored her emotional needs as a child, which explained how she approached things. With how confidently she carried herself, it never occurred to him she might be just as scared as he was.

Ugh, he was such an asshole.

Sebastian needed her to know how he felt about her. He wanted to tell her he loved her for how she was... The way they left things definitely didn't convey any of that. Even if nothing happened for them, Farren needed to know he believed in her and her dream.

"She thinks she's not good enough. She takes herself out of high-stakes situations so she doesn't disappoint anyone. As confident as she is—as she seems—she still struggles. Farren thinks she's not good enough for you, she thinks you're still hung up on your ex," Corinne said. Each word was like a drip of acid accumulating into a little pool of guilt he wanted to wallow in.

Of course, she was good enough. Farren was a better person than he would ever be. Sebastian should never even have put her in the same sentence as Ashley. Farren's perspective and how she looked at the world was brighter and more creative than anything he could come up with.

Anxiety built up in his chest, stacking against his lungs until it felt harder to breathe. He had to find her. Sebastian tried calling but it just rang until the now-familiar voicemail greeted him.

Can't get a hold of her.

Either she's not hearing/seeing my attempts to contact her or...

Or she doesn't want to.

I don't know what to do.

Corinne was probably so tired of him already.

Check her Instagram stories, idiot. She's posting which games she's playing as she plays them.

Of course. It hadn't occurred to Sebastian. Her handle was punny, and he didn't expect any less: @ImAMeeplePerson posted multiple stories highlighting the day.

Her stories were vibrant; the con looked so different through her eyes. To Farren, this wasn't too much, cacophonous and claustrophobic. To Farren, this was where she could be herself and enjoy getting lost in something fun for a little while. Where she could meet people and make new friends.

Her most recent story showed her in a room playing about twenty-five minutes ago. Sebastian struggled with the glacial pace of the internet, trying to look up how long the play time was so he could gauge just how long he had to find the gaming room she was in.

Maybe. Maybe he'd have enough time if he hurried.

He wove between people, stopping and starting as his flow was interrupted by others going in the opposite direction. Groups of con-goers walking together made it even harder to get through. The first room was small and devoid of her beautiful dark blonde curls.

The second was much larger, but despite him scanning every face he could see, walking around the edge to make sure, still no luck.

The final room was on the other side of the exhibition hall, the maze of people and stalls exhausting to try and snake through. His heart thundered in his chest, breath huffing in and out. Sebastian was vaguely aware of the beads of sweat trickling down his spine. Somehow, he heard the squeak of his sneakers on the exhibition floor as he stopped and started, pivoting around people meandering their way around.

He made it to the room, wooden doors shut against the din of the main floor. Sebastian pushed his way inside, a few heads turning at the influx of sound, but most remained focused on their tasks.

Farren included.

She faced away from him, on the edge of the room. Technically, her back was to him, but he knew it was her. Blonde hair was bundled into a barely contained bun, wavy tendrils escaping to curl against her neck. The curve of her cheek and the sharp wing of her eyebrow were all he could make out from here, and even so, he felt like she'd knocked the wind out of him.

They seemed to be finishing up, and she chatted excitedly with her opponent, gesturing with her hands as she spoke. Beautiful. So fucking beautiful.

He'd missed her so much. This glance. This tiny sliver of her was the best thing he'd experienced in weeks.

But she didn't know he was there, and the last thing he wanted was for her to turn around and for the smile to disappear from her face. Sebastian backed out of the room, his nerves skittering so close under the surface of his skin, he could have sworn he felt them physically.

That's why his hands were shaking, right? Why his sternum felt like it was about to crack under some kind of pressure?

He leaned against the wall near the door, trying to talk himself into walking back in there and approaching her.

She's going to think you're crazy, or scary. She's going to be mad. Farren doesn't want to see you. You're being so fucking stupid. Just go home. Just forget this ever happened. You don't deserve her anyway. Leave her to her happiness.

It was hard to ignore the stream inside his mind, the never-ending thread of thoughts serving no purpose other than to make him feel worse about himself. That voice was so hard to drown out.

Just a few minutes. I'll go back inside once I've caught my breath... Once I've figured out what to say.

He'd found her. Now he just had to find the right words. He'd be back inside that room talking to her as soon as he did.

It was a plan. Not the best, but a plan, nonetheless. Sebastian was sure it would've been pretty good, except he hadn't accounted for the chance she might leave the room right after her game. The possibility slipped his mind until a small throng of people exited through the doors, and the familiar sway of her hips was right in front of him.

"Farren!" It was out before he could think about it. His hand wrapped around her wrist. Not unlike their first meeting.

Like then, she turned to face him, astonishment giving way

to something else, something not—happy. Farren pulled her arm from his grip.

"What are you doing here?" It was difficult to hear her over all the noise.

"I needed to talk to you."

She shook her head. "I don't want to talk to you."

"I needed to apologize. Please." His voice cracked as he begged, emotion sitting close to the surface, leaving the words hoarse. Desperate not to lose her again.

Farren seemed to consider his words longer than was comfortable before she nodded. She gestured for him to follow her to an escalator nearby, leading up and away from the main floor. Sebastian followed, tethered to her by some unfathomable thread of feeling. The urge to reach out, to touch her skin again, was colossal.

He followed her through more of the colony, people converging toward their hive. They got to an empty hallway between multiple conference rooms that weren't being used for this convention.

When she turned to face him, it was with a carefully neutral mask, a few feet away, but it might as well have been a hundred. Farren stared at him, wordless, waiting for him to make the first move. Sebastian supposed her arms were crossed over her chest to look closed off or intimidating. All it did was highlight her waist, the soft swell of her chest under her sweater. God, she was beautiful.

This was it. His chance.

"I fucked up."

Shit. Way to ease into it. He cringed, wincing, unused to being this direct about his feelings... his shortcomings. Well, nothing to do but muddle right through the middle.

"I was afraid. You made me feel—so much. More than I

thought possible. More than I'd convinced myself I could handle."

Her arms loosened, dangling at her sides, her face pinched slightly.

"I'm so, so sorry. I messed everything up, and it was all my fault. I let my fear get in the way. You didn't deserve what I said... the way I acted. You deserve so much more. I know I hurt you, and I can't fix it with words."

God he wished he could. Sebastian took a deep breath before forging on. "You—you're everything. The last thing I want is to leave you with the impression that I don't think you're fucking amazing. Because you are."

Sebastian dared to step closer, aching to hold her. The hallway wasn't romantic in the least. Generic carpeting, harsh overhead lighting. The area smelled slightly dusty, nothing but a long hallway bracketed by closed doors. This wasn't what he'd planned. He didn't know what he'd planned, but it was supposed to be better than this.

She deserved better than this. And yet.

This was possibly the only chance he'd get.

"You had a funny way of showing it." Her voice was clipped, and she swallowed hard after she said it.

"I wanted to show it differently, planned to. Then I fucked it up."

"How would it have looked then if things had gone 'according to your plan?'" She rolled her eyes, and yeah... fair enough.

He was a planner. To his own detriment sometimes. It was how he controlled his environment, how he kept himself safe. But it didn't work, not always, not then. He hadn't reacted well to her showing up unannounced, to her throwing his whole life off its axis.

Sebastian shrugged the strap of his backpack down, turning

it around so he could open it and pull out the pale blue box. Once empty, his bag hit the floor next to his feet with a soft thud.

"In a perfect world, in a scene where I wasn't a dick, I would have given you this." Sebastian held the box out to her with both hands, willing her to take it, to hold the manifestation of just how wonderful she was, how fantastic her ideas were.

"Sebastian—" she whispered, hands wrapping around the square.

"I had it made for you. I'd been taking notes every time we worked on it together. The night after you left for home, I took pictures of the mock-up. I found a crafter and ordered it while you were in New Hampshire. I wanted to have something special waiting for you. Even though logically, there's no way it would have come that quickly. We'll blame my overzealousness." Sebastian ran his fingers through his hair, nervous, wanting nothing more than to pace and expend some of this frantic energy building within him all day.

She ripped through the paper, blue shards of wrapping hitting the carpet. Farren clutched the box to her chest, watching him with wide eyes that looked slightly glassy with emotion.

"I wanted to give it to you so many times, but I was so angry. Angry with myself for what I thought was a mistake. But I now know it was just a sign of how little I cared about what happened. If the job really was the be-all and end-all, I would never have taken the risk in the first place. Part of me knew that." Too bad he'd ignored that part for way too long.

"I got demoted at work because my boss saw me ordering this and thought I wasn't working hard enough. It wasn't my finest moment, but it was a turning point for me, and I didn't see it. Not then."

He'd been so stupid, holding on to a scrap of what he thought his life was supposed to be. Rigid, unrelenting. His goal was hollow. Sebastian didn't realize it until Farren opened his eyes to other possibilities. Something he'd never allowed himself to think about.

"Then you told me you loved me, and it devastated me. I wanted it so much. Needed it. And it terrified me because it tore through who I thought I was and what I wanted. I felt it too, how deep things were between us that night in Maryland under the full moon... before then, even. But I was a coward."

She shook her head at him, her frown carving deep furrows into the space between her eyebrows. Her lip trembled, fingers tightening on the stiff cardboard.

"I made a mistake out of stupidity and cowardice, Farren. I ruined the best thing that ever happened to me. And this doesn't make it right. This doesn't excuse what I said and did. But I thought you should know I believe in you. I've always believed in you. The proof is right there in your arms."

She looked down at the game again, fingertips ghosting over the glossy surface of her name on the front.

"This isn't me asking for you to take me back. I'm not—The way I... It's not about us right now. I know I'm pushy and an asshole, but I hope you'll get over being mad quickly because you have a slot in about fifteen minutes."

Her mouth dropped open, jaw slack with shock.

"A slot?" she asked, dumbfounded.

"Playtesting."

Her eyes widened, head shaking no in little jerks.

"Sebastian. I can't. *Are you out of your mind?*" It was a little panicked, a whispered shout, and he chuckled in response.

"Evidently. But love does that to people. Or at least, that's what I've heard."

The words seemed to permeate through her freak-out.

"Lo—" She started and stopped, the word dying on her lips.

Sebastian stepped toward her. His hands rested on the

outside of her arms, the box still clasped to her chest. He rubbed his thumbs against the soft material of her shirt and lifted one hand up to cup her cheek.

"I love you, Farren. I do. It doesn't fix anything. It doesn't mean anything between us changes. But I do."

"I love you. You lo—you love me. Of course this changes things! You insufferable, wonderful—" She sputtered, seconds away from what he assumed would be an insult, so he closed the distance between them and pressed his lips to hers.

Sebastian's hand tangled in her hair, the other still cradling her cheek. Farren's hands were trapped between them, hugging her game to her heart, but she leaned into him, returning his kiss with a passion that seemed to spread through his veins.

He pulled back slightly, breathless.

"I can't play this. Are you kidding me? Here? There's no way I can playtest this here," she muttered against his lips, and he captured hers again to shut her up.

"Farren," he warned.

"It's not ready."

"It's not supposed to be." Kiss, lips trailing over her jaw and up to the shell of her ear.

"How do... It's no good. No one has played it. I have no idea if it even works." She kept talking, her worry leaking out through her mouth in a stream of words he knew would just keep going.

"It does," Sebastian reassured, confident.

"How do you know?" she challenged, taking a step back, presumably so she wouldn't be distracted by him.

"I played it with your friends."

The words were out before he could even think about it. Farren wasn't supposed to know about that. He didn't want her to feel like he'd gone behind her back.

"What?" It dropped between them, heavy, loaded.

"You wouldn't take my calls, and rightfully so. I was losing my mind. I quit my job. I needed something to occupy my time." Sebastian shrugged, mentally thanking her friends for helping him through one of the worst periods of his life. They were kinder than he deserved, and all this... Her game... This hobby she loved kept him going and kept him positive, ensuring he could pursue the right path.

"Wait, you quit your job!?" The emotions flitting across her face were impossible to read in their entirety. He guessed there was shock, a little anger maybe. A touch of breathlessness under it all. Sebastian wrapped his hands around her biceps again, needing to touch her, stroking his thumbs across the softness to ground himself.

"Farren. Focus. Playtesting."

"But..."

"We can talk about it after if you want." He bent down to pick his backpack off the ground, shoving the bits of gift wrap into it. Sebastian zipped it and slung it over his shoulder as she stood there, slightly dumbfounded. Farren held onto the game like a stuffed animal, close to her breast, and cradled it as if to protect it.

He placed a hand on her lower back, urging her forward, and her feet seemed to obey even though he could tell she was still reluctant. He rubbed soothing circles into the dip in her spine, gently steering her back toward the play rooms. The first one—the one she hadn't been in—the smaller one was in front of them in no time.

Sebastian pushed on the handle, opening the room up to her.

Corinne kept to her side of the bargain, thankfully. Even though she wasn't convinced this was the best way to do it, she'd gone along with his plan.

A table was set up with another copy of the game, laid out for people to see. A banner hung off the edge of the table, the design and name boldly displayed. Under it, just as significant, just as bold... Farren's name.

"Sebastian..." She gazed up at him with tears in her eyes before looking back at it.

Another table was set up behind it, ready for players to jump right in. At the table, standing up when she saw them enter, was Corinne. She rushed toward her friend, her dark bob swishing around her face, and collided with Farren, wrapping her up in a huge hug.

Farren freed one of her arms to return the embrace, a watery smile on her face and a chuckle-sob forcing its way through her lips.

"I can't believe you did this," Farren said, and Sebastian wasn't sure if she was talking to him or Corinne.

"I'm still mad I found out about this through lover-boy," Corinne said as she pulled away, gesturing at the manifestation of all Farren worked on for so long.

"I'm sorry. It was a pipe dream. I never thought it would ever see the light of day. It always felt so silly, so small." Farren's lips folded into a sad line, and the tears she'd kept at bay all this time dripped down her cheeks.

"Babe, I'm so glad to tell you that you're wrong. We've all played it. Heck, I've played it multiple times to get ready for today, so I could help with the demonstration." Corinne elbowed her as if to say, *Look at this. Look at what you've done.* Farren's shy smile made Sebastian fall in love with her all over again.

"I can't... This is amazing." Farren sniffled, flicking tears from her face, smiling at them both.

"You're the one that's amazing," Sebastian said, pressing a kiss against her temple. "Now, are you ready to make your dream a reality?"

He walked over and pulled the chair out behind the display

set, palm out for Farren to step up and settle into her place as the game designer. Corinne walked over to Luis to give them some privacy.

"If I say no, will it make a difference?" she whispered.

"If that's really what you want, we can pack up right now. But I think you owe it to yourself to at least try. Even just once."

"I'm scared." Farren looked up at him, naked vulnerability on her face.

"I know, sweetheart." Sebastian kissed her forehead wanting nothing more than to comfort her.

But he understood. Going after what you wanted... what you thought you'd never get... what you'd convinced yourself wasn't for you. It was terrifying.

"What if it doesn't work out?" Her voice was small, the words wavering.

"But what if it does? Are you willing to take that chance, to miss out on something wonderful because you're afraid?" Sebastian felt the words come from deep inside, meaning very different to him after losing her.

"No." It was soft. Followed by a much firmer, "No. I'm not."

Sebastian's smile was so large, he could feel the joy bubble up inside his chest. Farren answered with one of her own, dazzling. They both had a long way to go, and it wouldn't necessarily be easy figuring out where to go next, but there was only one thing left for them to do now before they rolled the dice on another chance together.

"Then let's play."

Farren

The twists in Farren's stomach pulled tauter when the first child walked in, unease growing as they got closer to the posted time, and increasingly more kids filed into the room. Chairs were grouped around tables, different from the classrooms and similar, all at once. Only this time, it wasn't a particular grade or school.

"Welcome to the first of the Summer Sessions here at the Anacostia Neighborhood Library! I'm excited to see so many faces, and pleased to note we have some parents who've opted to join in on the fun. Are you all ready to get your game on?" Farren asked, excitement bursting past the nerves. She was greeted with a lukewarm chorus of yesses.

"I'm sorry, I didn't realize we were at a school assembly. I said, are you all ready to *get your game on*?" she urged, and this time, they mustered up some more excitement.

The anxiety in her loosened, the knots falling into relief and joy. Throughout the two-hour session, she walked around tables watching kids play and getting to know their peers. Luis, Corinne, and Alison sat at one of the tables with a small group, one of the younger-aimed games spread before them. Corinne was the one to find this place. The idea arose when she'd come home from the museum and passed the library on the way.

It was silly that libraries hadn't occurred to them right away, but it was the perfect solution, and after some talks and planning, Farren was finally kicking off her summer program. A few other libraries joined in, and it would fill Farren's schedule while schools were closed for vacation. Today was only the first of many, and it was lovely that her friends took the time to support the endeavor. A few game club members came to help and teach games.

The parents that stuck around joined in on the fun, and it passed in such a blur, Farren barely noticed. It wasn't until the library assistant peeked her head into the room and gave her a small smile that she realized time was up. When the group groaned in disappointment, their bubble burst, Farren's chest swelled with pride. They enjoyed it.

They would be back, she knew. Once the bug bit, it was over.

Corinne hung around until the last few filed out of the room, the friends sharing a hug and laughing excitedly as they discussed the future of the game clubs. But Corinne took a long lunch to be here, and Luis had to get Alison back home for her own lunch, or she would turn into a very cranky little girl. Farren was rewarded with a tight hug from her favorite little whirlwind and watched as the room emptied completely.

Packing up the games was strangely relaxing. The quiet after so much nervous excitement proved a welcome respite. Farren took in the striking mural, the bookshelves tucked into one corner of the activity room, and countless others just outside in the children's section. Posters and cutouts of riotous color filled the space with brightness, the perfect environment to encourage learning through play.

Her phone buzzed with a message, and she knew it was Sebastian before she checked.

Or thought so.

An email came through—one she needed to open with him.

The nerves returned in full force bordering on nausea, and

the ride home was a blur. Her game bag felt weightless in her grip compared to her apprehension. The packed Metro chugged along, a much further commute from Anacostia to Alexandria than her old walk from the board game cafe to her apartment. The journey through Old Town didn't calm her the way it usually did, and the white townhouse with the black shutters was a blip on her radar.

There was no neighbor on the stoop, no stairs to trek up, just their Tuscan Sun rose bush in full bloom, striking against the siding. She twisted her key into the lock on the front door, and when she pushed her way into the entryway, their mail was in a little pile on the floor, the brass slot on the front door serving its intended purpose.

"Babe?" Farren called out, dropping her game bag by the door and swooping down to collect the white envelopes off the wood floor.

"Sebastian?" she tried again, a little louder this time, kicking her shoes off and padding barefoot to where she assumed he was. Cool air from the vents hissed up from the floor, blissfully chilling after the cramped Metro, fluttering her sun dress around her knees.

His office door was ajar, the faint pulse of music from his headphones explaining why he hadn't heard her call out for him. Farren was careful to have her touch be soft when she placed her hands on his shoulders, not to startle him, but he jumped a little nonetheless, both of them dissolving into giggles at his gasp. He dropped the headphones onto his desk and turned in his chair to face her.

"How was it?" he asked, his smile coming so easy these days, that dimple peeking through the light stubble he had going.

"What are you working on?" she deflected. Her phone lay heavy in her pocket.

But he knew her by now; the months since the con were

filled with conversations and jokes, changes and growth. Farren couldn't hide from him.

Sebastian rose from his chair, cupping her face in his hands and kissing her lips with the barest of touches.

"Farren?" he asked, almost a warning, daring her to keep trying to sidetrack him.

She stared up at him, the warmth of his hands on her cheeks grounding her despite the swirling feeling in her stomach.

"It went really well." It should have sounded positive. It was supposed to, but he was here, and the email loomed. Farren worried she wouldn't be able to breathe properly until it was dealt with.

"Then why are you shaking?" Sebastian's thumb stroked her cheek, hand trailing down the side of her neck and coming to rest on her shoulder. His hazel eyes were soft with concern, worry dissolving his earlier mirth.

"I got an email," was all she said. All she had to say.

His breath whooshed out of his lungs, hope and fear on his face, likely an echo of her own.

"Have you opened it yet?" he whispered, searching her expression for something.

"No." She cleared her throat. "No, I was too scared. I wanted to do it with you."

Sebastian gave her a smile, sweet and understanding, before he nodded and held his hand out. Farren reached shaky fingers into her dress pocket, dropping the phone into his upturned palm.

He tapped in her password, pulling up her Gmail, thumb hovering over the unread email.

"Open it!" she urged, too chicken shit to do it herself, grateful she had Sebastian to help her with these things. He killed the spiders that came in after the rain, and he remembered to put the leftover Chinese in the fridge. Sebastian ran her bubble baths after long days of subbing and watched awful episodes of The Bachelor with her when she needed to escape her brain for a while.

He did the heavy lifting when it came to moving, initiating the search for a townhome. Humoring her after the move-in when she made him move her sectional multiple times to get the flow of their living room right. Sebastian helped her string up her fairy lights and kept his office door ajar so she never felt ignored or forgotten, even when he was hours deep in coding for his freelance jobs. The biggest difference was his pivot into app development for games, a far cry from the government dourness from before.

He tapped her phone screen, eyes roving over the words she didn't dare to read. Farren screwed her eyes shut, unease building in her stomach along with the sick lurch of hope.

"Farren..." he tried, and she shook her head. If she didn't read it, she could live in the happy spot between wondering and knowing, between hope and rejection.

"Sweetheart... you're going to want to read this," he said, and her heart jumped up into her throat at the light edge to his voice. She looked up at him, scared to let herself fall into the possibility. His face was open, smiling. Proud.

She snatched the phone from his hands, her breath coming in little huffs.

"Dear Farren... blah blah... thank you for your submission after our conversation at PAX East in Boston," she muttered as she read it to herself. The words dried up when she reached one particular sentence, tears choking what little vocal ability she had left. She cleared her throat, trying to force the emotion down.

"We would be delighted to set up a call at your earliest convenience to discuss the future of *Pitch, Please!* and look forward to hearing from you soon." The words were a whisper by the end, and the tears sprung forth, slipping down her cheeks with an incredulous chuckle.

What? What?! Was this actually happening?

Sebastian gathered her into a deep embrace and rained kisses all over her cheeks, both of them laughing in between. Glee dissolved as she saw the look on his face. The joy and something else lurking beneath.

"I knew you could do it. I knew it. I'm so proud of you," he breathed, his words forceful as if he could convey the depth of his feelings through will alone.

"I couldn't have done it without—" Farren started.

"That's a lie. You could have. I'm just glad I got to be a part of it." When she tried to argue with him, he silenced her with a quick kiss and a stern look, raising his brows when she tried again.

"You did it! *You* did it." Sebastian's voice was filled with wonder, and he held her close as he lifted her slightly off the ground, spinning them both in a little circle, worsening the dizziness when he feasted on her mouth. Farren sank into the kiss, into the happiness she was too scared to hope for for so long.

"You keep going like that, and things might get a little dicey," Farren said, breathless.

"Did you... did you just make a gaming pun in the middle of my very serious kissing?" Sebastian pulled back, looking at her in question. The corner of his mouth quirked up despite his attempt at being firm, his pretend-irritation at her silliness nullified. It hadn't been on purpose, but now that he'd put the idea in her head...

"Maaaaybe. You should give it a shot. Just *roll with it*." Her smile was massive, stretching her cheeks as she watched the disbelief bloom over his face, followed by him trying to contain his laugh.

"I swear to god. You're asking to get tickled." The words were a growl. Farren yipped as she darted away from him, out of the office, and back into the hallway.

His legs were longer, though, so she didn't make it too far before he caught up to her, wrapping her up from behind, fingers dancing along her sides, peals of laughter ripped from her body.

"Stop!" she wheezed. "Please." Farren managed to pull away, retreating upstairs into their bedroom, well aware it was a dead end.

"Make me," he challenged, following her inside and shutting the door behind him.

That look was back, the one hiding behind the pride: hunger.

Sebastian stalked closer, but Farren didn't try to get away this time. Her chest heaved slightly with the exertion of running away and the leftover breathlessness from laughing so hard she couldn't breathe.

"Oh, I can't wait to see how this *plays out*." The joke was little more than a rush of air and the anticipation of him taking the bait, which he did, of course.

Sebastian growled and crowded her toward the bed, nipping at her neck once the back of her legs met the mattress.

"You're going to regret that," he warned, his mouth laying waste to her neck and heat pooling between her legs at his touch.

"Just trying to keep you on your toes. Don't want you to get *board* with me," she huffed, knowing this was dangerous territory. Sebastian proved her point when he nudged her onto her back and dropped to his knees in front of the bed. His large hands snaked under her dress, pulling her underwear down over her legs, holding the fabric in his hand like a trophy.

"How attached are you to these?" he asked. His voice was

muffled where he kissed the inside of her thigh.

"My underwear? That pair or generally?" she asked, gasping when he sucked against her skin at her continued obstinance.

"Pretty attached, I guess. Why?" When his mouth reached her center, her gasps turned to a moan.

"I'll make you a bet. If I make you come within five minutes, they're mine." Intriguing, definitely not a bet that would be bad to lose. But she knew Sebastian—knew there was more to this.

"And if you don't?" she asked, back arching up when he sampled her.

"I'll get you the lemon honey croissant that started it all." It was a challenge, plain and simple. One that was a win-win as far as Farren was concerned.

"Deal!" she vowed, content with either outcome, though it might be better to lose this time.

"I'm going to keep them in my pocket, so when we go for dinner after this, you'll feel the summer breeze teasing where I've been, with nothing to cover you. And you'll remember that you're mine." Sebastian's large hands gripped her legs, the words rasped out between thigh kisses. Farren just wished he'd stop wasting time and devour her.

"I'm *playing for keeps*," he said, his chuckle piercing through the haze of her need.

His mouth slotted over her core, cutting off her surprised laugh. All thoughts of winning and losing fell away under his touch. They could take turns losing for all she cared, as long as they were together. As long as he didn't stop. Her impatience was rewarded, and although she lost the bet, she rewarded him in kind, both ruined by the time they left that room.

Sebastian took her to the bakery for game night afterward, underwear stuffed in his pocket, kissing her with honey lemon flavored lips that promised many more tomorrows. The sweet taste of victory.

ACKNOWLEDGMENTS

I've been an avid reader since I was gifted a Sweet Valley Twins book by my aunt somewhere in my tween years. This led to many sleepless nights of "just one more chapter" and spilled over into reading "covertly" at school during assemblies and in class—something I got in trouble for frequently—which my mom can attest to.

My love for stories only grew, fed by a gigantic shelf of Historical Romance novels that my mother kept well-stocked. I owe a lot of that foundation to her. Mom, you showed me how to escape into new worlds and I'm so thankful. You and those books made me believe in strong women and true love.

It was no surprise the bar for potential partners was super high because of that. Who could *possibly* compare to book boyfriends? Enter Tyler Crone. Comic lover, board game fiend, dad joke extraordinaire. My love, your support and encouragement have kept me going through many dark days. This story would not exist without you. I'm so lucky to say that what we have is better than the novels.

To my family, both in South Africa and in the USA: thank you so much for believing in me. My dad who gave me a love for music, which led to songwriting, which led to writing. My sister, who has been a constant support and kind smile (with the best dimples.) Tyler's family who have cheered me on from day one and accepted me as one of their own. There will never be enough words to convey my gratitude. I love you. I miss you. I am who I am because of you.

To my amazing friends: thank you for the game nights, sleepovers, and shoulders to cry on. You make every day better and I love you all. Your light, love, and late nights mean the world to me.

I probably wouldn't have gotten back into writing fiction if it wasn't for the Reylo fandom. Star Wars opened up a whole new world for me. Between multiple Discord servers (Reylo Creatives, 321 Write) and Ao3, I fell in love with writing fiction again. This particular story was written during sprints in the 321 Write server and wouldn't have happened without the support and encouragement there!

I've learned a lot, especially from wonderful and kind authors with far more experience (thank you, Liana De la Rosa!) I also found my CPs for this book through Discord and Twitter. They whipped this story into something passable and kept me going when I was ready to give up. Ana, Ashley, Nichol… You have no idea how much your cheerleading, advice, and unhinged commentary in the Google doc meant to me, from our early Reylo days until now. Jenna and Nichelle, your feedback was invaluable and taught me so much about how I can improve. I can't wait to hold your stories in my hand and say I knew you all back when.

Britt, Lake Country Press, and my author "siblings" WOW I never expected to find such a supportive and kind community during the publishing process. Thank you, Britt, for believing in me and Playing For Keeps. You have no idea how much that "yes" changed my life. I'm so thankful that my first foray into the publishing world is with you, Lake Country Press, and this amazingly talented group of authors. Thank you as well to Beka for your kind feedback and advice to help make this story shine!

Thank you to my editor Borbala Branch who took my messy, untidy writing and made it fit for reading. I appreciate the time and effort you put into my story!

Thank you to Vivian Rodriguez for the gorgeous cover art and to Emily's World of Design for the perfect accompaniments to make the cover and media kit so awesome!

Thank you as well to Dawn Lucous for the interior formatting to make this look like an actual book!

And one final thanks to you, beautiful reader. You taking the time and giving this story a chance is so appreciated!

ABOUT THE AUTHOR

Wife. Fangirl. Disney lover and belter of show tunes. Overall ball of anxiety. As a teen, Tristen escaped into her mother's trove of historical romance books and hasn't resurfaced since. Exploring new worlds through reading also fostered a hankering for travel. When she's not working or writing about two idiots falling in love, she is researching and visiting as many different places as possible. Tristen was born and raised in South Africa but now lives in Maryland with her husband and their ever-growing book and board game shelves.

You can connect with Tristen here:
www.tristencrone.com

ALSO BY TRISTEN CRONE

Coming Soon...

I Think Olive You